Praise for J.C. Hager's *Hunter's Witness*

*A novel of terrorism, courageous actions, Federal law and self-preservation:
set in Michigan's Lower and Upper Peninsula. Webb leads the usual
Hunter characters at his manipulative best. Terrorism becomes a two-edged
sword when you mess with a gangster's daughter. Thriller fiction, well-
researched, nonstop action and a surprise ending. Each of John Hager's
books in the Hunter series keep getting better. Just when you thought you've
seen "Islamic-terrorism," here comes a Hunter book with a new nasty twist.*
J.A. Greenleaf
Author, *XYY: Dead of Winter*, first in a series of Grettu Väyrynen
legal thrillers (also set in Michigan's Upper Peninsula)

*Hunter's Witness: A timely, sophisticated thriller. Physical details give a front
row seat for fast paced action.*
Joan Rust
Author, *The Anniecat Chronicles*

Praise for J.C. Hager's *Hunter's Escape: Quest for Freedom*

*Hager's best to date. 'Old friends,' familiar characters, return for more edge-of-
the-chair adventures. Matt is a long way from Michigan's Upper Peninsula as
he and his new bride face rapid-fire perils in what should be a tropical paradise,
except for a surplus of killers, narco-traffickers, Cuban gunboats and clanking
cell doors! You will definitely enjoy the read, but watch out for ricochets!*
Joseph Greenleaf
Author, *Sudden Light, Donegal's Novel*

Praise for J.C. Hager's *Hunter's Secret: Wreck of the Carol K*

When I finished J. C. Hager's first book, Hunters Choice, *I asked the
author, "Where's the next one?" I finally got my eyes on* Hunter's
Secret *and got by on little sleep until I'd read it. The locales depicted
are bang-on, the human characters are well-crafted and many return
as the reader's old friends. Now, John, where's the next one?*
Joseph Greenleaf
Publisher, Swordpoint Intercontinental Ltd

Hunter's Secret *has action, intrigue, spot-on descriptions, unique Michigan
settings....an entertaining and logical sequel to* Hunter's Choice.
Aubrey Golden
President, Michigan Karst Conservancy

Praise for J. C. Hager's *Hunter's Choice*

Superbly crafted, Hunter's Choice *documents Hager as a master storyteller whose attention to detail insures the reader's rapt attention from beginning to end.*
Midwest Book Review

John Hager knows the outdoors, he knows the human heart, and best of all he knows how to tell a hell of a story!
Steve Hamilton
Author, the Alex McKnight novels

In his debut novel, J. C. Hager has employed his expertise as a hunter to offer us quite a yarn that could probably easily make a great movie...What also shines in the novel is Hager's familiarity with the finer points of all things pertaining to hunting and boating that he cleverly interweaves into his plot.
Norman Goldman
Editor, BookPleasures.com

Hunter's Witness

Also by J. C. Hager
Hunter's Choice
Hunter's Secret: Wreck of the Carol K
Hunter's Escape: Quest for Freedom

Hunter's Witness
Trial by Terrorism

J. C. Hager

A Matt Hunter Adventure

Greenstone Publishing
Rapid River, Michigan

Hunter's Witness
by J. C. Hager

First Edition

Manufactured in the United States

Book and cover design by Five Rainbows Services
www.FiveRainbows.com

Information: www.GreenstonePublishing.com
1-906-280-8585

Publisher's Cataloging-in-Publication Data
(provided by Five Rainbows Services)
Hager, John C.
   Hunter's witness : trial by terrorism / J.C. Hager.
      p. cm. – (A Matt Hunter adventure, bk. 4)
   ISBN: 978-0-9797546-7-8 (pbk.)
   ISBN: 978-0-9797546-8-5 (e-book)
   1. Terrorism—Fiction. 2. Conspiracies—Fiction. 3. Michigan—Fiction. 4. Adventure stories.   I. Title. II.
PS3608.A44 .H865 2014
813`.6—dc23
                                    2014913598

To August "Augie" Altese

My friend and golfing buddy, now 92, who valiantly flew 38 missions as a navigator in the B-17 and B-24 during WW II. Then and now, Augie has been an inspiration to all lucky enough to know him. I am forever indebted to him for his assistance in the editing of this book.

The Imam

Standing high atop a large recreational vehicle, the tall, hawk nosed man surveyed his surroundings: an endless light blue sky, circling woods in brilliant colors, an isolated meadow showing no unwanted humans. The clearing, the object of his inspection, lay burnt by a dry autumn preceded by a hot summer. Short brown stubble spreading over several acres was framed by the colors and dark shade of the tall trees of Leslie Woods, one of many wooded areas in and around Ann Arbor, Michigan. After once more carefully checking that they were alone in the glen, he looked down at five men awaiting his orders.

"We are alone..." He spoke in winded, flawless English, his clear baritone voice showing traces of his schooling in private London academies. His full black beard, accented by a center patch of white, was highlighted by his white outer garb and matching crocheted cap, a brown embroidered vest over a flowing outer garment completed his clothing.

Removing his wire rimmed bifocal glasses allowed him to focus while looking down. He took several breaths, overcoming his exertion from the climb up the twelve foot chrome ladder and the precarious walk to the center of the motor home. He enjoyed this position of physical superiority; it complemented his established religious leadership as an Imam to the Islamic group. Lifting one arm, pausing for effect, he began addressing the men waiting below him, "This is our final rehearsal; we need the plane to get into the air within four minutes. Two weeks ago you achieved this goal twice, but without loading the canister and without using the cumbersome suits and masks. Today we use our protective masks and clothing and will be loading a canister filled with powdered lime. The next time we load the plane it will be with a very deadly powder which you must treat with great respect. One particle the size of a piece of dust brings death; make sure your masks and suits are well fitted. The killing powder and two containers have cost our leaders a fortune: it will rain death upon the infidels. We bring the wrath of Allah to the unbelievers. Fear will soon be their constant companion.

"Loaders, go through with your suit washing procedure carefully after the canister is unwrapped and then loaded. Be sure to put on the surgical masks as you leave, for the plane might leak powder as it takes to the air, conceal them with a scarf.

"I will start the stopwatch when I hear the rear doors open. Now, move!"

Four of the men ran to the rear of the large motor home, opening the back doors and lowering a ramp that defined the RV as a "toy hauler." Where many RVers stored their 4x4s or motorcycles, there was a large model plane, a *Telemaster*. Its fuselage was in two parts which the men quickly carried into the open. Their coordinated efforts efficiently aligned the three threaded metal structural tubes of one half, with the strong point holes of the other half. Large bolts were then placed and tightened; the two halves were solidly bonded together in a few seconds.

While four men worked on the assembly and the attachment of cable controls, one man worked his way up the ladder to reach the roof of the RV. He had a control panel secured by a canvas strap over his shoulder.

He carefully moved to the center of the RV, putting the strap around his neck and arranging the control panel comfortably in front of him.

With the plane completing assembly, two men ran to the RV's storage area, moments later emerging in white HazMat suits, carefully carrying an eight inch by two foot metal cylinder to the plane. Large side doors were held open, revealing a mechanism that was attached over a bomb bay like drop box. One man, now in a filter mask, lifted his arm, a signal to the man with the control panel, immediately came an electric motor hum: gears began to spin. The arm went up again and the gears stopped. With the circuit and servo motor checked for radio control, the cylinder was carefully slipped into place, meshing its gears with the previously turning teeth. Locking snaps clicked over each gear assembly, securing the cylinder. One man in his protective mask, suit and gloves, after tapping the metal cylinder several times with a screwdriver handle, unscrewed a metal covering from the top side, revealing a series of slits. The cover was carefully dropped into a heavy plastic Ziploc bag held by the other suited man.

The doors were quickly closed and latched, the plane held in place, engine idling. As the engine RPMs increased to a howling level, the large radio controlled model plane was released, it bounced across the field, the 12 foot wingspan gave it 21 square feet of wing, aided by large inboard flaps, it needed only fifty feet to gracefully take to the air.

The craft was bearing the University of Michigan's school colors—maize and blue: the wings blue, the fuselage starting in the traditional school helmet yellow pattern and ending in dark blue. The words, *Go Blue*, showed boldly in yellow on the underside of the wings.

After a smooth assent, gaining an altitude of a hundred and fifty feet, the operator maneuvered the plane over the nearby trees. When the distance increased to several hundred yards, he pushed two buttons, the hatch snapped opened, the cylinder slowly spun and the white powder came out in puffs as the cylinder's slits allowed wind and gravity to scatter it. In a tight circle, the powder was all dispersed in less than a minute. After two more circles, the hatch was closed, the cylinder mechanism stopped and the plane, under competent control, obediently returned to the glen. Flaring over the short brown grass, its' flaps activated, the landing was completed at walking speed.

The leader looked all around again, then after helping the operator down the ladder, slowly followed him to the ground.

He assembled his group, as the plane engine cooled.

He showed his stop watch, "You assembled the plane in two minutes, loading and testing took 40 seconds. The plane left the ground in three minutes and ten seconds after we opened the rear doors. The majority of powder dispersed in twenty-four seconds. The next powder will be much heavier and should come out more slowly." Turning to the operator, "You also need to adjust for greater weight, understand the wind, and get as low as you can to the stadium. Your position on the roof of the motor home and the low walls of the south side of the stadium will give you the necessary line-of-sight. There is no need to retrieve the plane; it can be flown off into the distance. A crash within the stadium will literally carry more of a message, however, the longer the unsuspecting crowd has exposure to the dust, the greater will be its effect. Also, we will have more time to escape without notice. Therefore, fly the plane away from the stadium. It will crash within the city."

The man reached into the traditional Muslim clothing of an Imam, and produced a 4x6 inch metal plate from his vest. "I want this secured inside the plane, it will clarify our message."

The plate had words etched on it, *Let them feast and enjoy themselves, and let hope beguile them: But they shall know the truth at last. 15.2*

"We will dress in college or football fan clothes. You may wear colors you would not prefer. As soon as the plane is airborne, all but Kassem, who controls the plane, will walk away to where we have vehicles waiting. Walk up wind for many blocks before going to the vehicles."

Turning to the two who carried the cylinder, "Do not use haste when getting out of your suits, be very careful you are free of any dust: use the water sprayers on each other. I wish we could disguise the suits, they are very noticeable, but you will be in public for only a minute or two. Finally, leave the suits and our weapons in the motor home; be sure to remove any fingerprints or materials that can identity you. Leave all the clothes and contents of the owners. They will be very surprised when they return from their Mediterranean cruise and find how we made use of their motor home. You will only take up your weapons if someone tries to stop the plane from taking off. Otherwise, act like you are enjoying the pregame festivities: smile, make anyone watching believe you are students enjoying a school prank. Kassem will have his bicycle on which he will ride away. He will change his clothes and appearance to avoid capture. He is the bravest of us all. He will be most noticed and possibly endangered by the dust.

"Now, come, see what we will rain on the crowd."

The Imam led the group into the RV. Opening a storage area, he showed a second metal cylinder, sealed in a thick transparent plastic bag.

"This contains pulverized Polonium-210. We have chosen this material because its alpha radiation is scanner proof, easily shielded by the container and plastic covering. Each particle is a million times more deadly than hydrogen cyanide. Death comes slowly but surely from the dust being breathed or eaten."

The Imam picked up the container. The men backed away. With a smirk of superiority and contempt for their fright, the Imam came toward them. "Control your fear. Knowledge, faith and care are your allies. Put your hands on the package. Feel the heat. The Russians use containers of this material to heat their electronic packages in their space vehicles. There are baffles and filler material inside to keep the cylinder from getting too hot to touch. Only a few grams are of pure radioactive material—but it will have great effect."

As one man touched the cylinder, he asked, "Is not this the material that poisoned Alexander Litvinenko, the traitor to Russia?"

The Imam answered, "Yes, and Yasser Arafat too. In fact, the poisoning is so subtle death is often attributed to other causes. Those two are notably famous deaths."

As he carried the cylinder to each of the men, the Imam continued, "Soon all will know we have quantities of some of the most dangerous material in the world and we will not be trifled with. The interminable news programs will fixate on and amplify the implications of our power. We can sicken or kill over twenty thousand, maybe more. Your actions will forever live in legend. "

After all had touched the plastic covered cylinder, feeling its heat, the group contemplated the package for a few minutes, and then it was returned to its storage area. When the Imam closed the storage door, he led the men into the forward area of the RV where he seated himself.

"Now let us put away the plane and leave. It is soon time to pray."

2

<u>Buzz</u>

Carla Webb walked hand in hand with her boyfriend, Dave Adams, through the shaded paths and around the many ponds of Leslie Woods. The tree colors were just starting to work their way up to the full glory of a Michigan fall. The ponds presented a double spectacle by mirroring the display of colors, with a frame of clear blue sky above and below. They had stopped twice to hug and kiss in the seclusion of the shadows and bushes. Carla had just started her junior year; Dave was a graduate student, three years older, completely in love with the beautiful Carla. He knew her father was a once powerful Russian gangster, a point always emphasized by her bodyguard that discretely followed them.

Kate Wilson leaned her back against a large oak tree, one hundred feet behind the loving couple. She felt a little foolish, but the shape and weight of the FN 5.7 semi-automatic nudged her thoughts back to her responsibilities. Her present duty was far superior to wearing a hot battle uniform, body armor, hydration pack, ammunition, Kevlar helmet and toting an M-16, as she had done in Iraq. After the army she was recruited by Blackwater, and then assigned to Webb's daughter. Webb subsequently hired her personally—avoiding the complication of several layers of security service management. She roomed with Carla, took classes and was closing in on a Bachelor's degree—all paid for by Carla's father. Although ten years older than Carla, her petite size, squeaky voice and always sparkling personality allowed her to fit into most university situations and Carla's busy and well funded life. Only a few people knew or even suspected her role as protector. On the very few occasions she had vetoed an outing or idea proposed by Carla as unsafe, her counsel was always followed without enmity.

A buzzing above the three forest walkers got closer and louder, they couldn't see a plane, just an occasional flicker of a shadow over the pond area near them. Kate caught up with Carla and Dave, as they too searched the breaks in the canopy that gave a small view of blue sky. Dave led them off the path and through the woods to a clearing. They spotted the maize and blue radio controlled plane bank in a tight turn, they also saw a small plume of white come from the belly, then the plane buzzed around over their heads, turning again to come in for a landing, into the very mild breeze.

Kate saw the two men on the top of the large RV. She noted the Muslim dress of one man. From some innate sense of caution, maybe a reflex from Iraq, she kept Carla and Dave within the dark shade of the forest. They watched the plane land perfectly. The rest of the group assembled and was listening to the taller, dishadasha dressed, bearded man. From their shaded position, over one hundred yards away, and on a small hill overlooking the glen, they could not hear any words. The look of intensity of the leader and the attention of his subjects made the three viewers believe this was not a fraternity group; but it might be a math or physics class. They saw the stop-watch raised and shown to all. Then the group of men, following their tall leader, went into the RV.

Curiosity was trumped by caution as Kate kept them hidden for several more minutes. Spying from behind trees, in dark shadows, the three watched the plane taken apart and carried into the large storage area of the expensive bronze, gold and black motor home. The plane, men and RV soon rolled out of the glen and onto a two track road that led east away from the woods.

Dave broke the silence as they returned to the prepared path, "That was the biggest model plane I've ever seen. They may be part of the pep rally Friday night."

Kate didn't respond, just slowed her pace to let the pair have their limited privacy as they slowly ambled their way back to the car. Her thoughts returned to a time in Iraq when her convoy passed a smiling native, who waved with one hand and with the other remotely detonated several large artillery shells under their lead vehicles, blowing them into smoldering shreds of metal and ripping apart the bodies and lives of seven friends. She knew her alarm was probably unfounded, but they were near the Islamic Center of Ann Arbor, and there were over 150,000 Muslims in the southern Michigan area. Having fun with a radio controlled air plane was certainly no crime.

For Carla and Dave, the men and their model plane was quickly forgotten, eclipsed by the beauty of the fall, the smells of the leaves, the ducks landing and taking off the various ponds and talk of the hopes for their futures, all spiced by the thrill of young love.

Back at the parking lot, Kate drove the Yukon, the seat and peddles suitably adjusted for her five—three height. Dave accepted this arrangement, he sat in the back seat, because he was going to be dropped off at his apartment, and not wanting Kate to feel like a chauffeur Carla took shotgun.

After dropping Dave, the girls went to their large, old, rental house. They had the whole house, basement and the two car garage. There was security in and outside the building and the Yukon was bullet proofed and had explosive countering floor and firewall plates. There had been no threats or issues for several years, but Carla's father called Kate once a month to remind her of her duties and admonishing her to stay focused.

Back at their house Carla and Kate began to work preparing the guest bedroom for Matt and Tanya, Carla's close friends. Carla had been Tanya's bridesmaid just over a year earlier. She had many adventures with Matt and Tanya. This would be their first visit to Carla's world at the large university.

Matt and Tanya were coming for the weekend's football game—Michigan/Michigan State—one of the great intrastate and Big Ten rivalries of the year. Carla had good tickets for them. Dave, Kate and she would be sitting in the student section. They were both looking forward to seeing their friends and catching up on the news and adventures of the couples' life in Michigan's Upper Peninsula. Tanya had graduated from the University of Florida and had never been to a Big Ten game. Carla had many plans to show them Ann Arbor's student fun spots: do some shopping, enjoy some great local restaurants and rub shoulders with the students at some historic beer bars, all culminating in the big game that Saturday afternoon. Carla was excited to share with her friends—pregame tailgating parties, later—the bands, and 100,000 plus screaming fans in the "Big House." A big university football weekend is an experience not to be forgotten.

Carla and Kate attacked the guest bedroom, which, until now served as a storage room for empty luggage, winter clothes, dozens of shoes, and a dusty treadmill machine. In an hour the room was cleared, cleaned and the never used treadmill was dusted and pushed into a corner.

Carla shoved a box of her shoes into an over filled hall closet, commenting, "Tanya and Matt should be here soon. Let's get the steaks into some marinade and up to room temperature. Matt is good with a grill."

Replying from the large kitchen/dining area, as she was putting a metal bowl of lettuce into the old refrigerator, Kate answered, "Steaks are soaking in red wine and spices on the counter and I've got the salad materials chilling."

As Kate closed the refrigerator door, a vehicle crunched on the gravel of their driveway. Both young women ran to the side porch.

Matt and Tanya had arrived.

3

Matt and Tanya

Carla hugged Tanya as Matt carried in their two bags. Kate showed Matt to their room. The four came together for a quick tour of the old home. Carla pointed out the 1920s wood work, the friendly squeaking parquetry floors, tall cupboards thick with many coats of paint, the thread bare—once very expensive—rugs, intricate windows with stained glass edging, thick doors with brass knobs, and finally, a back yard with neatly trimmed grass, a wide porch that stepped down onto a flag stone patio where a large charcoal grill stood beside an old, wrought iron table and chair set.

Kate lit the grill and Carla said, "This will take some time to get to grilling stage, would you like a drink before we put on the steaks?"

Soon they were seated in the courtyard, Matt with a bottle of beer, Tanya with a vodka tonic and the girls with red wine.

Matt started the conversation, "Carla, how's your dad and mother? We haven't seen them since the Dominican Republic, and we've only talked on the phone a couple of times."

"Dad's fine, he took mother to their cabin in Canada for the color. Manitoulin Island is a special place. They like the colors, the coolness and the fireplace at night. They talked about driving down to your place later this month. He's so busy with his DR estate, the hotel he opened in Luperon and various other little projects he always seems to have going on."

Matt thought about Webb, a Russian gangster, going straight—or at least not very crooked anymore. He was now in his seventies, but still formidable and always a little scary to Matt. They had been through a lot and forged a strong friendship. Webb always treated Tanya like a daughter, knowing her all her life, and before that—he partied with her parents, Cuban refugees in the 1960's Miami. Matt looked at Tanya talking with Carla, their coloring, hair and animation as they spoke to each other made him think they could have been sisters. They laughed the same and had a real affection for each other. A nearly twenty year age difference seemed to increase not detract from their friendship. Carla had a far easier life than Tanya, Webb and his beautiful wife—Karen—gave her everything within their considerable power. Carla still turned out respectful, considerate and appreciative. She had the lifetime of Webb's stories of growing up after WW II in a ruined Russia, the Communist's total control of a country, his education and eventual high position in the huge government administration. Webb, an Olympic level weight lifter and university wrestling champion killed a man in a drunken bar fight. He went to prison. In prison he earned the friendship and loyalty of members in the Russian Mafia. When Webb was released from prison his knowledge and contacts within the Russian Government and his underworld friends were a perfect combination for power and profit in a government and country that was crumbling internally. Webb had the means to expunge his criminal record, obtain authentic visas and a real passport and was able to come to the USA. Many years later in Paris, he met, courted and married a beautiful young Russian ballerina. Karen became the joy of his life and soon Carla was born. Karen's parenting influence included teaching the need for effort to achieve goals, the importance of physical conditioning, and a need for composure in any situation. Carla grew up in many countries, educated in the finest schools in Europe. She had the strength and courage of her father, the grace and elegance of her mother.

Kate brought Matt a second beer, and touched up the wine glasses, leaving the bottle on the table. Tanya said she was fine with her drink and would have wine with the dinner.

Tanya got Carla talking about Dave Adams—her boyfriend. They had been dating steadily for over a year. Carla was effervescent about her love and their future. Dave had met Webb during a brief spring break to the Dominican Republic; they had gotten on very well. Several of Carla's previous boyfriends had been very intimidated by Carla's family history, punctuated by an armed and vigilant body guard always a few steps away. Dave was older, very smart, a scratch golfer and a distance runner. His family owned a large trucking company in the Midwest. Dave grew up among blue collar workers, a no nonsense business environment and knew the value of a dollar and honest effort. He was completely in love with Carla and had questioned her about ring size. He would have an MBA next year when Carla would graduate with a BS degree in communication.

Carla turned from Tanya and included Matt in her conversation, "Dave works at the golf course twenty hours a week, he will be here after he closes up the pro shop this evening. I'm anxious for you to meet him. We can get supper ready whenever you feel like grilling steaks."

The steaks were soon grilled and served with the salads and other dishes that filled the patio table. The light was fading and the temperature dropping by the time they were finished. Dave came just as they had cleared the table and moved themselves into the living room. Carla had a plate ready for him; he ate as they talked about the next day's plans.

Matt liked Dave immediately and felt he acted older, more mature than he himself had as a college student.

The evening ended with Tanya getting their bed ready. Dave left to return to his apartment—he had an early class in the morning. Matt was pleased with the, "no sleep over," relationship, Adams was respectful and believed in eventual rewards. But Matt felt the love and comfort between Carla and Dave and knew the two couldn't have resisted each other at other times. Kate showed Matt the security system and set the various alarms for the night. The yards and doorways were all covered with motion activated infrared cameras, feeding a wireless CD system that would record weeks of activity without intervention.

Kate, sitting at the security systems screens and keyboard said, "This system works very well, it has alarms and a calling system to my cell phone. I can monitor it from my cell phone too."

Matt asked, "Any problems so far"

"Nothing really sinister—just some thieving kids a couple of times; I spoke to them over the built-in mics, scared the shit out of them.

"Kidnapping is the real threat to Carla and the biggest worry to her father and mother. We've been several years without a hint of trouble. Boyfriends were the biggest problem—with Dave now her steady, things are real peaceable. Dave is the only one around that really knows Carla's family and back ground. He is tough and smart and I feel good about him being around her. It helps that Webb is keeping a low profile. He calls me every so often to make sure I'm on my toes, or if he thinks of a new security gadget or threat. He doesn't come here, but flies Carla to him every few months. "

Matt left Kate to her final security duties of the evening and found Tanya in the guest bed.

After unpacking and hanging up some clothes in the old armoire that was full of the girls' coats and dresses, he got into the bed; the soft old innerspring mattress of the regular sized double bed brought him close to Tanya who welcomed him into her arms.

Tanya snuggled into him, "Feel like a college kid again?"

Matt looked around the room searching for hidden cameras, "I just hope we aren't going to be on You Tube."

4

Game Day in Ann Arbor

M att looked down at the brat on his "Go Blue" paper plate. He held his coffee balanced by thumb and forefinger, his plate supported in the same left hand by skillful leverage between the bottom of the plastic coffee mug and his supportive three remaining fingers. The brat had been boiled in beer and onions, then skillfully browned on a charcoal grill. It smelled and looked delicious, but he wasn't really hungry due to the previous day's tour of campus bars and restaurants that Carla, Dave and Kate had insisted they experience. They had enjoyed several parks that bordered the Huron River, then grabbed an early lunch at a crowded Zingerman's Deli Roadhouse. Matt picked up the impressive bill that followed the equally impressive food, and then the girls went shopping in the Kerrytown area while Dave took Matt to two of his favorite nearby beer bars full of fans and spirit on a Friday afternoon before a big game. They all ended up together at a little pizza place, where three pitchers of beer helped wash down the cheesy, crusty pies. Finally, after driving to and walking around some lighted area shops, the five got home happy with their shopping treasures and the effects of many beers, glad to find their pillows.

Tanya came over to Matt; they were standing in the Pioneer High School parking lot, southwest of the stadium area, full of tailgaters, motor homes, smoking grills and pregame camaraderie. Carla and Dave, always with a watchful Kate in the background, insisted they come to the tail gating party hosted by Dave's parents who, as Maize and Blue blooded alumni, came to most Michigan games in their impressive motor home.

"Let me hold your coffee so you can enjoy this great brunch. Have you tried the baked beans or the cheese soup? They've got jumbo shrimp grilled with some kind of ginger sauce," said Tanya as she took the coffee mug and delicately chewed on a bit of shrimp, on a wooden skewer held in a "Go Blue" napkin.

Matt, fighting carbs, took the brat out of the bun, it was still covered with onions and some dark stone-ground mustard, after a bite and chewing he mumbled, "Wow, this is delicious, and I'm still full of pizza and the great ribs I had at that deli."

As Tanya's shrimp and Matt's brat were dispatched, Carla and Dave came up, Dave announcing, "Time we leave, better make your pit stops here, traffic is impossible and we need to get to the other side of the stadium. I have a parking place at the golf course south of the stadium."

As Matt and Tanya gave their thanks to Dave's parents, Kate drove up in the Yukon. The four piled into their usual positions: Matt in front with Kate, Carla, Tanya and Dave in the back. Matt looked at the competent diminutive chauffeur/bodyguard and sensed Kate's nervousness at the tailgate gathering. While the backseat folks chatted with each other—his glance brought a response from Kate, "Security at that parking lot is impossible. The fact that the same people park and party together year-after-year helps some, but I'm always glad when we leave. Now we go among 100,000 wild, yelling people. They have inspections at every gate but it wouldn't stop anyone really prepared to do no good."

Matt asked, "Can you get in armed?"

"Yes, with a special pass and credentials from the school and local police. We go into the same gate all the time—they know me. I initially took a ration of BS from some guards because of my sex and size until

I got in their face about my war record and the approvals from several layers of administrators. Now we're all friends."

"We're going to be late for the kickoff," said Carla from the backseat.

"I can drop Matt and Tanya off as we go by the stadium. They have their own seats," answered Kate.

Matt spoke up, "We will stick with you so we know where you're parked."

The traffic poked along for nearly a half hour just to get past the stadium. They finally crossed the crowded highway, inched along the stadium's south side and then made a right at the driveway leading into the golf course.

The north end of the golf course had turned into a parking lot, cars lined the road and fairway paralleling the east-west highway that ran south of the stadium.

"Work your way straight ahead, Matt and I will move the portable gates and we can park on the far side of that building to the right." Dave spoke and gestured.

Tanya glanced at the lines of cars parked on the grass, "What do the golfers say about losing their fairway?"

Dave responded, "Michigan football comes first here. As long as it isn't too wet, the grass is fine. They don't let in the big campers or motor homes."

"There's one," pointed out Tanya. Directing them to a large brown and gold toy hauler parked along the edge of the fairway, directly across from the south end of the stadium.

"I'll bet they had to pay the parking cost of 8 or 10 cars," said Dave.

Kate paid no attention, concentrating on maneuvering the Yukon around cars bordering the driveway, dodging the few people left in the golf course area and stopping before a yellow wooden barrier. She drove ahead after Matt and Dave moved and began replacing the temporary road block. It was in three pieces that leaned and locked into each other and it came apart, Tanya jumped out to help the men. Then Kate looked to her right fifty yards down the newly formed grass parking lot they had just passed and saw the bus sized motor home parked close against the trees and fence that was the border of the fairway—and more importantly she saw two men in white HAZMAT suits hurry into the opened back storage area of the huge vehicle. She also saw several men working on a large model plane at the farthest end of the fairway.

Kate turned to Carla, "That's the motor home, the men and the plane we saw in the park last week! Those suits mean this is not a prank. Get out, call 911; say it is a terrorist attack. I'm going to stop that plane."

"I'm staying with you," said Carla as she began dialing with her iPhone.

"No time to argue…I know we can't let that plane get into the air, make the call, hang on and stay low." Kate turned her large vehicle right, plunged through a low hedge and over a mounded flower plot, toppling a Weber grill, and folding back the right outside mirror as she scraped a parked car. Matt, Tanya and Dave stood helplessly in wonder.

Band music and cheers coming from the packed stadium contrasted with the drama that played out on the golf course.

The Yukon's engine roared as the vehicle raced up the green expanse between lines of parked cars. The model plane had begun its take off run, the combined speed of plane and vehicle made their distance disappear in seconds. Kate noted the men standing where the plane had started. They had pistols and were firing at the Yukon, a glance at the huge motor home revealed a man standing on its top with a control plan. Shells hit and glanced off the front window of the Yukon, barely leaving a scratch. The plane was bouncing to get into the air. Then a startling staccato of thumps and impacts of automatic weapon fire came from the right side. Carla screamed, the window showed little circles and went partially opaque. Kate kept her focus on steering toward the model plane—now fifty feet away and climbing off the ground.

"Two men are firing machine guns at us from the side. The windows are stopping the bullets," yelled Carla. She had dialed 911 and hadn't made a connection yet.

Kate felt the right front tire go soft and she fought the wheel's wish to go to the right.

Carla gave up the call, switched her phone to filming and scanned the attacking men, and the eminent crash with the plane.

The maize and blue plane—its wings wider than the Yukon, crashed into the left front fender, turned over and completed its destruction on the windshield and luggage rack. Its high pitched motor whine quit as its plastic propellers beat upon, and then stopped on the Yukon's hood. When Kate braked the Yukon, the plane slid off the hood and supported by a broken wing, covered most of the right side of the windshield.

Another fusillade of shells hit the Yukon, the windows still stopped them, but Kate felt as the men got closer they would be able to defeat the windows and shoot into the vehicle. There was no time to back out of the attack. Her job was to protect Carla, she hit a switch that closed all outside air sources—proof against gas attack, it also pressurized the vehicle. "Stay inside and stay down," she yelled as she jumped out while locking the still running vehicle.

Kate brought her FN 5.7 pistol's front sight in line with the chest of the closest man with a machine pistol. He had paused, fifty feet away, putting in a new 30 shell magazine, thinking he faced a helpless little female that in panic had jumped from the vehicle. Instead, he was in the sights of a deadly handgun, aimed by a skillful, battle toughened warrior. In little more than a second three of Kate's high speed shells dropped him in his tracks. The other man with an AK-47 machine pistol was farther away. When he realized Kate was armed, he ducked behind a car, Kate anticipated his next move, as he looked over the car's trunk, Kate's shell hit him in the forehead , a spray of blood and brains flew onto the next parked car, he went down to stay.

Kate felt a tug at her left shoulder, a shot coming from the top of the motor home hit her. She was knocked back and down, into part of the plane's wreckage, she felt her hand sink into the yellow-gray dust that was spilling from the broken back and innards of the upside down plane. Another shot buzzed passed her ear. The man atop the motor home was lying prone, aiming a pistol with two hands, firing carefully aimed shots at her. She lowered herself against the Yukon, moving to the rear and working to a standing position on the rear bumper, on her tiptoes, she sighted over the top of the roof luggage carrier. Her elevated target was still watching the front of the Yukon; she took a breath, brought the white dot on the front sight blade and the two dots on the back notched sight into a horizontal line, identified the shooter's head and shoulders as the center of mass and put three bullets into the unwary, exposed terrorist. He rolled off the top and made a satisfying thud as he hit the ground 12 feet below.

Kate heard other shots being fired, they were coming from the fence edge of the golf course. There were two separate areas of shots, more than a dozen from each location.

All during the gun fight, Carla switched back and forth from her 911 call to taking pictures. Thinking—*If I die, at least there will be a record to use against these crazy people.* She got through just as Kate left the vehicle. She screamed with urgency to an operator that seemed to be a poster child for Prozac. The dialog could have made a macabre Saturday Night Live script:

"What is your emergency?"—"We are being fired upon by automatic weapons!'

"What is your name, location and phone number?"—Carla Webb, golf course south of the stadium, don't call me back—send help—lots of help!"

"Stay calm, Carla. Is there a street name and number?"—'There is only one golf course south of the stadium!'

"Does your location put you in danger?" —"Yes, they have fired a hundred bullets at us and are coming closer."

"Do you need medical assistance?"—"We could use the whole Marine Corps."

"Carla, would you like us to notify the proper authorities?"—Yes, please.

"Carla, please hold…"

Carla went back to filming mode—the side windows of the Yukon were dark—but Carla saw a flash of movement behind the motor home. A man was removing a white surgical mask and tossing it aside, she recognized him as the leader of the model plane group from the park a week or so earlier. Despite regular western clothes—complete with a leather jacket and watch cap, Carla identified him by his full beard with a white patch in the middle and his hawkish nose. He was slinking toward the main northern gate. No one else was around the fence—he looked evil and was watching the action as he was sneaking away. Carla knelt on the back seat, moving to the right inside of the vehicle, she shot still and motion shots of him through the side and back windows. The filming was less than perfect because the flash had to be turned off, it had ruined several pictures. She put her hand on the door handle to get out and get a better picture, but stopped—she remembered Kate's instructions and she saw Kate at the rear of the SUV. Moments later pistol shots cracked over her head.

Carla's ears rang from Kate's fire from the rear of the Yukon, then she saw her appear outside the driver's window—yelling, "Stay inside, do not get out of the car. There is bad stuff spilled all over." Carla indicated she understood. She also noted that Kate had blood on her shoulder, gray dust on her right arm and side. Kate looked very worried. With her pistol in her hand, she was checking the area around the Yukon for more gunmen. Then, pistol extended in both hands, she carefully went to inspect the men she had shot: motioning to Carla with thumbs up after inspecting each of her targets. She came back to the SUV in time to intercept Tanya who was running up the fairway.

"Stay away from the Yukon and the plane. That powder is poison of some kind. We need to get Carla out very carefully," yelled Kate. Adding, "Where are Dave and Matt?"

Tanya stopped thirty feet from the Yukon—she could see Carla in the back seat, "Dave recognized the leader and he and Matt went after him. They are with the police out by the street. Are you alright?"

Kate held her weapon in her right hand, her left arm hung loosely, "I'm hit in the shoulder and I crawled around in the shit they were going to scatter on the stadium crowd. They need to treat this like a biohazard scene. Keep people away and call for lots of help. I'm contaminated. Carla must stay in the vehicle until it can be decontaminated. I'm feeling shaky—but keep people away from me too."

Kate leaned against a parked car; she slowly slid down its side and sat on the grass. She put her pistol in her lap.

Three police cars came racing into the golf course driveway.

Another cheer came from the stadium.

Deadly Dust

Carla watched helplessly from the Yukon as armed police officers converged on the scene. Kate put up her hands, the left arm clearly bloody and giving her pain. Carla yelled from the closed vehicle, "Stay away, stay away...the dust is poison!"

Kate, sitting on the cool grass, could hear the loudspeaker and fans at the game but could barely hear Carla. She leaned against the parked car, feeling hurt, sick and exhausted. She yelled at the approaching officers, "Stay back, I'm contaminated." Her voice didn't seem to be her own; her adrenalin rush that had peaked as she fought off three armed killers now ebbed, taking her strength with it.

There were four uniformed officers fanning out as they approached, their pistols in stiff arms ending in double hand grips, mechanically sweeping right and left. One approached Kate, stopping twenty feet away.

Kate repeated her warning, "This dust is some poison, they were terrorists, HAZMAT suits in the van..." Her voice faded with her loss of blood and strength. The stadium across the street overpowered her words with cheers and band music.

The young officer saw Kate's pistol, heedless of her words, he charged up to her and grabbed her right arm while kicking the pistol away from her. He rolled Kate onto her stomach, roughly pulled her left arm behind her, holstering his sidearm, he snapped on handcuffs.

Kate groaned with the pain in her left shoulder, crying out, "You asshole, you got my dust all over you now, check the van before you go near the Yukon."

The officer paid Kate no attention, he looked at the dead man crumpled in the grass by the Yukon, another officer stood over him, holding the AK-47 pistol. The officer by Kate yelled, "I've got this one. I see someone in the SUV."

Kate rolled on her right side, facing the Yukon, "Please stop and think before you do any more harm. The dust that is on you and me is poison. The dust is all over our vehicle, it needs to be cleaned off before you open it. I'm a professional bodyguard, I've got ID. Check out the big motor home—it has to have information in it."

The officer stood over Kate; he noticed the dust, her wound, the pain and sincerity in her eyes. As he was trying to think what to do next, he recalled a two hour class at the police academy on biohazardous material. Just as some of the lessons from the class were coming back to him, another office yelled from his left, "There is another man dead here, shot in the head and another on the grass by the RV."

Kate summoned enough strength to say with authority, "You dumb shit, you're probably dying right now, and if you don't close off this area, you'll take a lot of people with you. Those were Islamic terrorists, and the stuff they were going to sprinkle over 100,000 people isn't pixy dust. You're like officers I had in Iraq, every experience is new and they were always surprised and unprepared. Listen to me, I saw these people practicing this terrorism in a park a week ago, that's why I attacked them. There were five men and a leader. I got three of 'em."

Kate ended her speech with a fit of coughing.

The officer went over and picked up Kate's pistol, jamming it in his heavy, police tool cluttered belt. He returned to Kate and unlocked her cuffs, helping her sit up so she could breathe easier.

"Stay away from the SUV and the powder," the officer yelled to his companions. "Check out the van." He clicked on his radio's microphone calling for a biohazard team and more help to cordon off the area. Kate smiled at him.

Carla watched all the action, angered and frustrated by the hand-cuffing and rough treatment of Kate, she dearly wanted to rush out of the vehicle and help her, but the discipline and trust Kate had instilled in her kept Carla inside. She finally called Dave's cell phone. There was no answer.

More police—some in uniform, some is sport coats, a fire engine and an ambulance arrived. The area was roped off with yellow, "Police Area, Do Not Cross" plastic ribbon. Rubber necking fans were kept back over 50 feet. Two officers came out of the open back of the van—one held a white HAZMAT mask at arm's length by rubber gloves: a very serious look on his face. He kept a respectable distance between himself and the officer holding Kate. Announcing, "We got serious problems, the powder is probably radioactive, there's yellow signs all over and it came from a box labeled 210PO, whatever that is—it probably isn't healthy."

The game was at half time, bands played, announcements and former players were introduced and cheered, Kate and the young officer listened in silence, contemplating their own fate.

A supervising officer, in a suit, approached Kate and the officer. He stopped 20 feet away, he was wearing a surgical mask. "We have a bio-hazard team on the way, it will be an hour. The feds are coming too, homeland security, and every department that contains three letters. We are to make a 100 yard parameter and isolate the scene from public view. The radiation department from the University will be here soon with radiation measuring gear and knowledge about the dust—the best professors are at the game."

He moved to the side so Kate could see him better, "Your name Kate? We have your friends. They are safe and will be able to see you when we have you cleaned up. They captured our prime suspect. There are issues we need to work out. That's Carla in the SUV, we'll be careful getting her out—we are talking to her by cell phone."

Kate nodded her head, looking very relieved, she leaned into the officer as she weakened, content that her responsibilities seemed to be in capable hands.

Time passed slowly, Kate and the officer, who introduced himself as Jason, judged it by the cheers, and whistles from the stadium. The whole area in their view was circled by blue, brown and gray uniformed authorities from many branches of enforcement. They were approached by two figures of indeterminate sex, or age—dressed in plastic suits and covering masks, instruments were held next to them—they couldn't hear clicks or see the dials. The brief eye contacts were serious and sad.

A cadre of covered figures surrounded the Yukon. Conferences followed close examination of all sides of the vehicle. Finally decisions were made, a fire truck came onto the grass, a suited group sprayed down the right rear door area, more metering followed, more rinsing, after a final measuring the window was lowered a few inches and a plastic suit was given to Carla.

After struggling into the suit, Carla opened the door, she was escorted to a van that had parked on the driveway.

Carla waved at Kate, who gave another thumbs up.

A plastic suited figure shuffled up to Kate and Jason. Even in the all-covering suit and air mask—they could determine by the bagging legs and arms that he was small, his voice was of an old man, his eyes were kind and sorrowful. He carried a bundle. He spoke, "I am professor Zamitus, I teach nuclear science at the university. You have been exposed to a Polonium isotope. It is a relatively weak radioactive material, but can be very serious if it gets inside of you. The radiation only can go a few inches in air and a material as thin as a piece of paper it will not penetrate. You need to take off your clothes—which are contaminated. Put them in this bag. Next, I brought you robes, booties and masks. Don't touch your face, lick your lips or swallow. Don't breathe deeply until you have on the masks.

Kate felt sick, she wanted to take a deep breath, lick her lips and swallow. Her shoulder was bloody and numb. Jason looked to be in shock, but he still helped Kate to her feet. She stepped behind the nearest car and took off her clothes. Jason undressed where he stood. Professor Zamitus collected their clothes as they came off and put them into a heavy plastic bag, he carefully wiped their hands and faces with toilettes, also added to the bag. The bag was then carefully sealed with plastic tape. After they were masked and in the rather short robes and ill fitting plastic boots, they were led to another van whose back doors were open and its cargo area all plastic lined. They passed many plastic suited people busy with measuring and recording the area. They were met with quick glances and then eyes returning to their instruments and recorders. As they were about to enter the van, the air was filled with the sound of helicopters. Three large machines passed overhead. Zamitus looked up and screamed, "No, no, no…they will scatter the dust. Proving his worries, the first machine banked and flared on the nearest fairway. The dust from the model plane swirled and blew across the Yukon's hood and out on the grass toward the stadium. The picket line of officers in that direction ran in panic, blocked by the golf course fence. The professor hurried Kate and Jason toward the van. As he closed the van's doors he said, "You are going to our lab where we can clean you up—at least on the outside."

Action at the Gate

Tanya watched helplessly from an ever increasing distance as more law officers arrived and pushed her back from the Yukon containing Carla and from Kate who was lost from her sight behind parked vehicles. She had left her purse with her cell phone in the SUV. Soon the perimeter extended around much of the original parking area into which they had driven. She watched the team of plastic-suited scientists moving carefully around the SUV and among the parked vehicles. Then came more vans, a fire truck, scores of police, most in uniform and some in suits with their badges exposed, all were crowded into the driveway. She couldn't get across to the gate where Matt and Dave had confronted the escaping terrorist.

Tanya borrowed a cell phone from another spectator. She called Matt, who answered immediately. "Tanya, I've been calling you, got Carla in the SUV. She's OK but frightened for Kate who fought off the terrorists but was shot and got the stuff they were going to scatter on the stadium all over herself. Where are you?"

Tanya answered, "I'm across the parking lot from your gate. They keep pushing me back, and down the hill. I can just see the top of the Yukon and the yellow of the crashed plane. Lots of people are around it—all in space suits. I need to give this lady her phone back. I'll work my way around to you. Can you see anything?"

Matt reported, "We just saw two university vans come in and back up toward the Yukon. We can't see much either—trees in the way. We'll wait here. I don't think the police will let us go anyway!"

"What do you mean?" asked Tanya, the woman next to her held out her hand for the phone to be returned. Tanya held up one finger—indicating just one more minute.

"There are issues with the man Dave caught…I'll explain when we meet."

Tanya ended the call and returned the phone with thanks. She walked down the slight hill, away from the rim of watchers. She soon came to the second entrance, leaving the golf course she went back on the sidewalk, up toward the stadium and Matt.

Just as Tanya saw Matt, the helicopters came over. As she reached Matt and Dave, the police cleared the driveway and two U of M vans drove out—the drivers still in their plastic suits, looking like space invaders.

Matt came to Tanya and hugged her, his lower lip and the bridge of his nose were swollen. Dave was talking with three men who were taking notes. By-standers were backed across the wide street, toward the stadium. An Ann Arbor patrol car was parked partially on the sidewalk; inside there was a mean looking bearded man glaring at them from the back.

After a careful kiss on his unswollen cheek, Tanya asked Matt, "What happened to you?"

Matt touched his lip and nose, "I think Dave's head hit me when I tried to break up the fight."

"What fight?"

"While shots were popping in the golf course, Dave caught the bearded man, accused him of leading a terrorist attack, the man acted innocent and tried to walk away, there was a scuffle, then the man started screaming for help, two agitated policemen came running up and began to separate Dave from the wild, bearded man. Dave had him pinned against the fence, just holding him, trying to keep from being clawed, hit, kicked or bitten. The cops and the now crazy wild guy were all yelling. I tried to help and got head butted by mistake. With the men separated, ID's got checked—we found out that the bearded man is a Muslim leader, an Imam, not a citizen—comes from Syria, has a nasty attitude—he carried a mean looking knife, which didn't please the officers, but he really screwed the pooch when he called them fascist pigs. He ended up on the sidewalk, got cuffed and then thrown into a patrol car that had just nosed up to the gate area. It didn't take them more than five or six seconds from the, "Fascist pigs" phrase to having his sorry Syrian ass thrown in the vehicle. It was a beautiful athletic effort by the officers. The Syrian—I can't remember his name—was literally spitting mad—foam on his lips. We had a small crowd around us then, but now the cops listened carefully as Dave mentioned seeing men under the Imam's direction testing a model plane that dropped powder. While this was happening I got a call, Carla, from the Yukon, Dave's phone must have broken in the scuffle, I had her on speaker—she told the officers and us what happened. Dave went white with worry, we all knew that people were dead and this was major league terrorism. The police got on their radios to cops inside the fence and someone found the mask the Imam had thrown away—making Carla's story and identification of the Imam credible. I asked Carla where you were—she didn't know. At the same time the cop's radios went off with biohazard warnings. Then it has been a parade of police types and vehicles through this gate."

One of the non-uniformed men taking notes with Dave came up to Tanya, asking who she was, looking her over about ten seconds longer than Matt liked. Tanya, holding Matt's arm said, "I don't have my purse—it's in the vehicle that crashed into the plane. I'm Matt's wife—Tanya Hunter."

The officer wrote her name and said, "We'd like to get recorded statements from all of you. We'll have to drive you to our station—since how your vehicle is a crime scene."

Matt responded, "Glad to help, but we're worried about our friends that were in the Yukon. How are they, where are they?"

"I'll try to find out that information while we go to the station," answered the officer.

Dave, Matt and Tanya were escorted across the now closed-off high-way where dozens of official vehicles flashed at the curb. Matt looked back at the car holding the Imam—the Syrian had moved against the outside window—semicircles of white underlined his hate-filled eyes which stood out against the blackness of his beard and perhaps of his soul.

7

Polonium

Matt and Tanya stood in an atrium that was a sitting area at the end of a long, white, hospital hallway. Looking through the glass that made up three sides of the room, they saw the only light that remained of their long arduous day, an edge of gold on a dark streak of clouds lying on the western horizon.

Down the hall were isolation and intensive care rooms. There was a family standing area, a changing room and air locks within each patient treatment area. Visitors were able to look and talk only through closed circuit television. They had just talked with Carla, who was awake, and now was hooked up to a blood transfusion machine. Kate Wilson was now sedated with multiple tubes in her arm neck and throat connected to even more machines. The policeman, named Jason, was also on machines across the hall from Carla, he had police and his parents as visitors. Matt and Tanya had passed them in the hall but both groups were too much into their own problems to talk to each other.

Tanya's cell phone vibrated. They were in a cell phone permitted area. She answered, it was Webb. He gave no preamble, "We're in the city, be there in a half hour. How is Carla?"

Tanya answered, "She's on a machine that filters her blood, she didn't test positive for radiation, so far her urine is radiation free also. They gave her drugs to relax her while she's on the machine. We talked to her for some time; she is most worried about Kate—who is bad. Kate is sedated. She has radiation poisoning in her lungs, blood, and most likely in her bowels and kidneys, no way to stop it. The doctors don't give us much hope."

Webb broke in, "We can talk when we get there.

Tanya asked, "Is Al with you?"

Webb answered, "Yes, he's more than a great bodyguard, he knows most of the cops around here, and he's a good driver."

He broke the connection—Tanya looked at her cell phone. "They gave this back to me and the things in my purse—but they said the purse was too hard to clean or even take a chance of any dust on it—so it was destroyed." Tanya started to tear up.

Matt hugging her said, "We'll get through this. We got through four hours of police interrogation.

Tanya said, "The local police were decent, the feds acted like we caused the whole thing. And they aren't done with us. We're scheduled to be back there tomorrow—more questions. Poor Dave—they are still grilling him. He must be worried sick about Carla."

"I gave him my cell phone, but it must be turned off, or they won't let him use it." Matt added.

They heard steps coming down the terrazzo hall. It was an old man, walking purposely toward them. When he got close he offered his hand to Matt, "Hello, I'm Doctor Zamitus, you must be Matt and Tanya—Carla talked about you a great deal. I headed the University team that was at the scene in our hazardous material suits. We have prepared for an emergency like we had today. As you probably know, the University has had its own nuclear reactor. It is of the oldest technology, dating from the 50's and we have been decommissioning it for the last decade. Although our facilities are old, our decontamination procedures and equipment are very good. We originally took the three young people into our facility and cleaned them up, then brought them to this hospital."

Tanya gave the little man a hug, "You were there so fast."

"Yes," said the Doctor, "We work with the city and state police on any radioactive issues. Five of us were not at the game, as luck would have it, I had called a morning meeting with two other professors and two graduate assistants, we just received a five million dollar grant from the Department of Energy to find out where nuclear power plants break down and we faced a deadline on some paperwork needed to outline our projects. Another few minutes and we would have been rushing to the game or to TV sets. I have to say we were very surprised to find alpha radiation, we are used to gamma and really hot situations. Alpha radiation is extremely weak. Most instruments don't even read it. It doesn't show up on our film badges or our exposure pens we always wear. Luckily we had some broad spectrum Alpha reading instruments and we were told it was Polonium."

Tanya broke in, "What's going to happen to Kate and Carla? The doctors here only gave us a few minutes as they rushed between rooms and I didn't understand half of what they said."

"I'm an academic doctor—not a medical doctor. But I've directed our nuclear reactor activities for over 20 years and teach nuclear physics. The doctors here are using a technique called chelation—chele meaning a claw or to grab—using chemicals and filtering the blood they hope to capture the heavy metal—in this case polonium—that is radioactive. All they capture will not be going into the bone marrow and organ soft tissues where it will destroy cells. They will use several other drugs to slow cell damage."

Matt asked, "What are their chances?"

Zamitus looked at them, took a deep breath, "Miss Wilson has contamination in her lungs, digestive tract and from her wound with the most toxic substance I can think of. She was sick and throwing up by the time we got her here. But I'm pleased to say, Carla so far is not acting or testing positive, but still she was exposed and it is hard to detect—one advantage is we know what they were exposed to. Most victims of Polonium poisoning don't know what is making them sick and the medical tests and treatments go on for weeks or even months as cellular destruction reaches a fatal level.

"I need to tell you several things—one, I am not allowed to talk about this situation—the administration is worried about my putting two students in a hazardous, life threatening situation—they worry about lawsuits. The federal people have taken over the site and sent us away. They will have their team in tomorrow. They made it clear that we are not to make public statements of any kind. They brought up the various grants that have been our program's life blood for the last ten years. But I will tell you some things we learned or suspect anyway. First, the half-life of Polonium 210 is in days, not years—138 days is its half-life. The molecule gives off alpha particles and turns to lead. The samples we analyzed, by volume, were not very hot—that is radioactive—indicating that there is a relatively small amount of radioactive material mixed with a filler substance—probably Fuller's earth or chalk. Also, the ratio of PO to PB, Polonium to lead, is very low—indicating the original PO 210 is some length of time from its origin in a nuclear reactor. This is good news, but doesn't lessen the very deadly ability of even minute amounts; a dust particle size, to be deadly. We are working on these ratios now, and we sent a sample to Lansing—Michigan State has a world class nuclear program—and a mass spectrometer newer than ours. I'll know more in a few days. Of course I may not be able to discuss these things."

Matt asked, "May we call you?"

The professor took out a wrinkled card from his wallet, "Here are numbers you can try—the University number is where I'll be most of the time."

He formally shook hands with Matt and Tanya and returned down the long hall way.

8

Carla Care

M att and Tanya prepared to watch and talk to Carla via closed circuit television and microphones. Matt noted the room adjoining Carla's isolation room once had a large glass window; it had been walled up and replaced with a flat screen television. Cameras and microphones worked very well, the viewing perspective slightly above regular eye level, but the clarity and depth of field were excellent. A cadre of doctors and nurses left Carla's room, working through the airlock and clothes changing procedure, they asked if Matt and Tanya were family—without hesitation Tanya said yes, she was Carla's sister—then they spent a minute volunteering that she was doing well, not testing positive for radiation. One doctor, who seemed the point man on radiation poisoning, said that Carla didn't have demonstrable Alpha radiation, adding that they were still following an aggressive decontamination protocol. He went on, "She doesn't have any of the prodrome symptoms—nausea, vomiting, but we need to watch for latent issues—mostly hematopoietic, blood related —from bone marrow damage." He avoided making any such positive prognostications when queried about Kate, then he followed his colleagues as they pushed on to Kate's room.

Carla was awake, several tubes and machines had been removed, she spoke to her television that showed a wide angle view of the visitor's room, showing Matt and Tanya looking below the camera at their television screen, "How's Kate? They won't tell me much, other than she is getting the best of care. And where is Dave—is he OK?"

Matt fielded the easier, second question, "Dave is still with the police investigators, he saw the terrorists just like you and Kate when they were in that park. Without him the bastard would have slipped away. You three are very important witnesses. There will be people talking to you tomorrow."

Carla broke in, "What about Kate?"

Tanya answered, "She's not good, they are giving her lots of different treatments—filtering her blood, giving her chemicals that help lock up the radiation—but she was in a lot of the bad stuff. It got inside her and it is very deadly. We can only hope—and pray.

"How are you feeling?"

Carla touched her hair, "Other than being a human pin cushion and having my blood sucked out and put back and being intimately probed by several space men and now being alone in a sealed room, having my dinner through my arm and wondering if I breathed one little speck of Polonium which will rot out my insides—I'm fine!

"Father, Mother..." Carla saw Webb and her mother, Karen, enter the room.

Matt turned to see Webb and Karen enter. Webb looked tired and all of his 70 plus years. Karen, holding his hand, focused carefully on the television view of her daughter. Dressed in dark slacks and a red plaid cape, Matt thought Karen looked like a movie star.

Webb looked at the screen, "We heard the doctor's words—from the hallway—why are you in an isolation room?"

Carla answered—her words from the speaker had a hollow quality, "I asked the same question, they said I couldn't give anyone radiation, I'm in reverse isolation so no one can give me any germs—in case my body can't fight infections.

"But I feel fine, just worried and tired. They said, depending on more tests, I should be out of here soon. What's happening to Kate? She is a real hero: fighting men with machine guns, stopping the plane, she saved a lot of lives."

Webb replied, "Kate is in a bad way, the nurse that brought us to your room wouldn't go into detail—we aren't relatives—but they aren't very encouraging about her prognosis. I've sent for her parents, they will be here tomorrow morning."

Carla looked very sad, and then her expression changed, "Honey!"

Dave Adams walked into the now crowded room.

Matt asked, "They sure gave you the third degree."

Dave answered, "And a fourth and fifth after that. There are at least four layers of officials involved—local, state, federal and some people from the state department—or someplace high in the government, Homeland Security was there, they came from the airport. They all wanted statements—asked their own questions and usually asked the same questions over and over. They were really arguing about who is in charge. It seems that the FBI and the federal prosecutor will end up the lead folks for now. The prosecuter said he will come to see you here in the morning. I overheard him talking with the doctors; you should be in a different room by then."

Matt volunteered for Webb's benefit, "Dave identified and caught the Muslim guy that was the leader of the terrorist attack. Dave also gave me this black eye during a scuffle."

Dave came close to Matt and checked out the slightly swollen nose and the streak of dark under his right eye, "It's not so bad, be gone in a week."

Webb, ignoring the interplay, asked, "Where is the Muslim?"

"He's in the local lock up, he has lawyers and there will be a lineup of some kind after they talk to Carla. They want Kate's deposition or something, but can't get to her now.

"Did you know that the state police shot two armed terrorists—right off the fence—like something from a prison break movie—one is still alive—just. There were six men involved—the same number we saw in the park. Kate got three with her pistol. The only healthy one is the hooked nosed son-of-a—bitch I tangled with. I saw him briefly at the station—he's dressed back in some of his Arab clothes.

"Also, some of the police may have gotten radiation. Six or seven are in another hospital being checked. Everyone at the station is talking about it. All of them have kids and wives and no one knows anything about what to expect. Everyone is researching Polonium and it is very scary. Between interrogations I must 'a sat outside offices for over an hour, heard lots of talk. The two that threw the Imam into the car bought me coffee. They are Ann Arbor police. They said there is a press blackout, they are not releasing any news reports and the contaminated area is all blocked off."

Matt watched Webb listening to Dave. The love of a father for a helpless daughter and the responsibility of an employer for a bodyguard he personally liked very much seemed to be weights on his broad shoulders.

Matt and Webb looked at each other—the tired helplessness in Webb's eyes dissolved, replaced by resolve and quick, focused glances at everyone in the room. His scan finally ended on the television screen. He watched Carla's image for a full minute, then he took in a deep breath, "We've got a lot to do. We need information, answers. People have to pay for doing this."

"You'll get answers—and payback," said a large man who stood in and filled the doorway. He was dressed in a Michigan turtle neck sweater, a maize and blue nylon jacket, Levis and blue running shoes.

He spoke to the five people that filled the little room, "I'm Assistant U. S. Attorney James Koning—I'll be prosecuting this case. I've already met Dave, and I thought I'd see Carla before I drive home."

He entered the room, nearly a head taller than Webb or Matt, he was a big man. He nodded to Dave then shook hands with each of the other persons, learning their names and relationships with Carla. He finally said hello to Carla, who had watched and heard everything. Koning, looking at the screen, and talking to the group and Carla, said, "I've never been so intimately involved in any of my other prosecutions. As you can see I'm a Michigan fan, one time even played on that field, was at the game with my daughters, we might be on that side of the wall if it weren't for your courage and actions. I couldn't just sit around waiting for my FBI reports.

"I can have a grand jury convened in Detroit on Wednesday. I'll get subpoenas for all the witnesses. We need to present evidence that the Imam was involved in this attack. The fastest a formal grand jury can meet would be about a week after the subpoenas. We need you, Dave and Kate—if she can—to link the man to the plot and an attempt to kill thousands of people. At the grand jury I get an indictment, then an arrest and finally a trial and then we punish this malignant person."

His final sentence boomed in the small room.

Webb spoke up, "Who is this Imam? And where is he now?"

The Assistant U.S. Attorney went to a small note pad he had in a pocket, "The man's name is Ahmed Hussin Saleem Alikhan. At least as best we can determine—it seems his name is spelled Ahmad and Salaam on some of his papers. He's a Syrian citizen, here ten years on a work visa as a Muslim leader or Imam. He has no criminal record. He is presently being held in the city jail, to be arraigned Monday morning before a local judge. He will be charged with assault on an officer, and we are working on the other charges—terrorist use of a radiological dispersion device and a half dozen other charges that need to be sorted out."

Carla, pushing the side button that brought her bed to a sitting position, pleaded, "Dad, Mom—please check on Kate."

9

Hospital

Tanya and Dave stayed in the visitors area of Carla's room. They were talking about everything except Kate and radiation. The others followed the large attorney out into the hallway.

Matt and Webb noticed two men arranging a small table and two chairs at the head of the hallway. Koning anticipated their question, "They are FBI who will guard our star witnesses. The local press and television are reporting speculation, they have very few real facts, but the word is out among the Muslim community that their Imam is in jail and several Islamic students have been killed. His lawyers are very vocal and I'm sure will make his situation a *cause celeb* for a variety of injustices—profiling, police brutality, religious discrimination—in brief, many in the Islamic community are intolerant of any criticism. I'm sure in time there will be demonstrations at the courthouse. I don't rule out violence and pushback from the non-Muslims if the whole scope of their plan is publicized.

"I'm asking you all not to comment. We need to keep the attack quiet for as long as possible, therefore we can't counter the Islamic objections with facts—it would polarize the community and I'm afraid there would be more bloodshed. Anyway, it may all come out at the grand jury—which now, with the Patriot Act, isn't secret between government agencies anymore. Also, grand jurors have been known to leak information. We're probably in for a mess, whatever we do.

Karen, Webb's wife, spoke for the first time, "But they did the damage and were carrying out a monstrous plan!"

Webb moved near her, "It doesn't make any difference—most Muslims don't think like we do. They believe what they are told, that their community feeling is infallible, they will blindly support powerful, and to them, heroic leaders like this Imam."

Koning asked, "How do you know this?"

"I'm Russian; we have fought with Islam for a thousand years."

No one spoke after Webb's pronouncement. Koning moved toward Kate's room.

He opened her door, "I need to see how our brave hero is doing."

There were caregivers in with Kate; they were too busy to look up at their screen. Everyone moved into the visitors area and looked in shock at the monitor.

Kate slept. Tubes came from both arms, an airway was in and more tubes came from it. She looked like a small child, barely visible among the machines and multiple types of tubing. Her monitors were not readable from the visitors camera angle.

One man finally noticed the group shown in the visitors' area. He gave some orders to the other caregivers, checked her heart and chest with his stethoscope and moved to the airlock. After a full two minutes he entered the visitors' area. He was middle aged, trim and athletic looking. Before he could say anything, Koning showed him a federal investigator's badge and ID wallet and asked, "How's she doing? When can I talk to her?"

The medical man's picture ID showed he was Dr. Knox, he asked who everyone was, thought about what he could say. Then said, "She is in a very bad way, there is little more we can do except make her as comfortable as possible."

Matt thought, *I count 7 tubes coming out or going in, an airway and a urine bag.*

Koning asked, "When will she be awake and able to talk?"

The doctor answered, "We are taking out some tubes now, the effects of the radiation are massive and irreversible. She will be able to talk to you tomorrow. She will be very sick and without drugs very uncomfortable."

Koning responded, "It is vital we get her testimony, or at least a video questioning. She needs to be conscious and clear headed. What's done is done—now we need to make those who caused this tragedy pay the penalty."

The doctor sighed, thought, and said, "I believe you can see her tomorrow afternoon, she will be in another room and you can be with her. We are communicating with top radiation experts around the world, I'm afraid our procedures will only slow the inevitable. "

Webb asked, "How long does she have?"

The doctor shook his head, reluctant to make a pronouncement, finally he gave in to Webb's stare and the large attorney's badge that was still in view, "I don't know, days, maybe weeks."

Karen, tears in her eyes, spoke, "What about Carla? I'm her mother."

"Carla seems to be very lucky, the vehicle, Kate's action and the people that got her out may have saved her from contamination. We still have concerns about long term effects. Her blood work will tell us if she inhaled any radioactive material. We worry about leukemic like symptoms, radiation attacking her bone marrow—but her blood looks good at present. If her blood counts stay normal, you will be able to be with her late tomorrow."

Webb held Karen's shoulders, they both looked much relieved. Then they glanced at the pitiful sight of Kate and their happiness vanished.

Koning asked, "How is the policeman?"

The doctor weighed his words, "He's not good—that's all I can tell you."

The group moved back to the hallway.

"I'm going home, been a long day, and I know I'll have phone calls to answer when I leave here. This whole thing is awful, but I'm glad about your daughter. I'm sure I will have nightmares of what could have happened." The big man turned and walked away, stopping for a few words with the FBI guards.

Matt watched him go, and then joined Webb and Karen, in with Tanya and Dave. They shared the good news the doctor had given them, avoiding specifics about Kate.

Matt and Tanya said their good—byes after giving Webb directions to Carla's house. Webb had a rental car with a GPS so the address was about all he needed. He said they would stay just a little longer. Carla was ready to get some sleep too.

Hope and Despair

Sunday became an emotional rollercoaster of hope and despair. Carla gave hope and Kate brought crushing despair. All the plans for legal interviews were put on hold until the next day or two. Kate remained in her isolation room surrounded by doctors and technicians, Carla went to a large private corner room where her parents held her hands.

Matt and Tanya visited Carla then Kate going from room to room, floor to floor, checking through FBI guards. Carla improved immediately when she was allowed to change rooms. At each visit Kate had fewer tubes in her, but monitors still crowded the limited space of her room. She was occasionally looking around. She gave a weak smile to her camera and wiggled the fingers of one IV-filled arm when she saw Matt and Tanya in her monitor. Tanya smiled back and waved, Matt heard his wife take in her breath, controlling herself, fighting back tears.

Matt roamed the halls, drinking too much acidy coffee, his dry lips sticking to the Styrofoam. He went out to retrieve a pizza and two quarter pounders. When he returned with the food, he found he had missed the federal prosecutor who had come and went in the late morning, after conferencing with the doctors and Webb.

Tanya mostly stayed in Carla's room. Her quick trips to see Kate always ended in hallway tears and on one occasion sobs of utter despair.

Matt was amazed at Webb's ability to control and even manipulate any situation. He listened more than he talked, never made a demand, asked very considered questions, and with just his strength of presence was able to get doctors and nurses to talk and to act.

At noon there was a sort of conference outside Carla's room. The lead doctor informed them that Carla showed few if any signs of radiation poisoning. He went into some specifics of blood and urine tests. Then speaking directly to Webb and Karen, "The only caveat I see now is about her bone marrow. Her blood counts are trending downward in white cells, partially explainable by the drugs and procedures she has been through."

He went on to explain that the Polonium isotope in the body weakens quickly—in days actually—and it generally migrates from the blood to lodge in the soft tissues—kidneys, spleen, and/or the bone marrow where it kills cells like the yellow PacMan of the computer game gobbles the little white dots. The body fights back, making new cells where it can. If the dose of radiation is light enough, the body wins. In Carla's case the chances of the body winning seems generally positive.

Webb said, "What can we do about the bone marrow?"

The doctor responded, "Bone marrow replacements and blood transfusions are options if the counts get seriously abnormal."

The meeting ended and the doctor left the floor.

Karen had brought Carla a robe from her house. Carla with just an IV port taped on her wrist was free to walk with her parents to Kate's room. Matt and Tanya followed.

Kate was awake and recognized everyone. She pushed a button and the back of her bed came up. She spoke with words that were measured and slightly slurred, "I'm sorry I didn't have time to get you out of the vehicle. I understand you didn't get much of the bad stuff."

Kate's eyes were dark and sunken, her hair was matted from sweats and the oxygen tubes that went over her ears, her skin was as white as the sheets and she had red patches where the oxygen tube touched her nostrils. There were tubes in both arms, one had an IV dripping into her, the other went to a pain monitor and dose injection system. Her injured left shoulder was bandaged, her arm supported by pillows, an oxygen monitor glowed red at her finger tip. A urine bag hung off the side of the bed. Her lips were pale and cracked.

Carla, with teary eyes, replied, "I'm fine. You told me to get out, I didn't cooperate. You are a real hero. The men who cleaned us up said the radioactive dust would have killed tens of thousands."

Kate broke in, with a flicker of a grin and a brief sparkle flashing in her eyes, "I never had a spaceman give me a shower before, he sure didn't miss any spots. I know I'm sick, but I took out three of the bastards. What happened to their leader with the big beard? I saw him sneaking away by the fence. Figuring he was trying to flank me, I was watching him, never saw the guy on the motor home that got me."

Carla said, "Dave and Matt caught him, he's under arrest. We need to identify him for the police."

Kate replied, "Have them get done what they got to do," she coughed several times, wiped her nose with a tissue, took several breaths and ended with, "I'm ready."

Matt noted a dark stain on the tissue, he exchanged glances with Webb.

Webb spoke, "Your folks will be here anytime. They landed a few minutes ago. I have Al picking them up." Webb paused, extended his massive arms, " I'm sorry for all this…"

Kate said, "Forget it, I could have got it a dozen times in Iraq, this is a good trade. We anticipated just about every type of danger that Carla could face. Who would have figured an attack by crazy damn Muslims at a football game? There should be a bounty on 'em."

Kate started coughing again, Webb suggested they should let her rest before her parents got here. Kate smiled, nodded in agreement, showing relief and exhaustion, she settled back into her pillows and closed her eyes.

Matt, Tanya and Karen walked Carla to the elevator to get her back to her room. Webb said he would go to the lobby and wait to guide Kate's parents to her room.

11

Video Questioning and Line-up

Monday late afternoon had prosecutor Koning, several of his minions and an official court stenographer all crowded into Kate's visitors area. She was sitting up, hair combed, a little lipstick and some eye makeup brought back her lovely face. Her force of will ignored any pain or discomfort. A camera and microphone were placed in her room.

After establishing who, when and where they all were—Koning asked Kate to describe her actions involving the terrorists. Specifically to describe and identify the leader—identified as Ahmed Hussin Saleem Alikhan, AKA: Ahmad Hussin Salaam Alikhan.

Kate gave a very organized account of the actions she had observed at the park: the plane, the dust and the six men, particularly the leader— very prominent in his long shirt, full dark, white tipped beard and hook like nose. She described her reactions to the HAZMAT suits and how she knew something sinister was about to happen. Her instincts were confirmed when she drew fire from several men. At this point Kate seemed out of breath, she paused, coughed several times, moved the oxygen tubes, blew her nose, replaced the clear tubes under her nostrils, straightened her covers, folded her hands in front of herself, took several deep breaths and continued, She told of her fire fight, and seeing the man now identified by papers and pictures as Alikhan sneaking away. She positively identified him as the man she saw in the park and at the golf course.

Koning interrupted one time, to establish that Kate had picked the Imam's picture out of eight shown of various men in beards and of a general appearance of Alikhan.

Koning asked a few more questions and Kate answered them: general questions about her background, combat experience, eyesight, and time in an Islamic country, all adding to her competence and credibility.

After nearly twenty minutes of running video, Koning thanked Kate, the equipment was removed and the legal retinue filed away.

Matt and Webb came into the visiting room, having heard everything from the hallway where they stood with Kate's parents.

Kate seemed to deflate after her gutsy performance and testimony. She coughed and gasped for air. An attending nurse increased the rate of oxygen flow from its control gauge on the wall and monitored the blood oxygen sensor that was on her finger. Then she punched the button on the pain medication machine, and then fussed with Kate's pillows and angle of the bed.

Webb, in a choked whisper, said to the microphone, "Nice job Kate. You are the bravest person I have ever known." He acted like he would say more, but words didn't come out. He left the room. Matt followed him. Leaving the parents to watch their daughter smile and fall asleep.

Later that long afternoon, Dave and Carla picked the Imam out of a line up at the city/county building. The Imam had his beard trimmed so very little of the white showed, but Dave commented that his evil and arrogant eyes would have given him away if they would have been the only part of him shown.

Matt and Tanya watched the whole procedure. Koning officiated as first Carla, then Dave stood before the one-way glass, and made their identification quickly and positively. Matt saw a dangerous and fanatical man in the Imam. He could have picked him out if he was asked to choose the man you would least like to ride in an elevator with.

As Matt and Tanya escorted Carla and Dave through the halls, back to the parking lot, outside the main lobby they passed several bearded men in dark suits who observed them with undisguised hatred. One took pictures with a cell phone camera. Matt covered Carla with his coat, hoping to conceal her.

They quickly got Carla back to the hospital where she was still being closely monitored for blood counts and any Alpha radiation in her metabolic wastes.

A week passed with Carla showing no adverse signs of radiation poisoning. Her mood and that of Dave and her parents got better each day. Kate had a brief few days of improvement followed by issues with her kidneys and digestive tract. She was given dialysis and put on tube feeding. During this time, an embarrassed FBI agent delivered a subpoena to her room. Kate looked at it with a weak grin. Commenting, "It says—You are commanded to appear...—good luck getting me there." The FBI special agent explained he felt sure that her video would be considered sufficient in lieu of her actual presence.

Carla, Dave, Matt and even Tanya were also each given a one page, fill in the blanks, form AO 110: Subpoena to Testify Before a Grand Jury of the United States District Court at the Theodore Levin U. S. Courthouse on Lafayette, room 1056 (10th floor), in Detroit the next Wednesday. The papers said not to discuss it with each other; the plea for nondisclosure was totally ignored.

There was no word or contact with Assistant U. S. Attorney Koning during this time. The FBI investigators and guards were omnipresent and said he was very busy and would see them in Detroit.

12

Grand Jury

The Levin Courthouse filled the whole block in downtown Detroit. It rose like a gray limestone mountain as Matt walked with Webb. Ahead walked Dave holding Carla's hand, flanked by Karen and Al on the wide sidewalk that led to the entrance their subpoenas and accompanying instructions had told them to use. Also, per the instructions, they had left their cell phones and Al's pistol in the cars.

Webb spoke as they walked, "I don't like not having armed protection—Detroit has the highest crime rate of any large city; also the highest income and property tax in the state. We used to live in Birmingham, Al too, nice place. Driving in here—we passed manufacturing areas that looked like they could be used for zombie movies."

Matt added, "Detroit is bankrupt—I think all their mayors went to jail—it is a perfect example of government mismanagement: corruption, taxing, spending and greed and our federal government and more importantly, the voters, can't seem to learn one thing from it."

They all entered the building, a wide marble floored hall led to a bank of elevators. They went to the tenth floor, the top of the building, and began to look for room 1065. They found a chrome and glass entryway. The glass door labeled, "Grand Jury," opened to a reception area that branched into waiting and meeting rooms. The general impression was of a typical doctor's waiting room. The office and furniture looked out of place in the magnificent Art Deco building. A guard stood outside of the rather plain door which they would learn opened to the actual Grand Jury room.

At the same time Matt was checking out a five month old *Field and Stream*, James Koning—Assistant U. S. Attorney in charge of the grand jury proceedings was watching the group of grand jurors troop into the grand jury room through their private rear entrance. The fluorescent lights were still flickering to their full brilliance as he peeked into the large, marble and dark wood room. Three rows of jury chairs filled one end of the room to his right. Beside the jury entrance door was a desk for a stenographer and recording monitors. A very large oval inlayed wood table with chairs for the prosecutor and his aides dominated the middle of the room, it was placed close before the low oak wood divider that partitioned the panel area. There was a comfortably padded witness chair and several straight backed wooden chairs for support personnel to his left in the back of the room.

The foreperson and assistant foreperson, selected by a federal judge, were seated before the rest of the panels' chairs. Their jobs were to preside over the jury. The foreperson began working with the secretary to call and record the role of jurors. There were 22 instead of the usual 23. The secretary took note and would keep a record in his docket sheets. Note pads were passed to the jurors, they would be collected at breaks, lunch and at the end of the day. The notes were locked up, maintaining the secrecy under which the grand jury operated.

Waiting for the jury to be organized and seated, Koning entered the room and asked the foreperson if the jury was ready and got a favorable nod. He checked the papers that an aide had prepared for him and had marked and sequenced on the table.

An FBI investigator had a large diagram of the crime scene and several more pictures and diagrams mounted on large tack boards, all arranged on an easel now fronted with plain paper. Then he reviewed how he wanted the video presentations ordered and how he would signal one of his assistants who held the clicker that controlled the

DVD machine. A video would show Kate's interrogation on a large flat screen attached to the far wall above the stenographer.

After one more look around the room, he went with an aide to the main door to the hallway. He stepped out and the door was closed again and guarded by an FBI aide.

Outside the jury room was the waiting area and meeting rooms for grand jury witnesses and any lawyers they might have with them. No lawyers other than the prosecutor, his aides and witnesses were allowed to appear before the selected panel of citizens.

Matt and Tanya sat at a small table shared with the two city policemen that had thrown the Imam into the patrol car. Webb, Dave, Carla and Karen were sitting on the other side of the office area. Al was roaming the building looking for old friends. One patrolman asked, "How's the nose?" Matt smiled, touched his still swollen and sensitive nose, and replied it was fine. The nuclear physics instructor walked up to the group. Carla stood, went to him and shook his hand. Recognition slowly came over his face and he hugged her twice.

Then the professor made Carla blush when he whispered, "I didn't recognize you with clothes on."

Koning looked over the group in the waiting area, noted his FBI investigator just walking in, and said, "Good, you're all here. We will start in a few minutes, we will send for you one at a time. I'm sorry you need to be cooling your heals for awhile—but we can't tell what questions might be raised, and the proceedings are private for each witness. I don't think this will take more than a few hours, unless we go to a lunch recess."

Koning went to Carla, "We will try to get you in and out as soon as we can. I understand you need to get back to the hospital today. I'll show Kate's video before you are called—in case there are panel questions that you can answer."

Koning turned to the policemen, "I'll call just the arresting officer in a few minutes."

Satisfied he had his witnesses and presentation materials in readiness, he reentered the now guarded grand jury door.

He watched the jury talking to each other. Most were dressed casually in sweaters and shirts. The majority was women, two men wore suits, one man was old and needed help moving into his seat. They looked serious and expectant. He confirmed the count 22, not the usual 23, but he had enough present to proceed with the grand jury. This was not a trial—there would be no defense attorneys, the object was for him to present enough evidence for the grand jury—by majority vote—to find for a "true bill"—enough evidence to justify a trial, so the defendant could be charged and arrested. The Grand Jury was part of the Fifth Amendment to the U. S. Constitution and unique among all law systems in the world. It placed common people between the powers of the government and the efforts of legal prosecution.

The stenographer announced his equipment was ready and working.

The foreperson announced the panel, "…in session." With no fanfare Koning began. He was asking for an indictment against Imam Ahmed Hussin Saleem Alikhan, also spelled—Ahmad Hussin Salaam Alikhan. The indictment to charge him with seven counts: murder, attempted murder, terrorism by use of a radiological dispersal device, transportation and use of a weapon of mass destruction, attempt to commit mass murder, conspiring to aid terrorists and attempt to commit a terrorist act.

Koning thought as he looked at the list of counts—pausing while copies of the charges were being distributed to the jurors. *I mentioned terrorism three times, radiological device, and mass destruction, when I was strongly advised in two long phone conversations with the Deputy Attorney General to soft pedal those words. Keep the lid on he said, tone down the sensationalism—maybe think in terms of—unregistered destructive devices—conspiracy—grand theft auto. Bull shit, my daughters and I could be in a hospital bed right now, dying like poor Kate.*

Koning watched the jury. They froze in shock as his words and their printed form gained their understanding.

Koning smoothly went into an overview of the evidence he would present. A juror raised his hand—the foreperson recognized the man, who gave his name for the record—the man asked if this was what happened outside Michigan's stadium.

Koning said, "Yes." The jury all seemed to sit straighter—and perhaps think where they or their friends and loved ones were on that Saturday.

A policeman was called, administered an oath by the foreperson and gave his descriptions of the scuffle, the actions of the Imam, the cell phone call from Carla, the shots being fired. A juror asked him a question—an informal departure from a regular trial. He testified for fifteen minutes.

Next the FBI investigator testified. He clinically diagrammed the crime scene. Continuing with pictures and drawings of the model plane, the pile of radioactive dust spilled across the Yukon, which had bullet holes that numbered over sixty and also the stolen motor home with radioactive material packing boxes and a special container and lastly, a diagram of where the three attacking terrorists had fallen. He mentioned two that had tried to escape over an eight foot chain-link fence bordering the golf course, referring back to the original diagram. He testified as to all the names of the fallen and that one from the fence was still alive, but in very critical condition. Almost all the jurors were intimately familiar with the stadium area and the corner of the golf course shown in the diagrams. Two major roads crossed at the corner across from the southern end of the stadium. There was discussion between the jurors about the investigator's information. They had heard about the shootings but no information about a plane, crashed vehicle or chemicals—let alone radioactive material—had become general knowledge. Hearsay is admissible and recorded for the record in a grand jury session. Koning worked to get the session back on his track. He asked the investigator, "Did these men know the Imam?"

The investigator said, "Yes, we have documentation they studied together at the mosque and frequented a particular coffee shop where they engaged in long discussions. The FBI investigator was finally dismissed.

Koning then gave a description of the actions of the terrorists in the park, and on the golf course. He mentioned all the subsequent witnesses he would introduce in good time, and then talked about Kate Wilson. He flashed pictures of her on the screen in battle dress in Iraq and as a student cheering with friends at a football game. He left a zoomed in picture of her exuberant beauty on the screen as he went over her background, a detailed chronology of her actions at the golf course, the consequence of her actions, including the intercepted plane and the shoot out with three terrorists. He ended with the fact that she endangered her life without hesitation and most likely forfeited it to save thousands. Koning emphasized that she had seen the Imam clearly on two occasions: in perpetration for the crime and during the actual crime. She had positively identified him from pictures. Koning then presented on the screen a mug shot of the soon to be defendant. The vivacious beauty and the dower beast comparison had a palpable effect on the jury.

Then Koning filled the screen with Kate's testimony from her bed. For ten minutes her image and words tore at the hearts of everyone. When Kate coughed and fought for air, the jury took deep breaths in sympathy to help the struggling young woman on the screen. Even Koning, thinking of his own daughters, had to clear his throat and fortunately found a handkerchief for his eyes.

Koning thought bitterly, *an indictment is a no-brainer—a lynch mob could be a real possibility.*

When the screen went blank, Koning broke the heavy silence by introducing Carla. She was escorted in and administered the oath. Her positions at the park and during the attack were asked and answered. Koning returned Kate's happy picture to the screen. Carla, remembering what Kate looked like now and her fate, teared up and cried quietly in the witness chair. Carla's youth, beauty, innocence and crushing sadness had several men and women jurors dabbing at their eyes again—they were only separated by ten or twelve feet. Koning asked if anyone wanted a break, no one responded, everyone straightened up and got back to business.

No one interrupted with any questions as Carla described what she saw in the clearing and at the golf course. How she had no doubts as to the Imam being at both locations. She had mentioned using her cell phone and taking pictures with it. No questions came about either. Her rendition was so compelling and pictorial that the jurors accepted it without reservation or retort. Her digital pictures were not mentioned. Koning didn't think they were needed and they were still being processed. After nearly a half hour Carla was dismissed.

Dave was called and took the witness chair. He corroborated the statements by the officer, Kate and Carla, plus offering his individual perspective of actual physical contact with the fanatical man. The white mask was reviewed as a link without going into great detail. Without a defense objection to be overcome, it made a solid impression with the jury. One juror asked about fingerprints or hair on the mask. Koning responded that the mask was cleaned to get any radioactive dust off it, so no hair would be found, and prints were smudged and rendered useless.

The emotional strain and five witnesses took more time than Koning figured on. He suggested that the jury recess for an early lunch; they agreed to return in an hour.

Jim Koning ate with his legal team. Tanya and Matt ate with Webb, Karen and Carla. Carla enjoyed the non-hospital atmosphere and food, but she had to get back to the hospital where they were carefully monitoring for alpha radiation in any material that she would be eliminating.

Matt noticed that Dave and Carla had taken turns talking with the professor, while one or the other was testifying. The banter allowed Webb and Karen to also learn most of the facts that would be in the testimony of Dr. Zamitus and all that the University team had done to save Carla and help Kate and the policeman. All this discussion between witnesses was expressly discouraged by the rules of the subpoena, but there was a guard at the door that did nothing to hush anyone. Matt watched Webb listen carefully, trying to fathom what was in the tough Russian's mind. During lunch Webb announced, "I'm going to thank him personally tomorrow."

After lunch, Carla, admitted she was tired, Al drove her back to the hospital with Dave and her parents.

In the afternoon the jury was pronounced back in session.

The last witness presented was Dr. Zamitus. Koning had the professor give his impressive qualifications. He then had him summarize his actions and those of his staff when they arrived at the crime scene. With some prompting Dr. Zamitus continued to describe the actions of himself and his team with the transportation and decontamination of Carla, the officer and Kate. His testimony gave a chilling account of the deadly material that the Imam was attempting to release over the stadium filled with 100,000 people.

Koning asked the physicist, "How deadly is PO210?"

Dr. Zamitus replied, "PO-210, by weight, may be the most deadly substance on earth. A microgram—a particle the size of a piece of dust—will deliver a fatal dose of radiation. It is a whole scale of magnitude, 250,000 times more deadly than hydrogen cyanide."

Koning asked. "How much radioactive Polonium was in the material that was to be dropped from the model plane?"

Dr. Zamitus looked at some notes and said. "We estimated less than a gram of 210-PO isotope was originally mixed into the filler material in the drum that was to scatter the substance.

Koning interrupted, "How much is a gram?"

Dr. Zamitus thought for a few seconds, "There are 28 grams to an ounce. A dime is about one and three fourth's grams. I'd say the Polonium isotope that was originally mixed had the weight of half a dime. Like I said, it is very deadly stuff."

Koning said, "Thank you, continue."

"Well, if the drum we examined was full nearly to the holes used to disperse the powder when it rotated and under ideal deadly conditions of dispersal and ingestion or inhalation it could have killed over 30 million people. However, the radioactivity was significantly reduced by time; its half life is 138 days. This means it was some months away from its probable origin in a Soviet nuclear reactor. We deduced this by the ratio of the radioactive isotope and the stable lead it degrades into. We also can calculate the ratio of filler to PO 210 by the Alpha radiation per a specific volume of the powder."

Koning, "What would have happened if the powder would have been scattered over the stadium?"

The professor answered, "I have discussed this scenario with several colleagues here and at Michigan State, we can only guess—it is all dose dependent and has many variables. We estimated if the fans initially didn't know the air was contaminated, there could be over ten thousand fatalities in the short term and three times that amount within a year: given the best mobilization and availability of medical care and having the advantage of knowing what was sickening the people. By the way—if we didn't know radioactive material was involved, the death toll could have been double the numbers we gave."

To Koning the jury looked like they all had been dragged through an emotional knothole. They were not just hearing statistics and scientific speculations—he felt that the jury pictured the cheering fans, the pageantry, the clash of athletes, the traditions—and finally the horrifying images of friends and family cruelly dying by the actions of men whose motives were as illogical as their religious tenets.

Koning shuffled some papers, cleaned up his table area, basically to give the jury time to relax for a minute or two. He then made a sum up of the charges and a recap of the evidence previously presented, then he did one more, "show and tell." He opened his black leather briefcase and produced a metal plate with words etched into it. The tired jury jerked to attention at the dynamic finale by the prosecutor.

Koning brought the plaque, encased in a transparent sealed plastic envelope, before the jury. He showed them the encryption on it, then read it, "*Let them feast and enjoy themselves, and let hope beguile them: But they shall know the truth at last. 15.2*"

"This plaque was in the model plane that was designed to scatter deadly radioactive material over 100,000 innocent people. The verse is from the Koran, the holy book of Islam. It links the Imam—an Islamic religious leader with Islamic terrorism. His finger print is on this metal."

Koning asked the panel for an indictment. He said they would now be alone to deliberate in secrecy. The lack of questions or clarification of charges and options available to them left him with the feeling that the deliberation would not take very long.

Koning came out to Matt and said, "We didn't need you and I probably presented more than I needed to get the indictment. I have a worry, and I wanted to share it with you and Mr. Webb. I had hoped he would be out here."

Koning checked his watch, figuring he had some time to kill, he continued, "This grand jury finding will eliminate a preliminary hearing, but as we speak, the FBI evidence and terrorist technique is already being shared with homeland security, and there will be interest from several other government departments. The grand jury proceedings were totally secret for many very good reasons until 9/11. Now I am required to share grand jury terrorism data, including my witness list, with at least a half dozen departments beside my Department of Justice: DHS for sure, and with the radiological aspect—DOE, EPA, NRC, and DOD—also, if it comes from space—NASA. I worry about the defenses' and the terrorists' ability to learn about and to tamper with witnesses. It might be wise, particularly if the trial gets postponed or drags on for months, for any of a large variety of reasons, that you and Carla's father help us guard her well."

Koning thought, *every terrorist attack during the present administration has been down played and prosecution delayed, this will happen here also.*

"As a country, I feel, we have reduced witness security in order to strengthen national security."

He turned to Tanya, who was listening, "Literally for the record you were listed as a possible witness also."

Matt thought a while then asked, "What's happening at the golf course?"

Koning answered, "I'm not sure—the FBI treated it as a crime scene—lots of pictures and measurements. It falls under the FRERP rules—Federal Radiological Emergency Response Plan—basically an incomprehensibly complex flow chart of government agencies—they fight over who is in charge—or is the LFA, leading federal agency. Actually a team from the army, not even listed in the plan, is here now—they are decontaminating and destroying the scene. I'll go over reports this afternoon, but first I want to sign an indictment and bring federal charges against the Imam.

The grand jury door opened—Koning went back in.

The deliberation had taken twenty minutes. The foreperson announced that the finding was unanimous on all counts. The indictment, a "true bill," was issued.

No Crime Scene

Matt and Webb drove by the stadium on their way back from dropping off Carla and Tanya at the hospital where they visited with the ever weakening Kate. Carla had been released to her home for the last week. Karen stayed at the house today, cooking. Dave was studying. Michigan was playing away this Saturday and the stadium area was deserted.

Matt parked his vehicle down the street, nearly a quarter mile from the corner. He and Webb walked back through the north eastern golf course driveway. They got just past the club house and came to a plastic barrier fence. They could see activity where the Yukon had crashed into the terrorist model plane two weeks ago. A flat bed truck was backed into the fairway area, which looked like it had new sod on it. A large gray concrete box dominated the truck's bed. Soldiers dressed in military field uniforms, some carrying instruments resembling metal detectors connected to ear phones and all wearing filter masks were busy sweeping the area, others were dropping branches and occasionally globes they detached from machines that looked like vacuum cleaners into the box. One person operated a pneumatic arm attached to the truck bed that opened and closed the heavy concrete lid.

A soldier with a side arm came to them from the other side of the six foot fence. "There's nothing to see gentlemen. Please move along."

Webb spoke, "What happened to my vehicle? My daughter was in it during the shoot out."

The soldier, paused for a moment, and then replied, "I don't know anything about that, I just keep people out of the area."

Matt could see that the corner area had tarps over the chain linked fencing and was effectively screened it from drive-by view. He and Webb looked for another few minutes, then another soldier came over and stood in front of them.

Webb snorted, "This is useless."

Returning to Matt's SUV they drove off to the nuclear power plant—no longer in production, it held the offices of Dr. Zamitus. They had called ahead and the professor had agreed to meet with them at noon.

Dr. Zamitus met them at the main entrance to the huge four story facility and escorted them through multiple doors and long hallways. He took them to an observation area that overlooked the once blue pool that was the signature of the late 1950's era nuclear technology. He explained they were nearly done with the dismantling of the nuclear facility which had begun in 2003, and it would become class rooms and research labs. He mentioned the University still had one of the world's best nuclear technology schools. Adding that the 14,700 square foot facility would be renovated and actually would add another 5,000 square feet of new research and classroom space.

They finally went into his rather small windowless office. There was scarcely room for his desk and a small couch. Before he had them sit he asked them for their cell phones. He put theirs and his into a heavy cylinder printed with a yellow radiation sign, then put on an equally thick and heavy top, and screwed it down. He then closed the door.

The professor began, "My motive for seeing you today is somewhat selfish, I needed to talk to someone about what I've seen, know and hold in speculation. I know you have many questions and just like me, you get very few answers.

"Initially my group and I were allowed, even asked, to help with the clean up. We had suits, monitoring equipment and radiological hazard techniques honed over many years on much more radioactive materials. We had isolated the radioactive powder material and bagged it. We dug up the relatively small contaminated grass area and put it into sealed containers. We were completing work on the vehicle and model plane when the army took over. They quickly pushed us out of the picture and swore us to secrecy. The army group had liquid filled portable vacuums—perfect for Alpha radiation collection and disposal. They swept, covered and removed the plane and car. The big concrete container was trucked in and all our bags and containers went into it. They have twenty workers—they were organized and competent. But they were not friendly. Everything was done under a cloak of secrecy. They had the area ostensibly cleared in a matter of hours—they didn't take any breaks. That was Monday, two days after the incident. I tried to enter the area yesterday, I was sent away. I believe they have spent the last week checking trees, bushes and any little hiding places for dust particles. They're just doing a final, final check now."

Matt spoke, "The press and TV coverage has been confusing—I saw you interviewed by the local television station and some national people—you made no comments. A spokeswoman for the U.S. Attorney said there was no danger and they were collecting evidence for an ongoing investigation and beyond that she wouldn't comment."

Zamitus replied, "She told me very bluntly not to comment. But did you see and hear the lady reporter from CNN? She asked, "… was it the plan of the armed activists to sprinkle ash from the Brazilian Rain forest over the stadium?" The spokeswomen said, "No comment at this time." The next day our picture was in the paper and the Brazilian ash quote went with it. The day after that the AP wire service ran it as a fact or at least a strong speculation. There we were, six spacemen, in plastic hazardous material suits, our helmets in our hands and the public was led to believe we were handling ash from Brazil."

Webb interjected, "*Credo quia absurdum.*"

Dr. Zamitus looked at Webb, "I believe because it is absurd—Exactly, the public, deprived of the truth, will believe the absurd…"

"There is much more—my staff and I have been reminded several more times that our funding comes from federal sources and federal favor is linked to the public not hearing about terrorism or our adding to the public fear of nuclear material. We just got a $5 million grant to study reactor parts exposed to massive beams of radiation—and projecting these studies to estimate when and where reactors will break down. We are working in conjunction with a working Russian power plant. You don't have to be a government rocket scientist—which we seem not to need any more—or a nuclear physicist to see how the information we produce can be used in arguments to continue the stagnation of the country's nuclear power program. But we need the money and the recognition of getting the grant."

Matt asked, "What are your other concerns?"

The professor held up several local news papers, "There are no reports of Muslim demonstrations—they will take to the street against McDonalds, a movie, or anything their community feels is unfair or prejudicial. There is not one word of their outrage in these local papers. I find this fact very unusual.

"There is a major political lid being put over this whole action."

Matt said, "According to the U.S. Attorney—we talked to him yesterday—the Imam is under federal arrest and will be arraigned next week—the indictment will be made public at that time."

"There is one more thing." said Dr. Zamitus. "I'm being followed and my phones are being monitored. I've seen people following me and I tested line resistance on a neighbor's phone and on mine. Mine reads like a party line. Also, my wife had a man following her—in very plain view.

"I came from Hungry; even as a young man I understood the power of a government to control what people hear and think. I see it happening in this situation and increasingly here—in this country. I'm trying to take the long view of what is happening. If this was a simple action—reaction equation—this attack should have been news all over the world… The Muslim community should be in apoplexy about five of their young men being shot and having their Imam in jail. As a reaction the non-Muslim community would be up in arms against the Muslims. We would have armed patrols forming a community buffer like Northern Ireland in the '60s. Major legislation might follow the interminable congressional investigations. The USA numbers over three hundred million non-Muslims versus two and a half million Muslims inside our boarders, our country would respond to this level of Jihad with strict immigration laws and harsh anti-Islamic actions.

But beyond the hand wringing political response to attacks, I fear what a continuation of 9/11, Fort Hood, Boston Marathon and other major organized plots that target our country's iconic symbols will eventually produce. I finally see a bloody response. Sooner or later many Muslims will die as a natural reaction to the deadly attacks of a few, thousands would be deported. Mosques would be supervised; many closed or maybe even bombed for instructing sedition. The Muslims must either stop Jihad or be vanquished.

"Maybe all the control that is being forced upon us is for a greater good."

Webb raised his hand, like a student, and summed up, "Your speculation is interesting, we should talk more—I have a Russian perspective where harsh actions haven't worked well—but for now the facts are: the crime scene is gone, the terrorists are called activists, the Polonium, bullet riddled SUV, and delivery plane are all somewhere in federal control. The plot to kill tens of thousands has morphed to a green peace operation. And with poor Kate dying, my daughter and her boyfriend will be the only living witnesses against the Imam."

Zamitus said, "I grew up in Budapest, my bedroom window looked up at the Old Buda Castle and I can remember swimming in the Danube as a child, those were good memories. I also remember that Russian repression can be very brutal. Oppression is an incubator for insurgency. I have followed the conflict and terrorists that has come from Chechnya, and I understood why my father and many Hungarians hated Russia. But we are the United States of America, the religious laws and legal practices of this country are neither brutal nor oppressive by any definition. I feel Islam brings trouble with its precepts and its leaders. Sooner or later we must recognize our basic conflict with their ideology."

Matt felt that Zamitus and Webb had more to say but they changed the subject and agreed to meet at Carla's home in three days to continue sharing information. Matt diagrammed directions on a yellow pad. They agreed not to communicate by phone. Webb was very knowledgeable with the security system at Carla's and told Zamitus he felt they would be safe from observation or eavesdropping.

As the meeting was about to end, Webb asked, "May I ask a few questions about Polonium?"

"Certainly, ask away, I've been studying the subject thoroughly for the last several days," replied Zamitus.

Webb held up three of his thick fingers, "One, where would these Muslims get it? Two, how would it get into this country? And three, what might an operation that they were attempting cost?"

Zamitus stood up; going to a book shelf he pulled out a thin document. "Here is a well researched paper on Polonium by one of my former students.

"Take it, I can get another copy.

"You'll see Polonium was discovered and named by Marie and Pierre Curie in 1898. It was found and isolated in very small quantities found in uranium ore. She named it after her native country—Poland. The deadly PO-210 is one of 25 radioactive isotopes of polonium. To answer your first question—where can you get it—I'd guess the best source would be a Soviet nuclear reactor. It has to do with their use of lead-bismuth liquid metal cooling—anyway, that's my opinion. The International Atomic Energy Agency doesn't even run tracking or safeguards on Polonium-210. If I was after the material without publicity or a paper trail, I'd deal with the operators of a nuclear power plant of the Soviet type."

Dr Zamitus picked up a stained tea mug from his desk, saw it was empty and continued, "Question two, bringing in Alpha generating radioactive material is simple—in a test tube, in water and nothing would be detectable. Of course it might bubble and give off a glow. It is a soft semi-metal—it evaporates unless it is in a sealed container. In the form we found it—I'd say it was mixed with the filler material and brought in as about a liter volume of powder. The filler material would control heat and any container would eliminate radiation detection."

Webb broke in, "Would this take specialized skills to assemble and mix?"

Zamitus answered, "Yes, air control and hygiene are areas one would have to know about. Just hand washing and showering along with a filter mask and good rubber gloves would allow a careful and respectful person to handle it with relative safety. Here we use a negative pressure glove box with high performance filters.

"Now as to your question of cost, I've never dealt with black market or illegal transportation of nuclear material. Getting rid of it is more my concern, not obtaining it. I would guess it would be very costly because of the small amounts available and the need for secrecy to obtain and transport it. But I couldn't hazard a guess."

Webb looked at Matt and said, "I know a little about international shipping—I'll look into this question."

Their meeting came to its end.

The professor returned their cell phones, nothing was discussed but all understood the security procedure of isolating the electronic devices and he led them out of the massive building.

14

Legal and Knife Points

James Koning, Assistant U.S. Attorney for the Eastern District of Michigan, closed the file folder that had arrived by special government courier an hour earlier. It came directly from the office of the Deputy U.S. Attorney in Washington D. C. and was marked Confidential and For Your Eyes Only. It was an inch thick with a label reading: George Webb.

Koning was shocked by the nefarious history of a man he had grown to like, along with Webb's wife and daughter. Webb had been a major underworld figure for a quarter century, indicted numerous times, never going to trial, let alone being convicted. The overview pages listed smuggling, multiple counts of various RICO acts: including extortion, arms trafficking and underground economy. Other charges or suspicions included; jury tampering, murder and attempted murder, interstate fraud, bribery, black mail—just to list eight on a crime list that went to a second page. The third page of the summary noted he had been cleared of any and all charges, had won on suits for false arrest and harassment and was presently a citizen in good standing.

The rest of the file contained case summaries and excerpts of court proceedings.

As Koning laid his large hands over the closed file, he wondered how Washington knew so much, so fast, about the father of one of his key witnesses. He wondered who was working with the Muslim community to keep their usual excited nature in check. He now had multiple contacts from the second highest person in the Justice Department. His case, that was so well documented and controlled such moral and legal high ground, seemed to be sliding out of his physical and legal control.

Actions and decisions were being made way above his GS-15 pay grade. He liked his job and was very willing to go along to get along. The decision between a military tribunal and the Federal criminal justice system was an easy one: the military is very slow, costly, has had lots of bad publicity within the U.S. and internationally for holding prisoners without trial, and a sizable percentage of their released prisoners pop up again as active terrorists. The federal system has much better facilities and a much better record for handling terrorists both in and after incarceration. The cost to house a prisoner at Guantanamo for a year exceeded $800,000 and there are 170 of them. Federal prisons average $25,000 per year per inmate and handle over 300 terrorists.

The Imam had been arrested, the initial appearance before a federal judge took only twenty minutes—for a half dozen uncontested reasons—the Syrian accused of terrorism and murder was summarily denied bail. There was a longer discussion about where to detain the man. Local facilities lacked isolation and provided fertile grounds for gatherings and demonstrations due to the large number of Muslims in the area. The judge, previous to the hearing, had entertained several motions: one was where to put the Imam while awaiting trial. Terre Haute, Indiana or Marion, Illinois are federal prison locations, relatively close, both with the ability and experience of housing Islamic prisoners. Marion was 525 miles from Ann Arbor, Terre Haute was 458 miles—a seven hour drive, Terre Houte was chosen. The Imam would become familiar with the corn crops of flat land Indiana over the next many months.

In total time Koning had spent less than an hour in several meetings with the Imam and his legal counsel. The man was defiant, arrogant and spoke only Arabic—just to be troublesome. The Imam's demeanor didn't alter as the list of heinous charges was read to him.

He spoke only two words in English, "Not Guilty."

After the hearing, he was handcuffed and led away by U.S. Marshalls. He would be in isolation with very limited and restricted communication with his lawyers.

As far as Koning was concerned it would be several months before the next steps in the trial proceedings. The Attorney General had 90 days to decide if the death penalty would be pursued. The worsening daily condition of Kate Wilson and the policeman sadly would make a strong murder count. There were also several sick law officers who were exposed to the radioactive dust. Carla seemed fine, but there were still worries about her fluctuating blood counts.

His witnesses did not have to be revealed to the defense until their actual trial testimony began. The grand jury testimony was relatively safe within federal control. The Imam had never seen Carla. Kate would be just a glance at most. He had seen Matt and Dave, and maybe a glimpse of Tanya. He did not know their names or locations.

He had been avoiding Webb and his family until after the Imam's detention was decided and acted upon. He was scheduled to meet with them this afternoon to explain the next steps in the federal court system.

Koning's driver parked the black government SUV in front of the old house. He went up the steps and pushed the old brass door bell. He heard the buzzer and felt the approach of Webb—who opened the door.

The group was soon assembled in the large front room. Carla, Dave, Webb, and Karen more or less circled Koning as he sank into an overstuffed chair that was not new when Truman beat Dewey.

Koning explained all the events to date. Where the Imam was sent, the timetable and level of justice that now rested with the highest law enforcer in the nation. Also, that secrecy and their security was upper most in his thoughts and actions. That was why he had come to them versus calling them into the federal building. He felt they could go about their usual business until the trial began—which could be many months—maybe a year.

He looked at the group—he had expected relief, if not happiness. Instead he saw distrust and incredulity. Webb got up—walked to the mantle over the unused fireplace—he picked up a towel wrapped bundle and brought it to Koning.

As he placed the bundle in Koning's lap, Webb growled, "Don't touch this, just look at what was stuck in our door last night."

Opening the towel he exposed a double edged dagger; its curved 8 inch blade had Arabic script, and Webb said, "So much for your secrecy."

15

Leaks and Sneaks

Al shut the knife-marked door as the FBI men departed. Koning had summoned them to look at the scene and to take the knife that had been pried from the wood as a message to the witnesses in the house.

Koning was apologetic, the FBI agents had been very professional. They had stayed and worked with cameras and questions for a half hour. They seemed to feel that a knife in a door was not worth major crime fighting time. Al's ideas, formed by ten years as a detective on the Detroit Police force, were ignored. Webb said very little other than asking several times, in different ways, where the leak came from that targeted his daughter. Koning had no answers and wouldn't make even a speculation.

Koning and Webb stood on the porch as the FBI vehicles drove away.

There was an offer to park a car and officers in front for their protection. It was refused by Webb. "Why not put a flashing light or neon that reads- Federal Witness lives here. Some interested party already knows where we live and who we are. We need to leave."

Koning said, "Carla and Dave, federal witnesses, can't leave the country. I know you have a home in the Dominican Republic."

Webb added, "And a remote cabin in Canada- both would be a lot safer than here."

Koning shook his head, "Can't leave the U.S. I know your history and record, I'm sure you can protect your daughter very professionally. This is a job for the U.S. Marshalls and the FBI- I need to talk to some people about our next move, our options."

Webb broke in, "You make your talk, and we'll make some plans. I'll call you tomorrow at your office. Don't assume your line is clean. If we decide on something I'll meet you or someone you trust- person-to-person."

Koning looked at Webb; he saw he had lost the battle of wills and skills in matters of being clandestine. He left Webb on the porch.

Webb went into the house, got Matt and Al and led them through the big kitchen where Carla and her mother were making supper, he poured a glass of wine, Matt and Al grabbed beers and the men went down the old squeaky wooden stairs to the basement.

In the basement was the neat, fluorescent lit, security setup of black boxes, monitors and computers. Al had already accessed the recorder that had the infrared images of the knife sticking person that had sneaked onto their porch. The time date listed at the bottom of the screen read- 2:13 am, that morning. The black and white video could show action or be broken to individual frames.

Matt had assumed Al or Webb would have shown the FBI this digital recording. The investigators had commented about the cameras around the building. Just before Matt began to tell them about the fancy security built around Carla, Webb sadly announced that the cameras were not working because they were run by Kate who, they all knew, is in the hospital. In reality the system was motion activated, totally automated, each black box would record over 400 hours, if unattended then it recorded over itself. There were four banks of recording boxes, each selectively accessed by a large screen monitor. There were even battery backups to counter any electrical issues.

Webb answered Matt's unasked question, "I have found it advisable to not trust the government, most are ass covering bureaucrats who worry about fixing blame much more than fixing a problem. Koning and the FBI will spend many more hours documenting their actions than probing for leaks in the system.

"If we had shown this set up to them it would all be gone by now-carted away: the same as Carla's cell phone with its pictures. We will not make that type of mistake again. I've never been on this side of the legal fence before. It is all barbed wire and we can't trust anyone.

"We are going to make copies of the intruder video and leave all this for the FBI to eventually find when they come looking for us."

Matt asked, "We are going?"

Webb, watching Al selectively copying to a file then to a storage cube, said, "If I can get the ladies' cooperation, we're out of here after we do the supper dishes. Al will stay a while and be our liaison with Koning. Also, he may have some other jobs we need done."

Matt said, "Carla won't want to leave Kate. She still needs regular blood tests, and there's Dave and she's concerned about her classes too."

Webb replied, "Kate is almost dead, Carla needs to stay alive. Dave will understand. Survival calls for hard and sometimes fast decisions. We're all going to your home Matt. We can do a good job of hiding and protecting her up there. I hope you got some venison left from last year."

Matt took in breath and prepared to say something intelligent.

Webb instantly changed the interest and subject as the picture of the person on the porch flicked by on the monitor screen, "Stop… play that back, now, frame by frame. Freeze frame, save each one as a photograph, highest resolution, and print them and copy them."

Al did as he was bidden. The images showed an average sized man, dark featured, no beard, long thick hair, ethnically inconclusive, in a long opened stadium coat with the collar up. The camera angle came from above and from his left. He used his right hand to draw the knife from his waist band. He searched in the dark with a gloved hand for a suitable wooden area on the door, then he viciously slammed the knife into the hard wood.

"There," Webb called out. "What do you see?"

Al cropped the picture and then zoomed in, finally touching the screen showing part of the grainy gray and white image, the man's extended arms exposed his wrists above the coat sleeves, "That's a watch on the left wrist and his right wrist has a bracelet of some kind."

Webb took the mouse and tried to get a better look, "This is interesting, jewelry on a Muslim man. I wish we had color to see if his watch or bracelet were gold. This man may not be a Muslim."

Al said, "Or a very smart Muslim that knew he might be recorded or it is a medical alert thing."

Matt looked closely at the man in the blow up and said, "Why would anyone do this? Maybe they want us to run: why a knife, why not a bomb or a Chicago style machine gunning or maybe a demonstration with fifty yelling fanatics on the lawn?"

Al answered, "Terrorists terrorize. The point was made, literally driven home, that someone or some group knows who and where we are. And that knife wasn't from the boy scouts. It had no finger prints on it I could find, it had been sharpened by someone who knew their business. Wear marks indicating it came from a metal sheath- another eastern tradition. It wasn't old or really very expensive. Probably hand made by some third world craftsman."

Webb finished his wine and said, "Let's wrap up here, leave it perfect, put the passwords where they can be easily found. Let's remember to aim the camera on the garage side away from our exit route. I expect supper is nearly ready."

Scram

The supper was strained and it wasn't the food. Webb led up to his decision over the course of the meal. Each course brought his summation of the facts that concluded with coffee and the pronouncement that they had to leave for their own safety.

Carla, bravely holding back tears, finally said, "Father, I'm not afraid of staying here. Kate and Dave are here, so are my classes. I feel fine. I don't want to hide."

Webb let her words expand in the room for some time, a sign he was listening and respectful of her point of view. No one said a word, then Webb spoke, "I know you are brave and there are many very compelling reasons to stay here—but that knife could be in your ribs or your stomach and you'd never see it coming in a classroom or in a crowded hallway."

Webb made a short jabbing motion as if holding a knife.

"I can't defend you effectively here unless you stay at home all the time."

Carla unconsciously put her hands over her stomach as a reaction to the knifing depiction.

Webb continued, "I'm more worried that the FBI may take decisions away from us and spirit you away. Your mother and I couldn't take that. Al and I both fear this will be the action that the prosecutor will propose in the next few days. You would be experiencing all the worst of the issues you brought up: no support to Kate, no contact with Dave, no classes. Add to that no parents, no Tanya and Matt."

Al, not to be left out of the argument, added, "And you would be at the mercy of people you don't know and we don't trust. If you will allow your father to outline his plan, you'll see it makes good sense."

Carla looked helpless and frightened—two very uncharacteristic emotions for her. She got up from the table, looked at everyone seated, saying, "I've brought danger to everyone. I'll pack." As she turned, Tanya, seated beside Carla, rose also and escorted her toward the bed rooms, saying, "We will be together. You will be safe and may be able to communicate somehow with Kate and Dave. Hopefully all this will be only for a short time."

Webb spoke as they left, "Take warm rough clothes, good for the woods, one bag only. We'll get more clothes and boots later.

"We need to be gone before midnight. We'll drive all night. I want to be across the Mackinac Bridge before anyone knows we're gone. Al will stay here, making it look like there is a house full. He will meet with Koning, help the FBI if they show interest, and I have several more missions for him in the next week or so."

Karen started to clear the table, rinse and stack the plates and utensils in the dishwasher. Matt helped.

Webb finished his coffee, brought the cup to the counter and said, "Right now, Al and I will take a walk around the block, make some plans while checking for people that might be watching us."

While the old dishwasher rumbled, rattled and swished, Matt and Tanya packed and took their luggage to their vehicle, now parked in the garage. They drove out and gassed up. When they returned they also made several extra turns, watching for any vehicle that might be following them. Matt backed into the garage, to speed their departure by eliminating a back out, stop and go maneuver as they left: less lights and engine sounds.

Webb and Al returned with a negative report about their being watched. They went to their rooms to pack.

Al had slept in Kate's room the last two nights. He was zipping up his rolling luggage when Carla entered the room. Carla looked around the room, picked up and replaced a picture, then a hand mirror, bringing a flood of memories about her friend and bodyguard. She had envelopes in her hand.

Giving one envelope to Al she said, "This is for Kate, please read it to her even if she's in a coma, and give it to her parents. Tell them I will talk to them when I can. Let them take anything they want from this room, plus Kate's clothes here and in the guestroom closet."

Al took the envelope, putting it in his jacket's inside pocket, "Do I need to screen this to make sure you aren't giving away where you are going?"

"It's not sealed, because I figured you would read it. Kate would have read it under the same circumstances if she was delivering it to you in the hospital."

Carla gave Al the other envelope she carried, "This is for Dave, and I've put his name and phone number on the outside. Please get it to him, he will be upset, tell him about the logic behind our action. Tell him I had to leave my new cell phone with you. Tell him to be careful too. The letter sends all my love. We are strong enough to get through this."

Al took the envelope. Carla left to lug her bag to the back door.

By 11 PM the SUV was ready to pull out, the luggage easily fitting in the large back area. Karen thought to bring pillows and also a soft sided cooler of sodas and sandwiches. The men in the front seats, Karen and Carla in the back seats, watched Matt fumble with the garage door opener.

Matt pushed one of the smaller of the three areas on the opener, he heard a click above him, then he pushed the large section and the door went up, no light went on. He drove out of the garage. Pushed the big button again and closed the garage door. Sliding down his window he dropped the opener on the grass.

As he raised his window he said, "It took me many years to figure out what the three parts to this style of garage door opener did. Al will find the opener in the daylight.

As they pulled away they could see Al's shadow in the window moving around and unpacking in the main bedroom of the well lit home.

Webb adjusted the Winchester 12gauge pump shot gun with a pistol grip stock to give him more leg room. He commented, "Kate had this under her bed, always the bodyguard. I can't think of any sound that will petrify an intruder more than a pump shotgun being racked behind him in a dark room."

At the mention of Kate, Carla stared out the window, her mother took her hand.

Matt soon had them on Interstate 75, north bound.

17

Al at Work

Al slept in the large master bedroom. He was up with the pale fall dawn. After making a pot of coffee and spooning down some milk and cereal, he started on his first assignment of the day—contacting prosecutor Koning.

He refilled his cup at the counter and returned to the kitchen table where he looked at three cell phones. He took a roll of masking tape from the kitchen junk drawer and labeled each phone—Webb, Karen and Carla adding their security numbers and their individual phone numbers taken from a notebook he carried.

He then punched up the utilities application on Karen's iPhone. Webb had recorded several messages for Koning on voice memos. Al practiced selecting the labeled recordings and playing each of them. The voice memo application showed recording time and each was labeled with its content and intended use. The response to the start and stop play function worked instantly. As the message played the screen showed a time line, easily allowing Al to anticipate interactive pauses and to select various messages. The audio quality was also impressive.

The application was equal to studio recording and play techniques, the digital technology had no start or stop sound distortion.

Satisfied he could make the technology perform as he and Webb wished, he punched in Koning's number that he read from the prosecutor's card. He got a secretary, explaining he was calling on behalf of Mr. Webb who wished to speak to Attorney Koning—who was expecting his call this morning.

Koning finally came on the line, Al said, "He's on now," and paused as if he was handing the phone to Webb. Al tapped the 1st recording and Webb's voice said hello and paused, Al stopped the recording until Koning answered and paused, then Al started the recording— Webb's message explained his concern for security and that he was going to move Carla, and that Al would be his liaison with Koning. The anticipated objection came from Koning along with the fact they were thinking of putting Carla into the witness security program and Webb should not hide a federal witness. Al played message two—Webb saying he wasn't going to argue with Koning or risk his daughter to government care. Koning responded, then Al played a message that said, "I hear you, but I've got to think about that." Then Koning listed several areas where information about Carla could have gotten circulated—the grand Jury, at the hospital, student friends, Kate's parents and more. Message three had Webb interrupting, "Listen, we will be leaving, Al will stay and work with you and your people. I promise to produce Carla for a trial. I really don't feel like discussing this anymore on a cell phone. Here's Al to talk with you about where you two can meet."

Al came back on the cell phone, Koning was sputtering—an Assistant U.S. Attorney is not used to be summarily dismissed. Al finally broke into Koning's threats and warnings, saying, "Sir, I'm a former sworn officer, decorated many times, you can find my record, I will be a solid and trustworthy link for you. If you try to arrest me you will be forfeiting your only connection to your witness."

Al gave his cell phone number and didn't wait for further comments.

Al thought, *Koning will have the FBI here in less than an hour.*

Al next took the three cell phones, looked for and found the garage door opener he knew Matt would have thrown on the grass, got into his rental vehicle and headed toward the largest RV dealer in the Detroit area. Koning called him three times during the half hour drive. Al never answered him.

Al and Webb had already selected and signed up for a three-year-old Holiday Rambler Ambassador 38PDQ RV. Nearly 40 feet long, like new, three slide outs and most importantly it would work in cold, freezing conditions and it had satellite phone capability that Webb had requested as part of the deal. The dealer technicians were doing the final dish installation and testing. Al left his personal luggage, his note pad and the cell phones in the motor home which was in the final stages of being road ready. He said he would be picking up the unit the next day. All the financial dealings had been electronically conducted by Webb's bankers from Gibraltar. Before he left the RV dealership Al made a cell phone call from Webb's phone to the car rental company arranging for them to pick up their vehicle at the dealership when he called them late the next day. He agreed also to have them add gas to the changes going to Webb's credit card on file with the rental company.

Then Al went to the hospital to visit Kate. He had been to her floor several times and was accepted as an extension of her family.

Kate was in a terminal coma. She was jaundiced from liver failure; her breathing was synchronized with the clicks from the heart/lung machine. Her parents were pitiful and it took all of Al's professional toughness to keep from falling into their morass of despair. He gave them the letter from Carla after he read it to Kate's inert form. The letter covered the love that Carla had for Kate. How they had so many wonderful times together, how much Kate's discipline and maturity had helped Carla. How she will always be a hero to Carla and that there is no greater love than to lay down your life for a friend. Al was just mouthing the words toward the end of the message—sounds were not coming out.

Al finally left the hospital—learning Kate's life could end any moment. He told Kate's parents that Webb would pay for all the hospital and funeral expenses and regrettably that he couldn't be at any services because of the need to protect his daughter. He told them to contact him with their needs and gave them his cell phone number. He drove back to the house, drained of emotion by several gallons.

At the house were three government vehicles. He took several deep breaths, put his pistol and its clip holster into the glove box and went inside.

The door was open; he had left it purposely unlocked. There were multiple FBI people inside, each identified by badges held by neck chains. Two uniformed city police were rubber necking from the driveway.

One FBI man came to him with a warrant in hand. He said, "I take it you're Webb's man. We have searched the house, no Carla, no friggin Webb, we have found recording devices in the basement, we found the passwords and are now looking up the record of the night the person put the knife in the door. Why didn't you tell us you have a video record of the incident? Withholding evidence is a crime. Lying to an officer is a crime. An ex cop working for a Russian gangster makes you a scum bag."

Al took a deep breath and calmly replied, "We didn't know how to run the stuff—it was Kate's system. I'm impressed and glad you boys are smart enough to make it work. Did you get anything off it?"

"We'll let you know—we're going to take all the equipment back with us."

Al looked at the warrant, "This doesn't say anything about taking personnel property—specifically video recording equipment and computers. I think you should leave everything alone until a judge signs the correct warrant. This limits you to looking on the property for Carla Webb."

The FBI guy moved into Al's personal space and looking up from a six inch height disadvantage said aggressively, "You know we can get a new warrant. Are you going to be difficult? We don't like difficult."

Al shrugged, "You represent the law, you should respect what you represent. I'm glad you can make the surveillance system work and I hope it helps find who threatened us, but that's expensive equipment and you can't just cart it away. I represent Mr. Webb and he paid for that equipment—just like he paid for the SUV that was shot up and has now disappeared and the insurance company can't even see it to work out a payment. Also, Carla is out a $400 cell phone."

Al pushed past the FBI man and went down to the basement. One man was at the keyboard, two men over his shoulder, they were watching the night visitor put the knife in the door. They didn't notice Al until he said, "That's a great picture of the man."

The FBI men turned on Al like alpha male wolves on a beta cub. They demanded to know who he was and why he was in the house. Al patiently showed his ID, including the Detroit retired law enforcement officer card. He explained he was Webb's assistant and had a notarized letter from Webb to act in his behalf regarding the house and property.

After the men viewed his IDs Al spoke, "You are welcome to work with this equipment, but you can't take anything away with you without a warrant. That includes the SD cards in the black boxes—in case you think I don't know this technology.

"I want you to leave now. When and if you come back, I want to see laws being obeyed and a level of respect for a citizen. And if you don't leave—because you have exceeded the warrant that got you in here—I'll go to the local officers who, I'm willing to bet, will be very happy to throw your arrogant federal asses out of this house. Now get up and get!"

No one moved, Al took out his cell phone, he punched 911. "I'm going to report trespassing, attempted theft, searching without a warrant and I'll name you all for the public record."

The men got up, Al stopped his call.

Al escorted everyone out. On the porch the man that presented the warrant still had a head of steam and got in Al's face, "You can win a round, but we will win the fight."

Al replied, "You're right, it's hard to beat the government, you run on our money, make your own rules and never read the constitution. I would have worked with you happily if you hadn't tried to run over me and called me scum. You get off the property too. I'm going to talk to the local police and let them know how pushy you are. When I served, we never liked the FBI, I bet it hasn't changed. Tell Koning we are not pleased."

Just then Al's cell phone chimed, it was Koning, "Speak of the devil, I am just saying good bye to your FBI storm troopers who were given a warrant for Carla and tried to expand it to take property. I would have helped but I don't like to be pushed around. Tell them to come back tomorrow and they are welcome to the pictures of the man that put the knife in the door."

Koning replied, "You are breaking federal laws and I intend to make sure you are held to account for your actions."

Al said, "We aren't messing up this investigation. You somehow gave away information that endangered your best witness. And now you are threatening the people who most want to help you make your case. Instead of understanding this, you are being demanding and bullying.

"I've just come from Kate's room, she was brave and competent, she gave her life to stop a terrorist attack. She very likely saved your life. She will probably be dead before morning. Then I come home to find your people all over the house, they called me criminal scum. They felt they were too good for due process. We've done nothing but cooperate until you or your system gave away our names and location. Webb said we will still help you punish the Imam. You should focus on terrorists not on alienating us. We keep our word. When you need Carla she will be there. Keep in touch."

Al ended the call.

18

More Al

Al slept later than usual for him, the house was unnervingly quiet, the only noises were the intermittent whish of the heater fan and the occasional noise of the refrigerator compressor.

During his breakfast he had made a list of to-dos for the day, it and the day would be a long one. He had just a fresh shirt and underwear and his Dopp kit in the house. After a shower and dressing, he put the kit, a few towels, sheets and blankets into a plastic garbage bag and put it by the back door. He went through the refrigerator and put foods that he could take to the RV—like breads, eggs and onions into a cardboard box, remaining items that would eventually spoil he either put into the freezer or into the outside garbage can. After turning down the house heat, he then printed a note to the FBI and attached a house key and taped both outside the front door.

The note gave the FBI permission to enter and suggested they take the SD cards from the surveillance equipment instead of carrying everything up the steps. He said the key would mean they wouldn't need to break the door in. He asked they lock up when they left and to please put the key back through the mail slot.

Al next took his cell phone and photographed every room and the security system for the record in case the FBI people trashed the place. Although he knew complaining to the government was generally useless and pointless.

Al left the house a little after 9:00 in the morning. Worried that the FBI would be there early, he wanted to be gone in case they had an arrest warrant for him. Even without an arrest he wanted to avoid the hassle of dealing with federal law enforcement. Also, he wasn't sure he could keep his hands off the little shit that kept getting in his face.

He would use the next few hours to visit old friends in Birmingham, including returning the pistol he had borrowed from his former police partner. He had a noon appointment at a security firm. There was a long list of equipment he was to obtain and get instructions on how to set it up. His credit card would take a major hit. Next was Wal-Mart where he bought a coffee maker, a toaster, some essentials like flatware, a two quart sauce pan and a small frying pan and most importantly—eight cell phones. Back in the car, he freed the phones from their very stubborn plastic packaging, labeling them 1 through 8, recording their numbers and then he drove to Dave's apartment. Dave was home and Al explained that Carla was being hidden by Webb and she would call him on these phones. He was to follow the activation instructions, never call out on them and after each call from Carla he was to destroy and dispose of that phone. Al reminded Dave to be careful of what he said on the phone. Dave wasn't happy but Al didn't stay to listen to his arguments. He just warned Dave to be careful, stay around his friends and be wary of strangers. After that he had a few groceries to buy before he went to the motor home dealership. His list of jobs for the day was nearly complete when he arrived at the motor home dealership. Webb had previously taken care of the negotiations and shot the final deal— Al carried Webb's cashier's check to complete the purchase. All the paperwork: Michigan license applied for (LAF) for the back window, temporary title, and bill of sale were either ready or being quickly prepared or attached. He gave the rental car key to the dealership secretary; his next assignment would be to drive to Canada. He was glad he didn't have to pilot the monster forty foot diesel vehicle through any more traffic than he had to.

Four o'clock in the afternoon found Al high in the plush and comfortable driver's seat of the moving palace that was a 2006 Holiday Rambler Ambassador 38PDQ, in a traffic jam that went a mile ahead and some miles behind. He wanted to avoid the late afternoon traffic at the Canadian border but the people at the dealership were frustratingly thorough. The operation of the newly installed satellite phone took an hour of paper work and instruction. The steps for winterization and cold weather camping took an hour. Every switch, tank, jack, leveler, slide out, entertainment center, washer/dryer and multiple capabilities of the driving instrumentation was covered in detail. Every time Al tried to cut to the chase of an instruction—they started over.

Al felt that Karen would approve of Webb's rather quick decision to bring another bed room to Matt's home and an even quicker pick of a six figure used motor home. The unit had been very well taken care of and had only been on the lot for a few weeks. It had an upgraded Garmin and the Cummins 330 Diesel looked clean as new. The slow moving line of vehicles crossing into Canada allowed Al to program the GPS unit and play with some of its functions. The stereo unit was impressive. Al also had a screen view out the back from a TV camera which he could adjust up and down. He passed the time inspecting the switches and dials that surrounded the driver's seat.

After an hour Al came to the border. The U.S. side went quickly with his declaration and a wave through. Al wasn't too worried that the long arm of the federal judicial system could have moved fast enough to catch him, but it was still a relief when he drove over the Ambassador Bridge. Al figured they might still be having fun searching or trashing the house.

The Canadian inspection was far from easy, fast or cursory. He was ordered to a parking area. A uniformed lady came on board and started inspecting every nook and cranny. Then Al was called outside by a man and had to open every storage bay and the several plastic boxes that held the few accessories that came with the unit and two of the Wal-Mart kitchen purchases. Al asked what were they looking for and was told weapons and liquor. His chatty disclosure that he just bought the rig was totally ignored by the all business Canadians. Total inspection time was a few minutes under an hour. It was dark when Al pulled away from the lights of the border inspection complex.

Al found the light switches and headed east on the Macdonald-Cartier Freeway—Canada 401. He had topped off the half filled 100 gallon fuel tank in Detroit. Paying cash, he got $1.87 back from two crisp hundred dollar bills. He was instructed not to use his credit card; it would give away too much information to an interested party. He was told he would get about 7 mpg, so he had a 700 mile cruising range—500 miles before he needed to look for diesel. So he set the cruise control for 60 mph, 90 kph, and tried not to be overly worried about controlling the 33,000 pound monster he was driving. Happily the Garmin knew there was a Manitoulin Island and gave a color coded map with distance and time: 907 km, 9 hours 12 minutes. The route was easy due to the lack of choices offered by the sparse Canadian highway system. He would stay on 401 to 407 to 400 or the TransCanada Highway all the way to the Espanola exit onto Highway 6 that went down to the island.

Al would get fuel, coffee and donuts somewhere on the way. He wasn't going to rest until the rig was parked by Webb's beautiful cabin. There was only light traffic on the clear and dry highway. He would stop once to make calls on Webb's cell phone with a few more recorded messages. They would serve to confuse any cell phone traces that might be in effect.

Once safely on Manitoulin Island he would supervise the building of a hidden compartment to facilitate the smuggling of weapons south across the border when he drove to Matt's home. He had some ideas for a false back compartment: the large storage area above the queen sized bed looked good, under the bed or couches were too obvious, a neat little tool area on the steps was too small. He had a local cabinet making artisan available with tools and a variety of woods and stains. The man was well paid and kept his mouth shut. The hiding area would be foam rubber filled around the weapons, the paneling would be perfectly joined, a thin layer of copper foil and paper would mask metal and penetrating radar detection. Some blankets, towels and pillows in front of the false back would complete the desired effect.

Gliding down the road, looking through a huge picture window from such an elevated position with almost no vibration, wind or engine noise made driving seem detached. Al forced himself to concentrate on the moment and to stay alert.

19

At Camp

The Yukon crunched over a driveway covered with leaves and needles as it pulled into the garage at Matt's Upper Peninsula cabin at 4:30 am. Five tired passengers, after nearly five hours and 330 miles in the vehicle, stepped into the flickering lights that changed from bluish to pink to bright white as energy saving technology went on for the first time in two weeks in a cool room. They were all heading for the restrooms.

On the drive up, Matt had pulled off I-75 only once, at the second Gaylord exit, fifty miles south of the bridge. Finding an all night station, they had used the facilities and briefly stretched their legs. While Matt and Webb were gassing up, the ladies got busy buying milk, eggs, juice and bread. Carla complained of being car sick in the back seat, so she had moved up to the larger front passenger seat. Webb then moved back and crowded the ladies he shared the space with. Tanya and Karen took turns sitting in the middle—on a less comfortable area between the larger back seats for the last hour and a half.

In the house, Matt quickly turned up the floor and water boiler thermostats; he also lit a fire in the glass enclosed fireplace that dominated the wall between the main room and the master bed room. Tanya asked if anyone was hungry, no one answered. They all were carrying their bags to the two available upstairs bedrooms. Carla went to the smaller bedroom and closed the door. Karen and Webb made themselves comfortable in the larger guest bedroom.

Tanya sensed Carla's dark mood and busied herself with heating some milk for cocoa and opening a box of oatmeal cookies she had in the pantry. When the milk was heated, she added the brown powder and mixed it. Then she made up a tray with a large mug of steaming cocoa and a plate of cookies and carried it up to Carla.

Carla was just coming out of the upstairs bathroom, dressed in her night gown. Tanya led her into the small bedroom and put the tray on the table by the bed. Carla sat on the bed and seemed grateful for the cookies and the hot drink.

After a nibble of cookie and a careful sip of the steaming cocoa, Carla said, "I'm off my feed. I feel jumpy and sad at the same time. This tastes good, thank you. I miss Dave and I wanted to be with Kate even if she didn't know I was there. I feel so bad for her folks."

Tanya took a cookie too, "You did all you could for her. If Kate knew all that was going to happen, she would have done what she did anyway. Running away from what she felt was her duty would have destroyed her as surely as the radiation—just slower. Your staying alive is the best tribute to Kate."

Carla finished her cocoa and got under the covers. Tanya gave her a kiss on the forehead and took the tray away, closing the door as she left.

Matt was in the bedroom when Tanya came in to get ready for bed. Matt had done all the driving and was tired. He had a glass of milk half drunk.

Tanya said, "Webb sure has things planned out. The motor home Al's bringing isn't really necessary but it will make sleeping arrangements easier. Poor Al won't have to be on the couch. We're going to need more food in the house."

Matt finished the milk, "You were all sleeping while Webb and I talked—the motor home is more than a bedroom, he's bringing in equipment and weapons. Carla will be able to talk with Dave. We will have monitoring equipment, so hopefully, no one can sneak up on us. The satellite dish will allow calls that can't be easily traced, there will be cell phones that Dave will have and use once. According to Webb, the NSA, FBI or CIA can, with some effort, find us but it isn't likely Islamic terrorists have the necessary technology. And we will be well armed—if I know Webb and Al."

Tanya added, "All this is scary. It means if people come after Carla they are either from our government or they are Muslims with help or information from our government. That's a lot of potential enemies."

Matt thought about Tanya's words while he turned off the lights and snuggled up to her. The light from the fireplace gave a flickering warm red glow to the room.

Matt whispered, "I'm glad to be home with you, in this bed. We'll take care of everybody and try to get people's minds off the hell we've been through. I worry about Carla. She feels guilty for being alive. We've got to help her get past this and on with her life."

Matt felt Tanya relax and begin her breathing rhythm of sleep. He smelled her hair and slowly pulled his arm from under her pillow, then he found his own favorite sleep position. As he closed his eyes he noticed the sky he could see through his east window was getting lighter.

Prosecutor Problems

James Koning had dry mouth and acid stomach. He looked at the eight people gathered in his meeting room. He looked at the pictures spread out on the table. Each person had a laptop computer on the table; several also had yellow legal pads. All eyes were looking at him. He took a sip of water from a plastic bottle and picked up a grainy picture, "Who is this person? How did he know where Carla Webb lived? Who leaked her name and address?

"We've spent three days, and between you and your agents five hundred hours have gone into the investigation and questioning of every grand juror, every nurse and doctor that even knew Ms. Webb, let alone where she lived. We grilled Mr. Adams for four hours- nothing. I've personally talked to every person that had access to the Patriot Act reports I forwarded. No one had an address more specific than she is a student at the University of Michigan. I personally supervised the redaction of the grand jury records to eliminate noncritical witness information including full names and all specific addresses. I had a fear of this type of witness attack, and my fear was realized."

A man across the table raised his hand, "We have a list of twenty Muslims in high administrative positions many in Homeland Security. Homeland Security was sent the grand jury information and witness lists. It wouldn't take a genius to contact the University with their government credentials and get Ms. Webb's address. Also, for what it's worth, the assistant secretary of Homeland Security has the same last name as our defendant."

Koning responded, "Ok, check with the University, see if anyone had gone after any of Ms Webb's records."

Another man spoke up, "What about the Hunters? They have been involved in some major escapades with Webb. Mrs. Hunter- then Tanya Vega- was tried for drug possession as a student. Their activity with the DEA is sealed, but could mean they know their way around the edges of the law. They have come into seven figures of money in the last few years. He is a retired teacher and she hasn't had a job since leaving her father's marina business."

Koning said, "They were in the house during the knife incident. And Tanya is very close to Carla and the Webbs. But follow up more on them anyway. There may be some rivalries or issues we are missing.

"Anything on the knife man?"

The only woman in the room spoke, "We've done all we can on the pictures. The infrared and slow camera speed makes a blowup difficult, the facial recognition is inconclusive. We have determined the person is a Caucasian man, 25 to 30 years of age, dark hair, 5 foot 10 or 11, no distinguishing marks, 165 to 175 pounds, middle European ethnic background. The knife was made in India, common, imported by the thousands; you can buy it at a Pier One Imports for $35 in a fancy hammered metal sheath. It was sharpened on a fine grinding wheel by a right handed person."

A man interrupted, "What kind of after shave did the grinder use?"

The woman continued, "We know the oil used on the blade and that the inexpensive gloves were cow hide, tanned black and new. That's all.

"Oh, the equipment in the house was top of the line, current technology and professionally installed and operated. I couldn't have set up a better system with commercially available equipment. Ms Wilson, the bodyguard was very competent. Mr. Webb was taking good care of his daughter."

Koning spoke, "Kate Wilson died two days ago.

"Let's dedicate our time and energy to getting this case to trial and winning. I want good protection and supervision on Dave Adams, monitor all his communication for leads to Carla. Our two best witnesses are gone- Kate is dead and Carla is missing. Adams is important but not key. I want you to focus on convicting Imam Alikhan; I don't want Carla Webb's disappearance to dilute our efforts that are already challenging enough. I'm upset enough for all of us about Webb taking his daughter away; however, I can understand his concern and mistrust of our system. I'm sure he will contact us soon. At least I hope so. The knife incident is probably a dry hole unless we get more information or the man himself comes to our attention."

Another man put Carla's cell phone incased in a transparent evidence bag on the table and spoke, "We have the pictures of the Imam, some are fairly clear."

Koning picked up a folder, opened it and referred to several 5x7 pictures, "These are useful, but without Carla's testimony we can be accused of digital manipulation."

Another man added, "We also have the Imam prints in the motor home and on the chrome ladder going to the roof."

Koning continued, "Gentlemen and lady, we have a serious challenge to win what should have been an easy conviction. Unlike many Islamic terrorists that freely admit they are jihadists and proud of it- our Imam Alikhan denies everything and all involvement in the plot or actions. His lawyers are bombarding our office with motions and complaints: from no Miranda to unusual punishment because of food and worship issues. He has an explanation for everything, at least for the actions they feel we will charge. We will have trouble introducing Kate's video testimony before a jury.

"We have been instructed to limit the use of Islamic terms to avoid inflaming the Muslim community. For example a jihadist should be called an extremist. You all have those memos- read them over and be careful what you say. Better yet, don't say anything for publication."

Koning dismissed the meeting and called two investigators into his office.

In his office he addressed his men, "Check with the cell phone surveillance geeks, they have flagged all the phones of the people in

Carla's house, also Dave Adams. Get a bug into Dave's apartment with or without a judge's signature. We have a fleeing witness in a capital case, a possible kidnapping, and several charges of violating a federal order- just do whatever it takes to locate Webb and his daughter. Use my name and authority- just tell me what I'm agreeing to before I get a phone call. Don't let it get out that we lost our best witness."

The men left Koning's office. He sat down and stared out the window.

21

At the Quarry

Al sounded the twin-tone air horn directed at the red pickup truck that faced him and blocked the one and only road into Matt's 265-acre property. The road was narrow and absolutely straight for a half mile and was once part of a railroad bed used eighty years before when steam engines were the iron horses of the long abandoned limestone quarry.

Matt got out from behind the wheel of the truck and walked up to the door of the monster motor home. Al pushed a button and the door hissed opened. Matt smiled and said, "Bout time you got here. We've been cutting trees and trimming brush so you could get this bus in without ripping off your big shiny mirrors and the expensive new satellite dish. These are my good buddies—Dick and Billy—they did the cutting, sawing and snipping, I drove their truck. They run on beer, about a can every fifty to hundred yards. We opened up the road to at least eight feet wide and fourteen feet high. Can you back up a little so we can get turned around?"

Al looked at his rear viewing TV. It was only twenty yards back to the paved highway. He said, "I can go straight backwards, but I don't want to hang my ass across the road too long. This rig is really big."

Al closed the door and the motor home moved backwards. Matt followed and turned around as soon as there was space. He then began escorting Al to the house that was nearly a mile away down the narrow dirt road. Dick and Billy sat on the edge of the truckbed drinking beer they took from a red and white cooler.

At the house everyone came out to see the moss green and cream motor home. Webb and Matt gave a lot of gestures and shouted instructions which Al ignored as he backed into the parking place they had prepared east of the house, between the garage and the garden. The area was nearly flat, Al had the book in his lap and found and pushed the correct toggles and buttons to level the unit and support it with automatic jacks that came down. The ground was hard enough that the jack bases didn't need to be aided with the plywood pieces that the previous owner had thoughtfully left in the massive storage area.

Al then opened the hatch that contained the unit's thick electrical cable and Webb directed him to the 50-amp plug that a day earlier had been installed and was wired to a dedicated circuit in Matt's garage electrical box.

Dick and Billy shook hands with Al. They had met him initially several years ago but they had also met Tanya at the same time and couldn't remember much except her. They also had been at Matt and Tanya's wedding in the Keys where her backless, sideless, halter-top wedding dress caused them to again not pay much attention to Al. After a quick tour of the Ambassador motor home, and with appreciation and Mexican beers given for their efforts, they got in their truck and took off to enjoy the rest of the weekend.

Webb popped a beer for Al and explained that some of Matt's friends had to be told he was protecting Carla or they would be talking more than if they were in on the situation. Also, they would provide more eyes for strangers. He was impressed that they noticed every different vehicle, car or truck, the mud or dust on them, their tracks and even boot or shoe footprints. Matt's property was in the least populated county of the least populated part of the state. The point being—new was noticed.

Webb, Karen and Al had instruction books spread on the RV's marble kitchen counter. Al referred to notes in his police inspector pad. They got the unit leveled then activated the slide-outs. After they had checked out the beautifully appointed bathroom and large refrigerator/freezer, Karen, Carla and Tanya went through each drawer, cupboard and closet

Armed with his first sandwich and his second beer, Al ushered Webb and Matt past the women and into the bedroom at the far end of the 40 foot Ambassador. Al spread his arms, "You could search for a month or two, use penetrating infrared or radar and two big mean sniffer dogs and you wouldn't find the weapons and ammunition I have hidden."

He opened the two doors of the cabinet over the bed. The bed had moved back along with its slide-out some thirty inches. The recessed head of the bed now had windows located on each side of the slide-out. The wood cabinetry was stained as cherry wood, beautifully blending with the rich carpet and fabrics of the interior. Al took out two pillows and some blankets, exposing the plain empty back of the cabinet: perfectly empty and with edges perfectly joined.

"Check this out." Al said as he went to one round knob of several on the crown molding symmetrically incorporated into the side of the cabinet. He turned it and the top of the back panel popped open an inch. He carefully took the panel out; it had a thin layer of foam rubber on the inside. Now the cabinet exposed an area packed with weapons and ammunition. All were surrounded and supported with foam rubber.

Matt whistled, "I recognize the pistols and the M16, but what are those?" Matt pointed at black plastic shapes that resembled either a large Ron Popeil Pocket Fishermen, a two foot long roofing stapler or maybe a musical instrument with a barely recognizable barrel and a sight.

Webb chuckled, knelt on the bed and reached into the cabinet, taking out one of the two strange looking weapons. "This, my Yooper friend, is a FN P90. State of the art weaponry made in Belgium—used by the Secret Service and many discerning killers. Watch this."

Webb pushed buttons on the top of the weapon and a smoky plastic tray popped up. "Look—fifty rounds—they turn 90 degrees and feed the machine. Slick as shit. 800 rounds a minute—this magazine gets emptied in less than 4 seconds if you're pissed off and pull the trigger all the way back and hold it. If you're cool and just squeeze it a little, it shoots semi auto, very accurately I might add. Same cartridge as the pistol—5.7 x 28, fast and deadly—with the right shells you can go through body armor or a car."

Al reached in again and took a pistol in a nylon belt clip holster, handing it to Matt, "This is yours, it is like the one I gave you for a wedding present and you had to leave it in the Dominican Republic. It's not threaded for a suppressor and it is legal in the states. You can buy good Belgium shells again—they were hard to get for over a year. I brought a thousand rounds of the special shells, used only for the military or government -30% faster and bimetal—nasty little bastards."

Webb took down the other P90 and an extra loaded plastic magazine from the hidden compartment, and one of three remaining pistols. He also took out several boxes of shells. "Let's take all these weapons out of here; they're no good in a closet if we need them. I want to show the ladies this hiding place and then close it up.

"We have some planning and a lot of work to do, tomorrow we set up a security system. I'd like to be able to get a good night's sleep again. Matt and I have been doing four hour watches. Right now, let's get the dish working, Carla wants to talk to Dave."

An hour of studying instruction books and getting the extended rooftop antenna to search the sky, the carrier signal light blinked on. Matt called himself at his house. The signal went out hundreds of miles and back, the connection was perfect, the delay was almost unnoticeable and the conversation was two-way. Carla was involved and helped with the instruction, reading as Al followed her directions. After the test was complete and successful, Al gave her the list of numbered cell phones in Dave's possession. Webb sat at the dining area and watched everything.

When Al left, Webb began a serious conversation with Carla, "Don't mention this location, Matt or Tanya, the weather, the trees, the RV or satellite phone. Tell him to get out in the open when he talks to you. His room may be bugged. And he needs to destroy the phone when you're done talking to him. Set up your next call, he can't call you. I don't know exactly how long you should talk—but for now, let's make this first call less than three minutes."

Carla paid attention but paled at what all these procedures implied. She said to her Dad, "Isn't Dave in danger too? He saw most of what I did."

Webb answered, "He's got protection, but he didn't see the attack or the Imam at the attack scene. I'm betting your pictures also show the Imam, and you're the link to the cell phone. Take it from me, you're the key witness, Dave just is corroboration. You're being safe actually makes him safer. So be careful what you say."

Carla picked up the phone, paused and said to her father, "Thank you for all this. I have to know about Kate, I miss Dave so much I ache. I'll be careful, but I want to be alone. Trust me father."

Webb stood up, gazed down at his beautiful daughter; noticing how her eyes looked older, sad. He smiled down at her, stroked her cheek with his massive hand and left the motor home.

22

Organization

Carla made her call to Dave and came out of the RV, she had been crying but produced her first smile in several days. She went to Tanya and her mother who were waiting outside to hear her report, "Kate's funeral was last Thursday. Dave went and her parents got my letter and understood why we weren't there. Dave's fine, really misses me. He was questioned several times by the FBI people and the lawyers about where we went. They have people watching him, saying they are protecting him. They follow him to class too. He says the papers and TV have the Imam's arrest finally making news. Nothing mentioned about radioactivity, just suspicion of conspiring to aid activists and possession of an unregistered destructive device and public endangerment: like they lose points if they use the word 'Terrorist.' The Islamic community is asserting their peacefulness, supporting the Imam and so far hasn't taken to the streets. He says the government prosecutors' office has made very few statements and they were generally—'No comment.' The word on campus has as many rain forest theories as radiation rumors."

Tanya asked, "What are Kate's parents doing? Her father wasn't going to have his daughter's bravery and her death get swept under the political carpet."

"We didn't get to that, but Dave did say my dad should contact Koning. Al said we would be in touch, and that was over a week ago.

"Also, Dave's roommate found a bug in their kitchen overhead light—he's a conspiracy theory nut anyway and this whole situation fires his total distrust of big government and big brother. They went to high school together and have no secrets from each other. I'm glad he's staying close to Dave."

The women went into the house. The men had the storage areas opened and most of the boxes of security equipment spread out on the lawn and driveway. Matt had an instruction diagram in his hand and was identifying the parts that were packed in ten boxes labeled 'Wireless Surveillance Camera System' he said, "This is some technology, it says we need to charge each unit for twelve hours, then they can be maintained by their individual little solar panels. They have a maximum 500 foot range in the open, motion alert or continuous operation, all remotely controlled. That box has to be the controller." Matt pointed to a box near the twin stacks of the cameras.

Webb looked over all the boxes of equipment and said, "I've been thinking—we brought this motor home up here, among other reasons, for Karen and me to have a bedroom—I now think it should be for Al. That way we can put all the monitors and electrical stuff in this house with an engine and not clog up Matt and Tanya's space, or alert their visitors about our security system."

Al added, "Fine with me, also, this RV has six big batteries, a major league power inverter, its own 8 kilowatt generator and it's hooked to the house power. It's a twenty ton uninterruptable power source. And we would have lots of counter and table space to spread out the monitoring equipment."

The consensus silently agreed upon, the men connected the camera units to their little chargers and found ten outlets in the garage and RV. They set up the computer monitor and screen on the trailer's dining table.

Al made an observation, "I can monitor everything, sit in a super comfortable swivel seat, look out a picture window at the main approach and have ten motion sensitive eyes and ears all around me."

Webb asked Matt, "Where does the road going past us lead?"

Matt said, "It goes another half mile, then turns to a two rut, winds into a swampy area, then, if you can get through the mud and brush, it connects to a gravel road two miles north of our property. Snowmobilers use it occasionally."

Webb asked again, "Can you drop a tree or two across it?"

Matt answered, "Wouldn't do much good, only a few local people know about the road, they all travel with chain saws and would cut the trees up and pull them out of the way as a kindness to the next person. If they see the trees were chain sawed, felled on purpose—they would be pissed at me.

"Let's walk around a while before supper—figure out where to put the cameras. Figure a football field and a half. We've got cleared fields on the north, the quarry and its steep cliff on the west, the south is the only real way in here. There is a mean cedar swamp and a couple of creeks and real rough going on the east side—but someone could work their way in if they were good in the woods and real determined."

The men hiked through the woods around the cabin, Matt pointed out two deer blinds and the shooting lanes each observed. They ended up at the north end of the straight sand and gravel road that went back to the highway.

Al commented, "Unless you grew up here, this is the only way in by foot or vehicle."

Webb, picking round burrs off his pant legs, added, "That's why I forced us on Matt. We can defend this place with just a few of us. Carla will be safe here."

The evening meal was a reunion of sorts. The group of six had shared a 54-foot Hatteras on an adventure through the Caribbean several years earlier. They had survived many deadly attempts on their lives. They had fought and survived together. The dinner conversations never mentioned their previous exploits, but they were there in people's minds when dishes were passed and a joke was told or the next day's plans were made.

Carla excused herself early, looking tired; she went up to her bedroom.

When coffee was served Tanya made a comment, "Carla is under a lot of strain, also, we can still have some worry about the radiation. If we were in Ann Arbor she would be having tests being done."

Karen directed a question to Webb, "What about that? If she starts feeling badly we need to get some medical help. We would give away her location by taking her to a doctor or a hospital."

Tanya said, "She can go as me, get her blood tested, we know what to look for as to various counts. If there is a problem we can step up to it then."

Webb nodded, "Good idea, Monday you can drive into St. Ignace and go to the clinic, I'll have a doctor call in the tests order for Carla, now that I have a phone. I don't think it will be a problem using her real name and we'll pay in cash."

Karen added, "We can get groceries too."

23

Security System

At the end of a pancake, eggs and bacon breakfast, Webb and Al brought out a box of little Midland radios and chargers. They each had an initial on them painted in red nail polish.

Al took the one with an A, passed the one with a W to Webb. He pointed at the button that made the radio turn on or off, then the thumb switch to make a call. After he and Webb pushed their 'on' buttons, Al called Webb at the other end of the table. In the small, quiet kitchen everyone could hear the transmission.

Webb said, "We want to be off the grid, but when we get spread out here—these will help us communicate. They are all set up—on Channel 5—a long range channel. They will work all over this property, except maybe in the quarry under the cliffs. There is a charger for each pair. Charge them on your nightstands, keep them on when you leave the house. Al in the RV will have a base station on all the time; he can also scan for other radios in the area."

Al passed the initialed radios to their respective person. He held his in an open hand, "These are simple, but they work fine. We have the 'roger' beep turned off and it is configured to be silent—no beeps or tones, Matt said this is how to set these radios for hunting. Don't hit the call button unless it's an emergency, then push it three times, it rings loud. Otherwise just push the side button and speak softly into the little hole at the end of the Midland label. It is one way, so let up to listen. Remember all of us can hear what you say—no gossip."

As the group broke up, they began radioing each other as they went about their day.

Matt said to Tanya, "The novelty will eventually wear off. These radios will become a pacifier to the cell phone withdrawal they were all experiencing."

Al moved toward the kitchen door, "Let's load up the Yukon and start putting out the cameras along the road and trails. I've got a ladder strapped on top."

Matt took Al and Webb to the main junction of several trails and the road. There, they carefully put out three cameras, cognizant of brush, trees and wind movement, also the fact that a moving vehicle along the road would be gone and out of view unless the camera was aimed to see it after it passed. This knowledge was gained by Matt from many years of trail cam experience and it made the camera easier to hide. If you didn't think ahead, the buck or wolf would be gone after it set off the motion sensor; all you would see were redundant animal-free pictures of the same trees or field. Matt also estimated the level of snow that might come in the next month, they set up a northerly angled view of the straight road and the two side roads that eventually branched off it to the quarry or eastern low lands. They concealed the solar panels and secured them in trees, facing south west, out of view from the road. Matt had some dull brown spray paint which he used to break up the dark green color of the camera mounts and the solar panel cable, also to cover the white phone wire staples that they used to secure the cables to the tree trunks. Two cameras went along the path at the quarry edge, two along the road leading north, two hidden in the only low brush of the open field north of the house. For the last camera they hiked into the thick cover east of the house and put it viewing the junction of the widest game path and the nearly over grown shooting lane.

Matt and Tanya drove up and down the road to test the system for Al and Webb who were in the Ambassador. Their Midlands worked perfectly even when the women were breaking in with cross talk.

At noon, Karen gave three call alarms and announced, "Lunch would be on the table in fifteen minutes."

Webb spoke to Al, "So much for the agreed to radio protocol."

Al asked, "You going to talk to her about it?"

Webb replied, as he left the big RV, "I'd rather fight a bear with a teaspoon."

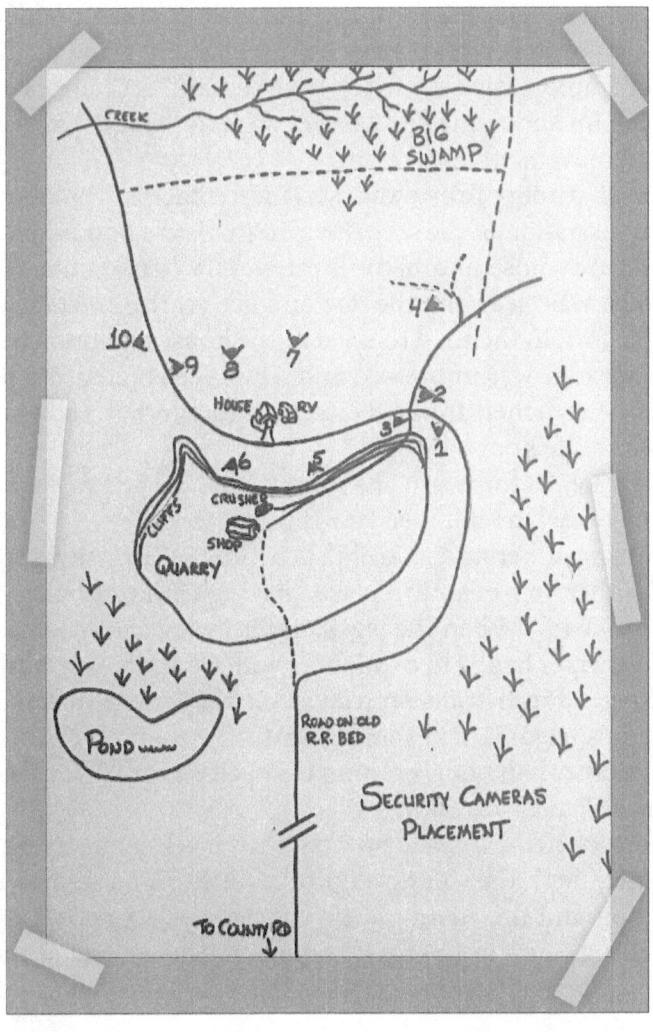

After lunch, Carla and Tanya took a walk along the leaf carpeted trails. Karen worked in the RV to make up Al's bed and get the kitchen and refrigerator stocked with some snacks and sandwich food, coffee and tea, for him or whoever manned the security system.

Al and Webb tracked Matt and Tanya as they drove and walked around the security system. The system showed color in daylight, but would be black and white infrared at low light or night. The recording system technology eluded them for the time being. Al said he would read more about the connections. Al made up a diagram of the grounds and placement of the cameras. It corresponded to the number on the screen that they could selectively bring up. The computer could automatically switch between and activate cameras, or could bring up and name any camera on standby that woke up when it detected movement.

By midafternoon Tanya and Matt were back at the house. They got a demonstration of the security system. And a bonus; one camera showed a fuzzy nose and behind the nose a curious doe. The computer screen was clear and the doe and her yearling were wandering around the fork in the road that led to the house and branched to the quarry. Everyone was impressed and Al was celebrated as a technical genius as he switched from one camera to another and showed all areas around the house.

Carla spoke, "If this wasn't so serious it would be fun. I want everyone to know how much I love you all."

Webb hugged her and said, "This is fun, we are with people that love each other, in a beautiful place, playing with technology."

Matt broke in, "When the legal stuff is over, I know some hunters who will be super happy to drink beer with a brandy side while watching all the good deer trails on television. They use trail cameras, but this system is instant, next century stuff."

After another half hour, nothing changed on the various views and the group talked about taking walks.

Matt suggested they should now test their marksmanship. The Yukon quickly filled with the smuggled pistols, little blue and gray boxes of ammunition and the weird plastic rifle things, six people crammed in—including Carla in the back cargo area and several of the empty security equipment packing boxes balanced on the luggage rack.

The quarry was perfect for shooting—flat and expansive, surrounded by uninhabited forest. Matt set up several boxes and slapped onto them round targets that stuck and also showed where the bullets hit by displaying an easily seen yellow splash.

The group's first shots were to be with the pistols. Al delivered a lesson; he took one apart and reassembled it. Pointing out it was all covered with polymer, with the exception of the bore, no exposed metal and it couldn't rust, the inside has the finest steel, even a chromed barrel. Al explained, "This is a single action semiautomatic pistol. It holds twenty cartridges in its magazine. You need to cock the action and load a cartridge into the breech. The safety is by your finger not your thumb. It is ambidextrous—a lever on each side. You can't see the hammer, but you know it has a chambered round and is cocked when you see the little chrome pin pop up by the breech."

Al showed a cartridge, "This is the power of the weapon—the 5.7 x28 cartridge—it is a small rifle shell—makes the weapon very powerful, reliable and accurate. Fifty yard head shots are very possible for an experienced shooter. It had 30% less kick than a 9mm, buts it is loud and had an impressive muzzle flash. It is vastly superior to the 9mm. It had been adopted by over 300 law enforcement agencies in the US and by our Secret Service."

Matt passed out two pairs of ear protectors—the other four had to use their fingers. Everyone fired the pistols and, with some instruction from Al, had very credible shots. They were taught to use the straight arm, two hands, thumbs touching technique. The 5.7 pistols were appreciated: light, controllable and easy to sight. After three fifty round boxes of shells, everyone had shot the pistols enough. All the women were, with a little encouragement, strong enough to work the slide on the single action weapon.

After pistol practice, Webb went to the vehicle and picked out the plastic rifle thing, "Now for the real deal. This is a P90, used by many bodyguards, including our Secret Service and by many nations. It is only six pounds, twenty inches long, fifty shells in it magazine, ambidextrous, a sight that lets you keep both eyes open, accurate to 200 meters, very reliable and easy to clean. Be very careful, this can go full auto and the muzzle is only inches from your fingers. It may look like a plastic toy, but it can cut a person in half. The two stage trigger is another issue—it takes finger control and practice, a touch gives one shot, pull it far back and it is fully automatic. It will empty the fifty shell magazine in less than four seconds. It uses the same 5.7 x 28 cartridge as the pistols."

Al fired first: accurate, aimed single shots, then a burst from an aimed shoulder position, followed by a burst firing from the hip.

Matt fired next, did the same sequence as Al, and out shot him. Matt laughed when he shot full auto from the hip. He said, "I've gone nearly a decade of hunting seasons on the same box of 20 shells and I just fired fifty. Seems so wasteful. But thank you!"

Carla shot and had a fun time, she commented as she handed the piece to Al to reload, "I really like that, easy to cock. Did you see the flame come out? Call me Bonnie!"

She walked over to Tanya, "I wish Dave was here."

Tanya shot, and then Karen was given the reloaded weapon, Webb's wife studied and weighed it, then handed the rifle to him, "I guess I don't like shooting as much as the rest of you, I hate to waste the shells, my husband does my shooting."

Webb took the weapon, worked the slide, moved to forty feet from the pile of now shot-up boxes: from the hip, ignoring the multiholed circular targets, he drew a line through all the boxes, then traced his line back. His trail of bullet holes was perfectly level, controlled and evenly spaced. For several seconds the echo of the long burst of firing lingered in the quarry and rang in the spectators' ears.

Matt whistled, "I never saw any shooting like that. Where'd you learn?"

Webb, popping the magazine out, replied, "I fired many automatic weapons in Russia. I was in charge of arms shipment for a few years. Had to test them. I learned from people who worked with Kalashnikov, the trick is to be strong enough to hold it steady against your hip and watch where the shells hit. Then it is a hose."

Matt thought, *Easy as piss'n in the snow, if you're a world class weightlifter and wrestler.*

They left the limestone quarry floor littered with brass, piled into the SUV and went back to the house, happy with their shooting experience.

Back in the house, waiting for a chicken casserole, cocktail hour started. Beers were limited to four bottles and two cans, vodka was domestic, three or four shots of brandy remained in the Paul Masson bottle, blended whisky was Canadian Mist and wine was a nearly full gallon jug of Carlo Rossi burgundy.

Matt, apologizing for the limits of his liquor cabinet, "We weren't expecting company, and there are lots of bottles down at the hunting cabin in the quarry—usually the best stuff. I'd be happy to run down there again."

Karen answered, "This is all fine, we can stock up tomorrow, the company is more refreshing than any liquor. I'm so happy we're together and safe. We will visit the clinic, shop and you men can stay here, shoot the little birds and drink up beers."

Webb spoke up, "Al will drive you, Matt and I will stay here. Tomorrow I'll spend time on the phone. We've been out of touch long enough."

24

Intruder Alert

Al was awakened for the fifth time that evening. Deer, wolves, bobcat and something that never showed on the screen all set off the system. He finally gave up the bed and just snoozed in the big driver's chair, waiting for the sun to start a new day. He needed some sleep so he would be sharp to drive the ladies to town. He had just dozed off again when the main camera alarm beeped. The screen showed a single brake light blinking before several particularly large holes in the road, a tail pipe glowing white in the infrared. Al became totally alert. Checking his watch—4:40 am.

He turned on the next two cameras on the road before they went on by themselves. They showed, in black and white, a pickup truck slowly and suspiciously coming up the road, continuing toward the house.

Al hit his Midland radio call button three times. By agreement Matt was to leave his radio on, the others were off. The alert would bring Matt in a minute or two.

The pickup went out of the camera's view, now close to the house. Al took his machine gun, a flashlight and went out of the motor home making sure the lights were off and the door closed. He met Matt slipping out of the darkened garage, pistol in hand.

"What is it?" whispered Matt.

"Truck with no lights coming up the road, can't see how many in it."

Matt and Al fanned out across the road across from the house. They stood behind large maple and beech trees. They could hear the truck in low gear coming closer.

Matt fingered the Five-seveN pistol; the little pin was up on the left top surface across from the breech opening, confirming a shell in the chamber. He used his right index finger and pushed down the ambidextrous safety lever. He forgot a flashlight, but his eyes were getting used to the dark and there was some moon above the low cloud cover, he could discern the road and the moving black mass of the vehicle.

Al was closer to the approaching truck, about three trees away. Matt decided to follow the former law officer's lead, let him make the first move.

A hand held spotlight suddenly flashed out of the pickup, it illuminated Al, who was partially hidden behind a tree. Al ducked behind the tree, out of the light. Matt moved toward the truck, kneeling behind a bush next to the road, drawing a bead on the source of the light, his finger tightening on the trigger.

The light blinked off after two seconds of illumination, still enough light reflecting back off the smooth gray bark of the beech tree to allow Matt to make out the vehicle, an old 150 Ford, rusty and dark brown, its engine knocking and straining to move the truck, the gear too high for no miles per hour.

Matt shouted, "Don't shoot!" as he stepped into the roadway.

The man in the truck, now close, said, "I won't shoot Matt—Sorry, I didn't think I was so close to your house."

At the same time Al shoved the machine gun into the truck driver's window.

Al said, "Don't move a muscle. The, 'don't shoot' was for me."

Matt walked up to the truck. He recognized the old Ford, as he got closer, he could smell the pipe tobacco, and finally, he could see it was old Walt, the glow of the loose tobacco of his hand rolled cigarette and the light from a dust covered instrument panel showed his old wrinkled face and crooked smile.

Matt said, "Kind of early to be partridge hunting Walt, and that 300 Savage beside you will just leave some feathers and a bloody spot."

The old violator looked at Matt and the funny looking gun five inches from his ear. He looked at Al, figured he didn't know him or couldn't remember him. After a few seconds of silence, he said, "Just checking on the deer herd Matt. Sorry to get you guys up."

Matt said, "Walt, this is Al, he's from the big city, a light sleeper and worries about people driving by at unusual times. He doesn't know that you are always checking on the deer herd. You might want to look at other areas for a while."

"Sure thing Matt, sorry to bother you, can I turn around in your driveway?"

Matt patted him on the shoulder of his worn army jacket, "Sure. See you around, maybe during hunting season."

The old truck's groaning tie rods registered their protest for a sharp turn, still with no lights, Walt made the turn around and headed back, this time he used second gear and a little more speed. After fifty feet down the road he turned on his lights.

Al commented, "Man's got good night vision for an old guy. He saw me cross the road a hundred feet away in the dark. Got the light right on me."

Matt chuckled as they walked back to the house, "If you had been a deer, you'd be getting gutted about now. He is a legendary violator, feeds a lot of people."

Al opened the motor home door and paused, "Funny he didn't say anything about your pistol or my weapon."

Matt went into the motor home behind Al. They turned on the cameras and watched Walt slowly drive back to the highway.

Matt commented, "That man was a friend of my father as a boy and hunted with my grandfather. His old Savage lever action dropped more deer than most men have even seen."

Al questioned, "In daylight or at night?"

Matt said, "Dates and daylight are complications that don't seem to clutter Walt's life. There's a story that one night he shot a goat on an old lady's front porch, commenting to his hard drinking cronies in the car with him that the eye color didn't seem right at the time."

Al asked, "Did they eat the goat?"

"Don't know, too many facts ruin the story."

The screen finally showed nothing as Al put the system on standby, he said, "You know this system isn't really suited to your property, too many creatures running around at night. We need to reevaluate how we use it. I didn't get enough sleep tonight."

Matt suggested, "Why don't you go the bed, I'll stay up and watch the system. I'll turn the beeper down and play with the cameras. You can get in three hours if you hurry."

Al gratefully went to the bedroom in the back, closing a dividing door to keep the light and sounds out. Matt played with the switches and keyboard, trying to understand what and where he was looking. He tried to be quiet for Al's sake.

25

Webb on the Phone

M att awoke from the knocking on the motor home door. Webb stood outside with an insulated carafe and a coffee mug. Matt was sleeping in the comfortable driver's chair. The parade of camera activating critters let up after dawn and he had nodded off.

Webb entered and said, "Wake up sunshine, morning in the swamp, burning daylight and every other daybreak greeting. It's going to be a beautiful fall day—up to over fifty and sunny.

I've got a lot of phoning to do. Why don't you and Al go have some breakfast?

Matt made a shushing sound and whispered, "Al needs sleep, our spy system is literally inhuman up here. Poor Al had animals at one or another camera almost continually during his watch. We had a human deer violator come by around 4:00 am, the system picked him up perfectly, I was on call and came out, I happened to know the hunter and got rid of him. Al said he hadn't gotten any sleep. I took over and actually had a good time. I don't know how to record yet, but I saw wolves at almost every camera—working the whole area. There will be a legal hunt for them again this year—about time. They are big and spooky. The deer are jumpy and for good reason. I saw a doe and two yearlings go by and seconds later—three wolves following them."

Webb wasn't interested in wildlife stories, "We can give Al another hour of sleep, then he needs to eat, get cleaned up and drive the ladies into St. Ignace. You go have breakfast and I'll wake Al in a while."

Matt went in for breakfast, joining Tanya and Karen.

Tanya brought Matt a plate with scrambled eggs, toast and heat-and-eat sausage.

Matt had gotten his own coffee.

He told the two ladies about the adventures of the night. He asked where Carla was.

Tanya answered, "She's still in the bathroom, not feeling well this morning. I think it's nerves. We'll cheer her up in town. She can't eat anything because of the blood work we hope is approved for this morning."

Webb came in, "I talked to my former doctor in Detroit—explained everything and he agreed to call and fax a blood work order to the clinic. He has their phone and a fax number in his records. Tanya knows the directions—she's been there with her parents."

Tanya spoke, "That reminds me, I'll have no issues with my parents. I usually call them several times a week. They are on a cruise through the Greek Islands for three weeks. My dad was complaining about being charged for every little thing—Wi-Fi, $7 a drink, a $50 coupon for soda—and you need to carry a special cup, and they charge for phone access. He said only call for an emergency. They will be back in the Keys in a month."

Webb answered, "You and Matt can use your cell phones now, you should check that all your location services are still turned off. I expect the government will be on to us fairly soon anyway—but at least now we are set up to protect Carla. We're on familiar ground, hard to find, we have surveillance gear and we are well armed.

"I'm calling Koning this morning. I expect he'll give me a ration of crap, but bottom line he will be relieved, if not pleased, with the call."

Carla came in, looking beautiful, but pale. "I'm ready when everyone else is.

"I want a Big Mac, maybe two, when we are done with the clinic. Then we can do some serious shopping if we can find stores. I need some boots, a couple of heavy sweaters and maybe a down vest with a hood or neat collar. I've been using all of Tanya's boots and clothes."

Webb listened and smiled at his daughter, "No credit cards, your world passport to plastic wealth has just been revoked for now."

Carla looked shocked. Webb took out his wallet, "Here is a little used and soon to be forgotten means of exchange—cash money. You give the store people these green things and they let you buy goods and services. Sometimes, if the counter person is very clever, they will even give back money and round shiny coins, if their cash register knows how to make change and they know how to work it."

Webb counted out ten one hundred dollar bills. He gave another ten to his wife. They put the bills in their purses.

Karen said, "At least we are on the decimal system, unlike England and a few other countries where we had to play with their funny money. Thank you kind sir, we will return with treasures and food."

Al came in with clean clothes on, "Ladies, give me a few minutes to freshen up and we will be off to the city."

Al ate two, now cold, sausages off the service plate and went to the upstairs bathroom.

Webb watched the Yukon leave in a whirl of dust and colored leaves. Then he went into the motor home with a leather binder and his day planner. He laid out several papers and got a chair organized before the phone. He called the Dominican Republic and spoke to the managers of his properties there—one at his hotel and the other at his home.

He next called a man in Detroit, the phone was answered with a simple, "Yes?"

Webb said, "You know who this is?"

The man answered again, "Yes."

Webb went on, "Did you get the information I asked you for?"
"Yes."

Webb asked, "Give it to me slowly—I'm making notes."

The detached emotionless voice from Detroit began with an address, a house description: color and material, the yard, the trees, walkways. Then he went into the cars and finally the individuals in the house:

age, descriptions and some of their observed habits, school levels and activities. Lastly were a list of hobbies and the name, approximate age and breed of the family dog.

Webb asked, "Anything more?"

The man added, "The youngest daughter has an aquarium in her bedroom. A big fantail goldfish in it and the tank isn't very clean. The dog sleeps with the other daughter. They are both National Honor Society, pretty."

Webb ended with, "Oh, tell your actor friend he did a perfect job; the pictures from the porch served their purpose and are continuing to drive the feds in circles, keep them defensive. Double check that he lost the wig, coat, watch and bracelet. Give him a second envelope with the original amount in it. Tell him it is for continued treatment of his acute amnesia.

"You've got the bank numbers. As usual, all cash, no records on your end, I get itemized accounts from Gibraltar. Remember, I trust you as long as you live."

No one said good-by, Webb hung up.

Webb was now mentally and physically ready to call Koning when Matt knocked on the door.

Matt was dressed in camouflage clothes and Kromer hat. He had the FN 5.7 pistol clipped to his belt. Holding up his Midland he said, "I'm going for a hike around the place—maybe shoot at a bird if I can get close and it holds very still—like they like to do. Maybe I'll see a wolf, but I doubt it. I'm curious how all these wolves are affecting the deer. You can get me on the radio. I'll be back in a couple of hours."

Webb wished him luck and Matt went north down the road.

Webb again called Detroit—Koning's office. His first response was an automated phone answerer, he listened to and picked option 6 and got Koning's secretary's secretary. He tried to explain the call involved a government witness, however, that news didn't light any fires, he then tried Carla's grand jury subpoena number, that small dollop of officialdom got him to Koning's secretary—she answered with Koning's name and title. Webb explained everything again and was told Attorney Koning was unavailable but would return his call. Webb said he was also unavailable and would only call Koning personally and directly.

The secretary said that was not possible. Then Webb asked the secretary if the federal prosecutor was interested in winning at the trial of the Imam that tried to kill a stadium full of people? The line went dead for twenty seconds then James Koning came on.

Koning began, "Hello Mr. Webb, long time no speak. Where are you and more importantly where is your daughter?"

Webb replied, "We are safe from knife wielding fanatics and computer stealing federal officers. I'm calling you to ease your worries. You realize my actions were to protect my daughter. I'm sure you can relate to my feelings. You would be very concerned if your daughters were threatened in their home."

After a pause, Koning, waiting for more from Webb, finally spoke, "I have drafted warrants for your arrest. You just can't take a key witness away. We have laws…we have U.S. Marshalls; we know how to deal with witnesses.

"I know you're in Canada. I told you not to leave the country. We are working with the Royal Canadian Mounted Police; you'll be caught and handed over to federal authorities. It is just a matter of time.

I've read your record, you think you're too smart to live within the law, I'm going to show you that your actions will have jail time consequences."

Webb interrupted, "Skip the tough talk, you're in a hole and you keep digging.

"We have never left the United States. We are cooperating by promising to have Carla in the courtroom when you say. If your records are good enough you can read that once I was guarded by U.S. Marshals and so was another man that drove my car—he was killed and I barely escaped assassination. So I don't have respect for your protection system, particularly when my daughter's life is at stake and we were surrounded by one hundred fifty thousand Muslims. And I don't think much of your threats or lectures either. I can get very serious too.

"Is a trial scheduled, if so when?"

Koning, in a more civil tone, answered, "No trial date is scheduled. We're up to our five drawer filing cabinets in pretrial motions. It could be months yet."

Webb asked, "Who leaked Carla's name?"

Koning paused, "We honestly don't know."

Webb said, "That's too bad. It isn't very comforting. It strengthens my resolve to protect my daughter—your best witness. Believe me; I have many tools, people and decades of experience at my disposal. We are not one of your many problems. I'll stop at nothing to keep my family safe. Dig down into your heart and mind; if Carla was your daughter, I think you would do as much. I've got good advice for you. Put those warrants in a shredder and tell your youngest daughter to clean her goldfish tank. I'll call you in a week."

Webb hung-up.

26

Checking Leaks

James Koning looked at the cordless phone in his large hand; it just went dead when Webb hung up on him. He always thought a hang up without a good bye was very rude. He couldn't remember the last time he hadn't been the one to end a phone call. He carefully put the phone back in its holder-charger. He shook slightly, fighting to control the urge to slam it through the desktop.

He pushed a button for his secretary, she came into his office.

Koning rattled off a series of orders, "Schedule an afternoon staff meeting.

"Type up the agenda—in this order—Finding Carla Webb, investigating where our grand jury information went—I want specific offices and names of people who had eyes on the material—I want a technical type to report how we can trace the next call I get from Mr. Webb. I want to see a progress report on the knife guy. I want a report on our surveillance of Dave Adams. Then schedule another meeting with just the legal team on the Imam trial, make a list of all motions and pleadings and have someone speak to every point. Find out specifically what is delaying a trial date. Make this look like I'm in some kind of control."

Koning then put his suit coat on, "I'm going for an early lunch."

Koning then drove himself home, calling ahead to alert his wife.

At home before sitting down for a lunch he went up to his youngest daughter's room. The aquarium was in the corner, on a low book case. It would not be seen from any window. The large goldfish stared out at him through a green slime coated tank wall that did indeed need cleaning. The implications of Webb's advice chilled his heart.

Koning went down to lunch, without any appetite. He normally shared everything with his wife, but adding home intruding and heated verbal sparring with a Russian crime boss, on top of the worries she already had about his prosecution of an Islamic leader, was too much to put upon her.

Instead his wife added to his problems, "Right now there is a demonstration in front of the Ann Arbor mosque and at the city hall, police wives and the municipal workers and the police unions made protests against the lack of action and the cover ups of the terrorist attack. Several Muslims were attacked around the city. The policeman died and several are still in the hospital—not doing well. The University officials and the mayor are all pleading for calmness."

Koning tried to swallow the bite of food that had turned to sawdust and gravel in his mouth. He took a sip of milk, "I've got to get back to the office—the stuff will be hitting the fan for sure."

Trouble began as Koning was pulling into his parking place. Police wives with signs surrounded his car. They were demanding justice and action—two areas James Koning had always thought were in his job description. The local TV people were in front of the courthouse, Koning quickly went in through a side door as several people he knew called him by name.

In his office his staff was already assembled, even though it was still the lunch hour. His secretary headed him off before he could open his outer office door.

She announced, in a low voice, "There's a Muslim waiting to talk to you. I put him in the outer office. Here's his card."

Koning looked at the very plain card; it was in Arabic script except for a name and title. The name was long, the title was Community Services. Koning went into the outer office and ushered the man into his large office. After a poor attempt at saying the man's name, Koning asked him what he wanted. Both men stood on opposite sides of Koning's desk.

The Muslim began by pointing out there were many thousands of Muslims in the area and he represented them, he then smoothly segued into how blissfully peaceful were the precepts of Islam. He was into a second minute of the history of the Islamic community when Koning interrupted him.

Koning said, after looking at his name on the card, "Sir, I have many very pressing issues, what is your business with me?"

The Islamic leader said, "Muslims are being harassed by the police and by rude demonstrations. Your police are fining and arresting anyone they suspect is Muslim. Clearly this is profiling and police harassment. It must be stopped and those responsible held to criticism."

Koning answered, "I am the federal prosecutor, I don't deal with local law enforcement unless a federal crime has been committed. I will have these areas investigated for the grounds you mentioned."

The Muslim next said, "Are you not the person holding and prosecuting Imam Alikhan?"

Koning responded, "Yes, the Imam is charged with several counts of federal crimes."

The Muslim asked, "Would he be arrested if he were not an Islamic leader?"

Koning took a deep breath, hoping his answer would come out under control, "Yes, anyone leading an attempt to kill tens of thousands of innocent people would be arrested for many serious federal crimes. He will have his day in court to prove his innocence. I believe we are showing more tolerance and respect for the law than his native Syria shows to Christians."

The Muslim looked shocked.

Koning went on, "Do you have any more complaints? If not, I'll have FBI investigators contact you. Perhaps we can work together to keep peace between the various factions."

Koning opened his door and looked directly at the Islamic leader until the man broke eye contact and left.

Koning filled his large aluminum vacuum coffee mug at the machine in his secretary's office and headed for the staff meeting room. He knew his blood pressure was now another issue but he wanted coffee and action—they went together for him.

He was early in the meeting room, he consulted a phone number section in his day planner, punched in 9 and then ten numbers and got the Ann Arbor chief of police. They had been friends and golf buddies for almost ten years. They talked. Koning explained his last visitor's purpose, the chief told of the sadness of an officer's death and the tension added by several more men still ill and in hospital. The chief put the ball back in Koning's court by asking, "When do you go to trial and we get some justice? We are doing our best to keep the lid on. The harassment claim is bullshit. Some of the younger Muslims are just asking for an arrest to show they are not afraid of the infidels. I am personally meeting every week with an Islamic group to lower tensions. So far the general public hasn't been involved and the news has not been printing or broadcasting anything overly inflammatory."

They were still chatting when Koning's staff filed in. Koning ended the phone call and faced his group.

The agenda was passed out by Koning's always efficient secretary. The room was full, the October sun came in and it was a little warm around the table.

At the head of the long table, Koning picked up the paper. "OK, number one, where is Carla Webb?"

An investigator standing in the back spoke, "She has disappeared, we thought she was in Canada but further work proved negative. We think she contacted her boyfriend, we found he has several throw away cell phones and he seems happier now—probably because he has had contact with her: just a feeling by our observers. We have the cell phone numbers, we will be able to listen in on his next conversations. Nothing will be admissible."

Koning said, "Good, I'll worry about admissible, keep working the boyfriend angle. I spoke with her father he said they were in the United States and he would have Carla at the trial. He drives me crazy, but I believe him.

"Next, the grand jury information—really, where are the leaks that identified Carla?

Two men spoke at once—Koning recognized the closest one. "We don't think the leak came from above. After twenty interviews in Justice and Home Land, we feel they didn't share information of a personal nature."

After a brief pause, the other man took up the subject, "We feel the hospital and the local homeland security people had access to the names and locations of the witnesses. There was information in the Islamic community the day of the attack. There are many Muslims working both Ann Arbor's and Detroit's airports. Homeland Security personnel were present at the questionings of the suspect and several of the witnesses. They also knew who was in the hospital. There are many Islamic personnel that are valued caregivers in both hospitals—both doctors and nurses. We feel the leaks came from local sources due to the timing of the knowledge that spread through the Islamic community. Their people were under no confidentiality orders when the initial attack occurred. People will talk."

Koning looked relieved, "Good, keep following up on leaks, but it is back burner—water over the dam, the damage has been done—we need to look ahead for security of future information and the safety of Dave Adams. Double up on him. He is our best link to Carla. If you find out where she is hiding—come to me directly and immediately, it will not be a matter of bull pen discussion. Are we clear?"

Everyone nodded. FBIers understand security.

Koning continued, "Now, the knife guy."

A woman spoke, "Our initial position remains, the pictures are inconclusive. We thought we had a good suspect for a time, a young man at the model plane store—he is a Muslim, young, right height and features—but he had an iron clad alibi for the time of the door stabbing."

Koning said, "Take the pictures to the Islamic community—the leaders and some of the younger people. The fat's in the fire anyway—they may as well share in our search and see why they might want to continue to keep a low profile."

Koning slid a card to an older agent, "Make sure this man sees the pictures and video, ask him if he knows the person. Be professional—he's sensitive to police harassment and to ethnic profiling. Leave him with some guilt, tell him it would have been a real community service if the Islamic community had warned us about this major terrorist attack.

"Who do we have on phone technology?"

One man raised his hand, "We are as of now set up to trace any call that comes into you, even satellite can give us general information. A cell phone will give us the house. Do you want 24 hours?"

"No, a single daytime watch is enough. My bookie calls at night."

That got some smirks, but no laughs.

"Now let's take a break and I'll meet with the trial team. The sooner we have a trial the better."

27

Phone and Clinic

Matt was enjoying hunting on his own land. He planned to wander all the way around the old open quarry. Starting south of the northern stream that beaver work turned into a small lake and a large swamp, he walked west along a ridge. He kicked up several partridge too far ahead for a shot. Along the north and west quarry edge he hunted along the old overburden piles, material originally cleared to expose the limestone, now a thick forest. He worked through and around limestone out croppings and occasional sink holes and boulders characteristic of karst formations. He was hunting areas of wild grape, patches of clover and where the forest floor was carpeted with the little red berries of wintergreen, all preferred food of the tasty grouse. Quiet stalking brought Matt to his first decent target: a large male partridge perched on a branch of a skinny twenty-foot poplar tree. Matt took his time, steadying by bracing his left hand on a tree and putting his right hand with the pistol over it. Firing from forty feet, the bullet took the bird in the neck.

The crack of the fast little shell echoed over the quarry. Matt's target dropped heavily to the base of its roost overlooking the quarry. Matt picked up the bird, putting it in the game pouch of his hunting vest and continued his hunt around the quarry. At the south end it got swampy and cedar trees became common. Matt got two more birds—filling his personal limit for the day. He walked back to the main road and looked at cameras. Tiny red LEDs recognized his presence, he wondered if Webb could see him.

Matt cleaned the birds along the trail, carefully checking their crops to confirm their feeding choices. He finished by putting the gut piles where the camera would betray what creatures came to eat them. Matt hoped Al would crack the technique to record the wolves.

Matt used his Midland radio. "You read me?"

Webb came back immediately, "Just ready to call you. I heard the shots and the cameras picked you up when you hit the road. The system works well."

Matt waited, Webb didn't say, "over" and the beep was turned off, "I'll be back soon, I'm circling back through the woods, checking out our east camera, over."

Webb, "I'll be watching, I've still got more phone calls to make."

Matt put the cleaned birds into a large plastic bag; happy with his pistol hunting and his head shots. Also pleased because he didn't have to ruin the perfect meaty breasts by cutting out shotgun pellets and pulling out feathers the shot forced into the flesh.

He worked his way back through the woods east of the house, waving at the camera as he walked through the game trail. With his handgun in the holster, Matt could use both hands on branches and sticks to work quietly through the heavy brush.

Back at the house, Matt waved at Webb—in the RV—busy on the phone. In the kitchen Matt got out the cutting board and prepared the breasts and thighs for cooking. He put them into salted water and hunted around for his favorite roasting pan. It was old and beat up, Tanya kept it way back in the corner cupboard. Then Matt rummaged in the pantry and the refrigerator to make sure he had the ingredients for his partridge cooking. Satisfied, he made himself lunch.

Webb came in and joined Matt at a late lunch. Over soup, crackers and cheese Webb related most of what he had covered with Koning. Matt was interested in when the trial would take place.

Matt washed down a bite of cracker and horseradish cheese with a long swig of Coors light and said, "We will get busy around here as we get into November. You know most of the people that will come to camp; I don't think we will have any new folks, most of my friends' kids are in college or have families and don't hunt with us anymore.

Still we will have six to eight hunters come in for opening day. Most will also show up sometime soon to fix their blinds or just walk around. How do you think we should handle it?"

Webb said, "We go with the flow, I've never hunted white tail deer, Carla and Karen have never been around a deer camp and Tanya wants to hunt. Dick and Billy were clear, they will do everything for her, they have a blind and a plan all figured out. I think we can all fit in. I'll help with the food."

Matt smiled and added, "I'd love to be in the woods when you rip off fifty shells from your butt ugly plastic machine gun."

Webb smiled, "I'll get another rifle."

The SUV wasn't back yet when Matt decided to start his partridge cooking. He took the old aluminum 9x13 baking pan, covered the bottom with a layer of dried beef, using most of the package, next the six hand sized breasts wrapped in bacon, then he poured on a can of mushroom soup and spread a couple of scoops of sour cream over it all, a little white wine for moisture, directly poured from a gallon jug of Carlo Rossi Chablis, got splashed on and then a layer of grated cheese, finally ending with a light sprinkling of a partial envelope of onion soup mix. Then he tightly covered the pan with aluminum foil. Setting the oven for 325 degrees, the timer for two and a half hours, chef Matt opened another cold beer, grabbed a second one and went out to bother Webb.

Webb took the beer and popped the top just as the camera buzzed and the side of the Yukon came into view on the computer screen.

Webb commented, "We need this system to record, so we could stop it and get license numbers and such."

Matt said, "I've read the instructions, they're in some kind of literal translation from the Chinese, verbs and pronouns are optional. Al said he would call the store manager as a last resort. I think Microsoft might be an issue too."

The Yukon crunched into the driveway and the garage door went up. Matt and Webb went to greet them.

Carla was happy, handing her father a McDonald's bag, "Here—these are cold but full of delicious food, all bad for your arteries and heart.

"We had a good day. The doctors and nurses were friendly and we found stores."

Webb and Matt were loaded with boxes of boots and clothes and a cargo area filled with plastic bags of groceries. Everything was carried into the house, bags into the kitchen, boxes to bedrooms.

Webb, noticing a band aid on Tanya's arm, asked, "What did they do to you?"

Tanya answered, "We all had a meeting with the doctor about radiation and transfusions and bone marrow. I said Carla and I had the same blood type and I'd be happy to help her any way I could. He said being a blood donor was easy, but a bone marrow match is a much more complex and difficult matter. We decided to have blood drawn to check on compatibility. It takes several tests and lab work."

Webb glanced at his wife, then asked, "When will you know about the tests?"

Carla answered, "They said a week or so. I told them I've felt tired and my stomach was upset sometimes. I said it was just nerves and stress, sadness about Kate and from being away from Dave and school. They gave me a good going over. The doctor said I was very fit and looked healthy to him."

Tanya broke in, "Have the two papa bears been in my kitchen? I smell cooking and the oven is on."

Matt said, "Partridge for supper, brought to you by a mighty hunter and the electric can opener."

Tanya opened the oven, "You're using that old pan. But the birds smell great."

Matt said, "Yes, bacon—culinary duct tape—fixes everything—and don't open the tin foil or you'll let out the steam."

Webb spoke, "I talked to the prosecutor today, he said the trial is not even scheduled yet, it could be some time. I hope Matt and Tanya can put up with us for a while."

Tanya, closing the oven, said, "We love you all. Fall in the U.P. is magnificent, a great time to be with friends. Everywhere you look is a picture. We're in one of the most beautiful spots in the world. There is a lot we can do."

Al, who had also found a beer, added, "You sure have enough creatures running around. How are we going to monitor the surveillance system? The person on duty can't get any sleep. I'll be burned out in two more days. We need to set up watches or the system won't work."

Webb, in a serious tone, "We can work it out. I know sooner or later there will be harmful people coming up that road. They will be working for the government or part of a jihad or even people that are both."

Matt asked, "Explain that last part. Both?"

Webb sat at the table, people moved around to hear him, "I spent most of the day using our marvelous satellite phone. There are elections coming, the administration would rather have a dozen trivial issues on the news programs rather than hear the words—terrorist attack. Our present administration was elected by a majority formed by minorities. A lot of votes will be jeopardized if the Muslim community is targeted or if the country's security structure seems inept. This significant attack in the heartland of the country is a two edged political sword. I know people will come for Carla. That's why we are here—lots safer and a hundred times more defensible than being in a suburb."

There was silence in the kitchen. Carla went over and hugged her father.

Webb continued, "I figure they—whoever they are—will try for Carla first. Failing to get her, they may get rid of the nasty Imam. Either way the trial will never take place in their lifetime. We will learn the timeframe of one or the other of these actions if Koning ever sets a trial date. Of course a date can be set and then get changed, but each time would risk more headlines and the chance of some real reporting kicking in. I believe all this will be history by the end of November; at most it will never make it to the New Year.

Carla said, "What about Dave?"

Webb answered, "I'd bet he is being closely watched to find a link to you. He has protection, but he is not close to being as important a witness as you. Don't let him know where you are or he will be in even more danger, and so will you."

Karen spoke, "Tell the whole story. It's not just Carla, you have enemies too."

Webb looked at his lovely wife, she looked back with icy blue eyes.

Webb took a breath, "Do you remember when we sat around the table on the Hatteras? We...really, I was fleeing for my life from certain drug dealers. Behind their angst was the fact I had a great deal of evidence and names about their activities. Well, that information touched—actually grabbed—many high government officials in the Department of Justice and various court systems. Those same people are now several steps higher in their respective bureaucracies. I got a pass, if not a presidential pardon, when Clinton left office—along with a dozen others that had influence and money. I left the country at that time, and a standoff was achieved. Now I may be on their radar again. I know this terrorist situation is at the Attorney General's desk and when they see my name lots of alarms will go off. The publicity of a spectacular trial just won't be allowed."

Tanya spoke, "Well, we are all in the same boat again."

Matt added, "At least we don't have a drug cartel after us, just the leaders and followers of our vast federal government and the world of Islam.

"If I was coaching a football team right now, I'd say—play hardnosed defense and hope for a break."

No one said anything. The kitchen smelled of the birds, bacon and cheese, the silence allowed the sizzle of the cooking to be heard. Outside the sun was setting and the trees were illuminated in colors of gold, brown and yellow. All seemed to be waiting for Webb to cap his announcements with wit or wisdom. He just read the fine print on his can of now warm beer.

Carla broke the mood, pouring a glass of white wine, she happily announced, "I'm going to try to talk to Dave, he's out of class by now. I'm early, but I really want to hear his voice."

Carla left for the motor home.

Tanya began supper cooking. From the freezer she took green beans, from the garage baskets she had Karen retrieved two medium-sized butternut squash and red potatoes; all food grown in their garden.

An hour later the food was cooked and served. Green beans, creamy white partridge meat, orange squash and a salad bowl made a colorful table. Glasses of white wine and fresh hard rolls accompanied the meal. Carla gave a positive report about Dave and the generally stabilized politics in Ann Arbor.

Al made a couple of trips to the motor home to check the system. The meal ended with a watch schedule. Al would get two four hour breaks, relieved by Matt and Webb tonight, and Tanya and Karen the next. Al and Matt felt they would have the recording issue conquered by the next day, also they could have the alarm system call the cell phones of Matt and Tanya so they could have freedom from being in the motor home and still have alerts.

A fireplace and conversation ended the active day for the six people.

28

Location

Koning heard a knock on the frame of his open office door. His top surveillance expert rushed in. She put a map copy on his desk. It had a magic marker circle on it.

The happy FBI investigator said, "We found Carla. She is in the Upper Peninsula, at Matt Hunter's.

Koning looked at the map, asking, "How do you know?"

The investigator replied, "Yesterday she called Dave, we listened in. She said a lot of mushy stuff, but mentioned she went to a clinic. She gave her doctor's name. We located the doctor in a clinic at St. Ignace, just across the bridge. Today we had two very dashing operatives call on them and they finessed the address where they were to send the lab results. With no court order in hand or overtly causing a violation of patient confidentiality—they just used sweet talk, 20/10 eyesight and the ability to read upside down.

"Do you want to send marshals?"

Koning thought, then said, "No. Locate the property from the air, get some pictures. Build a file on the Hunters—back to their birth. Get court orders for cell phone surveillance. This is a priority assignment, get some help and get information on everyone and everything on the property. Put some cars on the road, be very careful. I don't want Webb running again. Be clever—find a ploy—like UPS, mail, something plausible—use your head. Remember, Webb is very smart and has instincts and powers you are not used to."

The FBI woman asked, "When do you want an update?"

Koning said, "Every afternoon, schedule with my secretary. And I'll buy you, and your significant other, a dinner if you can find Webb's satellite phone number."

With the best news he had had in a week of frustration regarding the prosecution of Ahmad Hussin Salaam Alikhan, Koning call the Deputy U.S. Attorney. He had known that Carla Webb was missing and had sent almost daily barbs to that effect.

Koning got through to the second highest person in the Justice Department. He began, "We've located our star witness. You can stop the memos."

The Deputy replied, "Good, are you going to put her in custody?"

Koning replied, "Not at this time, she is safe and not a taxpayer burden. We will watch her and her father closely.

"I feel we can schedule a trial, the Imam's defense team is running out of legal chaff."

The Deputy said, "This is off the record, don't be too quick to go to trial, make sure you have all your ducks in a row. The longer we wait, the more the religious tensions have a chance to relax. I understand the city police and administration are being quite vocal about the incident."

Koning said, "Incident? Killing a girl and a policeman and nearly killing tens of thousands isn't an incident."

The Deputy cut him off, "Be calm, see what I mean, we need to handle this with care. Now is not the best time for a high profile trial involving an Islamic scholar. We have the holidays coming up; maybe after the first of the New Year would be more appropriate for your staff and the jurors. You have our full support, whatever you decide."

While the Deputy babbled on, Koning thought, *he called that hateful, blood thirsty Islamic fundamentalist a scholar.*

At the conclusion of the political babble the Deputy ordered, "Send me a report of Ms. Webb's location and your actions to make sure she doesn't flee the country with her father. I may be questioned on this subject and I want to be onboard with all the current facts."

Koning said, "I'll have it sent this afternoon. Thank you for your interest."

The Deputy ended the call, "Thank you for the update. You're doing a fine job out there."

Koning hung up second, again wanting to put the phone down hard enough to crack the plastic.

He thought, *I was just reminded I'm...out there, I serve at the pleasure of the President and the people that are...in there, also, I have a gangster who knows my daughter's goldfish bowl needs cleaning. One wants me to postpone the trial until after the fall elections and the other will protect his daughter at any cost.*

Koning called in his secretary, "Have the surveillance team send me an update on the Webb situation by this afternoon. Make sure all the facts and planned activities are included. Keep it brief and pointed. Make them aware I'll be forwarding the information to Justice in Washington."

29

Issues Galore

After a week of daily exercise walks to the mailbox, Carla and Tanya finally got mail. The weather had gone from cool to cold as October turned to November. Boots, down jackets and warm hats compensated for the cold 35 degree wind gusting to 20 mph out of the northwest. Skiffs of snow and frost accumulated on the north side of trees and brush. It froze every night now.

Five days earlier an impatient Webb had been on the phone with the Detroit doctor that ordered Carla's tests. The doctor had insisted on talking to Carla privately. After fifteen minutes she stood on the steps of the RV with a shocked expression.

Karen looked up at her, "What did the doctor say?"

Carla looked at the group standing outside the garage, "I've got good news and unexpected news. There are no issues with my blood counts, they are a little low, but within normal ranges, and I'm expecting."

Everyone paused for a ten count.

Karen, reacting first, hugged her, Tanya congratulated her, Webb blew his nose.

Matt said, 'Somewhere we have champagne."

Carla smiled and said, "I can't drink now, make mine milk.

"I need to call Dave, we only have one phone left. We've been saving it until he gets some more, haven't talked to him for four days. He doesn't have class this afternoon. I think this is important enough. He was so worried about the tests, thinking about radiation."

Webb came to Carla, gave her a hug and said, "We love you. Things will work out. Don't be afraid of anything."

Carla kissed his cheek, "You're more afraid than I am. You should know I've got this great dad that does all my worrying for me.

"Now I've got to call Dave."

Carla went back into the motor home and called Dave. No answer. She tried four more times that night. In desperation she came to her father, "What can I do? The phone rings but no one answers. I can't reach him."

Webb said, "Try again tomorrow and if you don't get Dave I'll call Koning, I said I'd call him—he must have someone watching Dave. There is probably a good reason, the phone may be faulty."

The next day Carla called at dawn and several times later with no success.

At mid morning Webb called Koning, asking, "Do you know the whereabouts of Dave Adams?"

Koning cleared his throat, "I've got bad news, Mr. Adams disappeared six days ago. If I had known your number I would have called you. We are worried. I've got all the local police and my investigators all on his trail. Nothing. He went to class—actually he was in charge of the class and never got back to his apartment. His vehicle is parked in his space at the apartment. There are no signs or reports of a struggle."

Webb asked, "What about your watch dogs?"

They followed him until he pulled into the parking area. They remained in their car, watching the only way out of the covered parking area and his building's front door. He never came out the front and his roommate said he never came into the apartment."

Webb said, "This isn't good. He doesn't know where Carla is. If bad people have him, he will take a lot of punishment. You said the FBI hadn't a clue after nearly a week?"

Koning said, "Not a clue. There were no cameras around, our team remembers a van and two vehicles coming out of the parking lot, nothing unusual or attention drawing.

"On another subject, how is Carla?"

Webb replied, "Her blood is good and she's pregnant. Your news will not be taken well. Can't the government do anything well except spend money on incompetency?

Webb gave Koning his satellite number and with it a warning, "Call if you learn anything, I figure you can find us now, but don't send in troops without calling ahead or they will be considered trespassers and a danger to Carla. Hear me—I won't take prisoners. Also, the people I hire get their job done.

"Now I've got to tell my daughter the bad news, I have to look into her eyes and tell her the father of her child has been abducted. This whole thing really pisses me off."

The girls opened the mailbox out by the paved road. It was big, rusty and 'Hunter' that was hand painted thirty years earlier was barely discernible.

Inside was a 6x9x5inch cardboard box, two letters from the clinic and a Cabela's catalog. The catalog was addressed to Matt, one letter to Carla Webb c/o Matt Hunter and the other letter to Mrs. T. Hunter. The box was hand lettered and addressed to Carla Webb at the Hunters, there was no return address.

The wind and cold precluded opening anything at the mailbox. Carla and Tanya started back to the house. Tanya used the Midland to call for the Yukon. She said, "Walking into the wind with bundles is too much for a mother-to-be. Please have the staff send the carriage." She repeated the request in Spanish just for effect.

Matt picked them up halfway down the straight road. They appreciated the heated vehicle. When Matt went to the paved road to turn around he noticed a gray vehicle he had seen a day earlier following him from Naubinway where they had bought food and drink at the general store.

In the Yukon Matt said, "I think we are being watched. That car has been around here too much. We need to tell Webb and Al."

In the house, at the kitchen table, Carla read her report, "All within normal except the hCG, human chorionic gonadotropic hormone. I am truly with child. It is good this isn't a bad report—it took so long to get here that if I was serious for radiation poisoning I'd be a goner."

Tanya asked to see Carla's report. Carla gave it to her, Tanya studied it carefully.

Carla said, "I can't wait to tell Dave, he will be surprised but eventually he will be pleased."

Webb saw the set of Carla's jaw, she was fighting tears.

Tanya opened her letter, "Ah, I have blood, it took four pages and I believe $500 to tell me that." Tanya scanned the numbers and verbiage as she spoke, flipping back and forth between several pages. She also looked at Carla's report again. After almost a minute she glanced at Webb who acknowledged the look with a thin smile."

Matt asked, "What about the package?"

Both Webb and Al came forward to look at the package. Al said, "This isn't good. Only the clinic knows you are here, and this doesn't look like it came from any medical lab, its post marked Dearborn."

Webb picked up the package and took it to the garage work bench. He put it down and turned on the bright florescent light.

He said, "This needs to be opened carefully."

Webb and Al had everyone leave while they slowly worked on the package. Cutting a small hole in the side and using a fiber optic attachment to a Maglight they carefully increased the hole until they could make out a DVD in a plastic container and a cell phone. Bubble wrap protected the contents. They cut open the end and wearing rubber gloves they extracted the two items.

They opened the unlabeled DVD. The anxiously awaiting Matt, Tanya and Karen followed them to the entertainment center in the large living room. Al put in the DVD and hit the play button.

The screen was filled with a spot lit Dave Adams taped to a gray metal chair. A voice came over the sound system, "Call Dave and listen to him. The phone is programmed with his present number. Failure to do this will be fatal for him." The unaccented voice ended but the video of Dave continued. He looked hurt, his lower lip was split and bleeding, he had bruises on his right cheek and chin. His left eyelid puffed half over his eye. He looked into the camera. He was blinking from the strong light in his face.

Before anyone could stop her, Carla ran out and came back with the small cell phone, "We must call him. He's been beaten."

Matt spoke, "Stop, put the phone down. Play the disc over."

Al worked the control for the DVD, the image went backwards, then forward.

Matt said, "Watch his eyes, his blinks. They are regular, controlled. It is code."

Al said, "I agree, I'll run it several times."

Matt said, "It is dash dot and dash dash dash, that's 'no' in Morse Code. He's shaking his head between the two letters. He was a Boy Scout too."

Matt took the cell phone from Carla, "We need to treat this carefully. The last thing we will do is turn it on, because it could be the very last thing you do."

Carla burst into tears, she sank to the floor, her eyes on the screen showing Dave blinking at the light. He was hurt but still defiant. She took the control and played the macabre scene over and over. Tanya and Karen stayed with her.

Matt looked at the cell phone. It was labeled 'Alcatel', all black with a chrome rim.

Webb looked at it, "Well they know where we are. Why didn't they send people instead of a package? They gave up surprise. It has to be a trick or a bomb. I say take it out and shoot it."

Al said, "I think it can be snapped open . If they put something in it, it has to open. They can't be using it as a GPS if they already know our address."

Matt added, "Curiosity killed the kitty."

Al said, "Get clear and let me play. Maybe it will tell us who we're dealing with."

Webb said to be careful and he and Matt opened the garage door and stood in its opening. The cold air came in, Matt took a fire extinguisher off the wall.

Al worked with a tiny bladed screwdriver and his jackknife. The phone popped open.

Al said, "Look here—I bet this wad of putty was not originally part of this phone.

Al took his knife blade and carefully scooped out the gray putty material, scraping it off on the edge of the wooden work bench. He got most of it out.

Al smelled it, speaking loudly he said, "Smells like nitrates, motor oil, with just a slight bouquet of rotten eggs. When I was a detective I remember we had ScentKits that they trained police dogs with, they smelled like this, with more smell of rotten eggs. This is a binary explosive. This little dab would take half the caller's head off."

Webb and Matt came back into the garage and lowered the door.

Matt asked, "Is it safe now?"

Al answered, "No, it could still explode and there's enough left so you would be picking plastic and parts out of your face. It is all battery and solid circuits, nothing I can see to cut, I just took out most of the explosive. The detonator part can be no bigger than a thread and I don't dare scrape away enough to see it or where it goes."

Webb asked, "What do you suggest Al?"

Al looked at Matt and Webb, "We have kidnapping and attempted murder. Our hiding place is blown. This was to get by our defenses, it was cold, clever and it could have worked if we weren't on our guard. I say bring the FBI in after we hide Carla again."

Webb thought, and then said, "I agree. Carla needs to see this cell phone. Al you need to explain to her. Be clear and graphic. Dave is either dead or not, we can't help him. He wouldn't be a bargaining chip if the phone had worked. He would have been a link to the killers, he was not blindfolded.

"What a day."

Webb went in to the living room. Carla was lying on the couch with a cold cloth on her forehead. He knelt by her and said, "Honey, you need to talk to Al in the garage. You have to face hard facts. You've got to be tough for yourself and for the miracle of life inside you."

Carla and her mother went to the garage. Webb turned to Tanya who was still kneeling on the floor beside the couch. She had made no effort to leave the room.

Webb sat in the chair across from her. He began, "What have you figured out?"

Tanya said, "I graduated with a biology major from Florida, also I have been studying about blood and bone marrow doning ever since Carla was exposed to radiation. The chances of a donor match between two unrelated people are 1 in 540. Carla and I have a match expected of sisters. According to my report, the human leukocyte antigen, HLA, protein markers in the screening process gave it away.

"Are you my father?"

Webb looked at her and said, "Yes, I knew Anita, your mother, in Miami before she married your father. She was the most beautiful woman in the whole Cuban group. She loved your father; he was away in basic training before they married. It was one of those parties and a night that went too far. He doesn't know. My Karen knows. There is enough going on, can we keep this between us for now?"

Tanya took his hand, "I've always known something was between you and me, and you and my mother. I've loved Carla from the first time we met. Now I know why you were always there and why mother didn't want you around."

Webb said, "Anita can certainly be feisty, unless she needs me.

"Let's go into the garage, we need to do some planning."

30

Nobody Move Nobody Die

Carla listened numbly to Al explain the intent of the DVD and the cell phone. She fought the realization of Dave's fate by asking how she could contact the people that abducted him.

Webb and Tanya had come into the garage and heard her sad questioning.

Webb said, "We'll call Koning right now, most likely we'll get a recording, but we need his help and his FBI staff.

Carla, Webb and Matt started toward the motor home to make a call. As they were leaving the garage all their Midland radios went off. As they opened the heavy RV door the alarm from the security system was buzzing.

Al rushed by the group and brought the camera generating the alarm to the computer screen. A man's shoulder went by as a ghostly infrared image, behind him another set of eyes glowed, reflecting as from a flash picture but showing up as white, a second man following along the narrow deer trail.

Matt said, "Two men, sneaking up from the east. Turn the lights off in here, put down the shades. I'm going after them. Don't follow me. I want only bad guys and me out there. I've hunted the area for forty years, from a time when I could look over the trees as a child."

Webb said, "Let's remember these could be government men just trying to spy or they could be Muslims on a mission to kill us."

Matt asked, "What's your plan? I'm frustrated with all this uncertainty and waiting. I'm happy to have someone to go after, some action."

Webb asked, "Al, make the call."

Al ordered, "Women inside, turn on the upstairs hall lights, wait downstairs, lights off, train your guns on the kitchen and patio doors. I'll stay here and whisper in the radios. I can cover both garage doors from here.

"Challenge them, shoot at the slightest movement that isn't surrender. Don't think about it or you'll be too slow. It's easier to explain an accident, if you're alive."

Matt started out of the RV, saying, "I'll put on camouflage, take my pistol, flashlight and my Midland, I'll keep it off unless I need it. I'll come in behind them. Honk the horn if there are more than two. If I call you, be quiet, yes is one, no is two taps. We use these to hunt with and we don't like to talk when we're in the woods."

Webb said, "I'll get the women set up, then I'm going on top, if we turn on the patio lights on the other side of the house it will give a large view to the north and it will make this side of the house seem that much darker. I'll have a good field of fire up there."

Matt changed into his soft felt bow hunting pants and jacket, he also had a net face hood that didn't impair his hearing or vision. After putting on light unlined Danner stalking boots, he checked the small Maglight and put it in his left pants pocket. He chambered a round in the FN 5.7 pistol, there were 14 more in the magazine. He put another magazine of 15 shells in his other pocket.

He left quietly from the garage door, disappearing into the darkness.

Webb put Carla and her mother in the living room, crouching behind the protection of the stone fireplace that protruded into the room. He armed them with a pistol and a shotgun. He stationed Tanya in the hallway off the kitchen, arming her with the deer rifle she had bought for the coming season.

Webb said so all the women could hear, "Don't come rushing to the sounds of gunfire. Stay at your stations, keep your fingers off the triggers and don't shoot anyone that looks like us."

The women settled into their positions and made themselves weapon supports out of chairs and throw pillows.

Webb then put on a dark brown leather coat and black Navy watch cap, took his plastic machine gun and awkwardly stuffed a second box magazine in the coat's cargo pocket, he worked his way to the top of the RV, he laid down, facing the east woods.

Al had the RV's door open, the interior lights off, towels over as much of the surveillance system lights as he could. He had the rear TV on, then decided it put too much light into the driver's area and besides Webb had that area covered, so he turned it off.

Meanwhile Matt had gone quickly north on the road then cut in on a familiar and long unused trail, he moved with his pistol holstered, using both hands to move, and return branches as he worked his way into the forest. The leaves were damp from the cold, the mud on the path hardening from the frost that was just settling in. Matt made little noise.

Matt knelt beside a large maple, he listened to the sounds of the forest. The snap of twigs and the brush of branches against hard cloth came clearly to his trained ears. He very carefully moved in a vector between the sounds and the house. He worked around pine trees, stepping on their needles and avoiding noisy leaves and twigs. He heard whispering fifty feet ahead of him.

A low red light came on. It was a great help to Matt, it gave perfect directions and outlined trees between him and the two visitors.

Matt fought back a chuckle and he thought, *I shouldn't be enjoying this, but I can't help it. I think I would rather stalk these men than a deer. They're looking at a map or aerial photograph, the assholes are lost.*

Matt watched the red light change to a brighter white light, quickly covered with a gloved hand.

They're using a GPS device or a smart phone with maps and GPS. Good technology, bad sneaking technique, might as well make a camp fire. A white light in a black forest sticks out like a flare.

Just as Matt was plotting his next movement, the house patio flood lights came on, they were on the other side of the house, but the light gave direction and also outlined the two men to Matt whose night vision was at full ability.

The men moved apart a few feet and toward the light, making enough noise that they couldn't hear Matt's careful approach. They stopped at the wooded edge, with twenty yards of mostly open yard to the motor home and house. One man, in a crouch, moved to a small bush that gave meager cover halfway to the house, the other stayed back, stood up and peaked around a tree.

Matt moved closer to the man by the tree. At twenty feet Matt stood behind a smooth barked beech tree. He took out his flashlight and held it in his left hand around the left side of the tree, he aimed the pistol from the right side. He wished he had a switch on the flashlight instead of needing to turn the top. With some dexterity he brought the beam to life.

Using his best Charlton Heston, as Moses, voice he said, "Don't move, put up your hands."

The man closest to Matt spun around, he pulled a gun from a belt holster and tried to roll out of the light. The flashlight's brightness made the man by the bush harder to see. That man clearly did have a pistol in his hand. He tried to duck down on the other side of the bush from Matt to escape the light.

Matt thought, *bad move, now Webb could see you.*

Matt's glance at the farther man, cost him a split second, his man fired. Matt could hear or maybe feel the bullets hitting the beech tree. Matt kept the flashlight on the man and fired back. He couldn't sight, he just pulled the trigger five times in the general direction of the now prone, rolling man. The tongues of fire coming from his pistol lit the area. The crack of the little powerful shells was deafening. But Matt still heard a grunt and yelp of pain from his target.

From the edge of his vision Matt realized the man in the yard had stood up, perhaps to also fire at him.

At that moment Webb's P90 stitched the ground two feet from the standing man's leg. He dropped his gun, raised his hands and shouted, "Federal Agents, Federal Agents, don't shoot!"

Webb, in a much more authoritative voice, said, "One move, you die right now."

Matt's man raised his hands from a now sitting position, also dropping his weapon.

Matt came around his tree, still with the flashlight out at his side, approached the closest man, "Keep your hands up, get up and lean on the tree."

The man complained, "I've been shot, and I think you nicked my heel."

Matt said, "Do as I say or you get more than a nick—move!"

The man had watched enough cop shows to do the right thing. As Matt came up behind him he said, "Relax, we are federal agents."

Matt countered, "If either of you move wrong, you'll be very dead federal agents."

Webb ordered his man to lie down, the man thought too long, Webb fired another near burst. Matt was relieved to see that no blood was coming from multiple holes in the man under Webb's weapon, as he quickly got on the ground.

Matt's man jumped then returned to tree pushing. He didn't quiver a muscle as Matt found his empty holster on his belt and removed a small revolver from an ankle holster.

The garage driveway and the southern outside lights came on. Matt figured Al must have done this.

Matt moved his man toward the house, and on the way searched and removed a second gun from the man that Webb had controlled. Matt got him up and moved them both to the house.

Al met them with his P90 leveled at them. Matt thought, *it didn't look much like the fearfully deadly weapon it is, a pump 12 gauge was a lot more impressive.*

Al, the excop, took over. Matt decided there is a protocol for moving prisoners through a door. Al waited until Webb was off the motor home and was positioned inside the lit garage, then he guided them inside. Fifteen feet seemed to be the closest you wanted get to a prisoner.

When Matt got into the garage the men were sitting on the floor, their backs to the workbench. One man started to speak and was told be silent.

Al stationed Matt and Webb at good covering angles and distances. The Yukon in the two vehicle garage took its share of space. Then Al went into the house and relieved the anxiety of the women as they must have heard the small war going on. He sent Tanya to man the surveillance system in the motor home in case there were more people coming.

Carla came into the garage and glared at the sitting men, "Where is Dave?"

One of the men replied, "We don't know. We are with the FBI."

Matt thought *that about sums up the state of the situation.*

Karen came out to get Carla, she glanced at the men, took a step toward the nearest one and looked down.

Webb said, "Don't get in front of me, stay away from him."

Karen said, "He's bleeding."

Matt noticed the blood on the gray painted garage floor. He also noticed the men had on bullet proof vests under their dark jackets.

Al was back from getting Tanya set up on the camera system. He went from man to man, taking off their jackets and giving them a further search, finding identification, radios, car keys and jack knives. He found change in one pocket, as he put it with the other items on the workbench he said, "You don't sneak with change in your pocket," One started to talk and Al back handed him. "You talk when we tell you to talk."

Al looked at the ID's, matched man and pictures, went through any papers in their wallets and checked the weapons that Matt had put on a small table that was just inside the door.

There was silence until Al said, "These guys are feds."

"You guys can stand up, but we are going to keep you covered until you tell us what you're doing and why."

The older of the two, who Matt had wounded, was named Stan. Matt noted he had two hits on his vest and a chunk out of his heel and didn't have a shoe on that foot.

Stan took off his vest, checked the bullet hits, one was close to the neck, he looked back at his heel. Holding up the vest, showing the mark near the neck, he said, "That was close and you blew off a laced boot."

Matt replied, "I was doing the best I could to kill you, you fired first. Why are you sneaking on my land without notice or warrants? We told Koning we wouldn't take kindly to him sending people.

"You're real lucky Webb is such a good shot when he fired that warning burst."

Webb snorted, "Warning shots my ass, I was trying to cut him in two, we need to practice night shooting and I'm sending for lasers for everyone.

"Actually you came at a good time, we're glad we don't have to get rid of your bloody bodies. We need you to take evidence of a kidnapping and attempted murder back with you.

"Now tell us why you're here."

The men talked about their assignment to watch the house. They said they knew the location because of Carla's slip about the clinic and doctor.

Webb interrupted, "Don't say that in front of my daughter or you won't have teeth."

The men said they were told to get as much information on the house and motor home as possible. They got bored with sitting in the car, watching deer cross the road, people rubber necking as they drove by, and having two stop to ask if they needed help. They didn't intend any arrests or to take custody of Carla."

While they were talking, the pointed weapons were lowered, but not put away. Karen came out with sudsy water, towels and bandages. Matt left the garage with a larger flashlight and found the agent's shoe, the back was sliced as neatly as could have been done with a razor.

Returning to the garage he handed the high topped rubber soled shoe to the agent who viewed it and said, "I'll have to make up a better story than having someone sneak up on me and shoot me three times in the dark."

They completed examining the cell phone. Then they went in to see the DVD. Carla came downstairs when she heard the DVD. She cried quietly and didn't want the men to take the disc.

Webb assured her it was the right thing to be done. The agents said they would keep it safe and even make duplicates. The unsaid feeling in the room was that it was so terrible that she should never see it again.

After an hour, all that needed to be said was said. There were no more threats by Webb or claims of governmental authority by the agents. The agents gave Webb their cards and direct numbers. Matt had the agent he had shot sit on the work bench and duct taped his boot back on, over his bandaged foot. Matt and Webb drove the agents back to their vehicle, where Webb gave them a box containing their weapons and all the mailed material.

They agreed to call Webb immediately with any and all useful information.

Webb, Al and Matt sat at the kitchen table with Karen. Carla had gone to bed where Karen had stayed with her until she had cried herself to sleep. Tanya was in the motor home.

Webb said, "I wasn't joking about lasers, and I wasn't trying to miss that guy. I should have shot horizontally but I didn't know where you were Matt. The man was aiming toward you.

Matt said, "The whole thing came out better than it should have with thirty or forty shots being fired. I thought my shells would go through body armor."

Al answered, "No, not these, they tumble and mushroom, very deadly but not armor piercing—you need a different, hard metal core and from your range it would go right through both sides of his vest. I'll make some calls tomorrow to Detroit to get overnight delivery of some night fighting sights and lasers. I should have thought of them. I'm not used to having the night be so dark."

Webb said, "Carla can't stay here anymore. Let's talk about a new location tomorrow. Those guys got close, people with lots of firepower and suicidal tendencies could get to us. I doubt that we could stop a half dozen with body armor and AK's. Let's think and talk about this in the morning."

AL said, "I've got the watch, Tanya can relieve me at 4:00 am."

Except for Al, everyone found their pillows.

Matt showered, getting the fear and cordite smells off himself. He quietly slid into bed beside Tanya.

Tanya turned toward him and gave him a warm kiss, "I need to tell you something, seeing how I don't go to confession anymore."

Matt kissed her again and put his hand on her hip, saying, "Have you been a bad little girl, do you need to be severely punished with a mink whip or some other fiendish torture?"

Tanya pulled away, "Be serious. I lied to my father."

Matt questioned, "When did you talk to him tonight?"

Tanya went on, "You remember when I came home from the clinic with the bandage on the IV spot? Webb questioned me about it and gave Karen a look. I figured something wasn't being said between them. Well, when the reports came they really didn't say much more than Carla and I had some similar blood proteins. There were no DNA results or anything about matching ratios. I've felt for years there was a dark secret between my mother and Webb. The more I'm around Carla I see myself twenty years ago. Her hair, skin, even her cuticles are like mine. So I played a trick on Webb. I led him to believe the reports told me the fact that Carla and I are sisters. He admitted it tonight. He said Karen knows and of course my mother, but absolutely not my dad—that is George Vega."

Matt, now wide awake, whispered, "That explains a dozen things I've thought about from when we first met. A crime boss would never go out looking for a small lost shipment of dope; he did it because you were on the plane that crashed. He should have killed us both when we were on the boat and he was running. We were a problem and a link to his disappearance. He came after you when the Canadians took you—jumping at your mother's command.

"How are you going to handle this news?"

Tanya answered, "I'm still thinking about it. I won't ever tell George Vega, it would literally kill him, his heart barely works as it is. I might tell Carla, she needs all the love and support she can get, but I'll talk to Karen and Webb—I will still call him that."

Matt kissed her and found her hip again, saying, "Good plan. You sleepy? Shooting people always makes me horny."

Tanya whispered as she slid closer to Matt, "You get horny if it snows or you hear an owl."

31

Plans

Tanya slid out of their bed before her alarm went off—set for 3:45 am. Matt reached over and touched her breast, and then came closer and said, "Who…who-who."

Tanya whispered, "I don't need a horny owl at four in the morning, thank you. You were wonderful, but I've got responsibilities and horny owls aren't a help to me."

She dressed and went to the RV. In the Ambassador she found Al and Webb drinking coffee. They stood when she entered, Tanya was honored by their courtliness.

Webb spoke, "Want some coffee?'

Tanya said, "Yes, please."

Al served her coffee in a plastic mug.

Webb said, "We have been up all night thinking about Carla, the baby and Dave. We have a plan, or more correctly a start of a plan."

The computer buzzed, they jerked their heads toward the screen, a large, thick coated wolf went by camera 3.

Al said, "They hunt all night, sleep in the daytime I think. I'd hate to be a deer or a rabbit."

Tanya asked, "Didn't you sleep?"

Webb answered, "I slept a few hours. There are too many time sensitive problems. The number one is Dave Adams who we saw taped to a chair, the father of my grandchild may be in a dumpster right now. I want to be smarter than these people that send a cell phone that was intended to blow my beautiful daughter's head off. I want to get that Imam and make his death so exquisite that when his followers bow to the east they will think of it."

Tanya sat in the driver's chair, sipped her coffee and scanned the monitor, looking at her biological father—who sat with resolve and action infused in every muscle, she said, "What are your thoughts?"

Al answered, "There is a leak between Koning and somewhere. We need to use it."

Webb followed, "Koning is the law, we can be justice, and they're not the same. You can help us. I'm going to call him at his home right now, his youngest daughter will answer, you say you are Carla Webb and must speak to her father immediately. When Koning answers, hand the phone to me."

Al made the call, punching in a number written on a memo pad that was in Webb's hand. He handed the phone to Tanya.

There were many rings then a sleepy voice answered, "This isn't funny Glen."

Tanya said, "I'm not Glen, he would be very rude to call you so early. I'm Carla Webb and this is a life or death situation. I must talk to your father. This isn't a prank, please get your dad."

A minute passed, Tanya could hear a door opening, quick steps on carpeting, another door opening and the Koning's daughter shaking him awake.

Koning spoke, "Yes, what is this. Its four o'clock in the morning."

Tanya handed the phone to Webb, who said, "Koning this is Webb, get out of bed and get your brain going. I'll give you a minute."

Thirty seconds later Koning said, "Go ahead Webb, I'm awake."

Webb described the actions of the previous day: every detail of the DVD and explosive laden cell phone and the fire fight with his FBI agents.

Webb went on, "The FBI has all the material that was sent here. You should be getting a report later today. We need your help to try to save Dave. You need to make a report based on the agents' information that Carla has been moved and with Dave Adams missing you've lost your best link to finding your witness. Mention the DVD and that the cell phone didn't work. Say your technical people found explosive in the phone and its chemicals corroded the circuitry."

Koning said, "Slow down, I'm making notes."

Webb waited, then said, "This is about our only chance to save Dave, if it isn't too late. If they send another message or recording at least we've bought him some time. If they let him go they will be using you to find Carla again. Mention you have a trace available on Dave's last cell phone that is in his apartment. Then watch the phone. It is all we could think of at this time. Any thoughts?"

Koning replied, "I'll need to get to the agents right away so our stories match. That shouldn't be hard. We can put an active GPS signal in the phone. We can play cell phone games too. I'm going to have my offices swept for bugs, if we find them we won't take them out just yet.

"For your information, we traced Adams' abduction to the van that left the apartment parking lot. His finger prints were in the van, and no others. It was stolen then abandoned in a Wal-Mart parking lot."

Webb said, "I'm sorry I woke your daughter, I couldn't take a chance with your office phone and we had to have these actions in place when you go to work today."

Koning asked, "How did you get her number?"

Webb answered, "Verizon and money."

Koning asked, "Do you have my cell phone number?"

Webb replied, "Everyone has your number, that's why I didn't use it. You can use your land line and call this number. Keep up the cover story. Use your daughter's phone from home for the whole truth."

As Webb concluded the call with Koning, there was a tapping on the door, it was Carla with a coat over her flannel pajamas.

Carla came in, "I saw your lights from my bedroom window, it seems you can't sleep either. All I can see when I close my eyes is Dave in that chair."

Webb took her to the couch and found a blanket to wrap her feet and legs. He gave her a detailed report of their thoughts and plans.

Webb said, "You need to keep calling the last cell phone. Dave's roommate was probably asked to not answer it, but if he does, just honestly tell him your worries and about the DVD. Say the cell phone wouldn't work."

Carla was given a half cup of the last of the coffee, she sipped it and said, "Doing something is better than just worrying. Do you think there's a chance?"

Al said, "Sure, Dave is a means to an end, you're the target. The people that have Dave went to a lot of trouble to take him, make that cell phone bomb, get our address and get the package here so fast. They aren't dummies and they are connected to government sources."

Webb added, "If they kill Dave without killing you it will harden your heart and make your resolve to testify even stronger."

Carla nodded her head, "That's what I am feeling. I want that Imam dead. I could kill him myself."

Webb smiled, "That is the Russian in you."

Webb glanced at Tanya, who smiled back.

Webb stood up, "Now we should all try to get a little sleep, while Tanya watches the creatures of the night—or more precisely—the early morning."

32

Hide and Seek

Matt and Karen were alone at breakfast. The others were sleeping in after being up most of the night. The security system would send a call to Matt's cell phone if it sensed motion.

Karen served Matt toast and eggs, then put her plate across the table from him. She dunked a toast finger in her eggs-over-easy. After a bite and some coffee she said, "I understand we have a plan, which was all my husband said before he turned over and started snoring."

Matt said, "Tanya also said they had a plan, and she said we would learn about it later."

Karen added, "At least Carla is getting some sleep. Whatever the plan, it seems to have calmed her. I guess we were the only ones who got a night's sleep."

Matt, after using the last of his toast to clean his plate of egg, said, "I've got an idea for another hiding place. It is the opposite of here. No hundred thousand dollar RV palace, no electricity for surveillance gear or flat screen TVs, no road, no water runs or flushes, but it is homey. I'll check with the owner this morning."

Karen asked, "Sounds like a challenge, how far away?"

Matt answered, "Four miles or so, seems like a lot more. I'll make the call right now."

Matt went to a 3 year old phonebook; it had old phone books back pages stuffed in the back. He sorted through several loose pages and found the number he wanted. He went into the garage to talk privately without bothering any of the house's sleepers. After he talked for a half hour he came back to the kitchen.

Matt poured a second cup of coffee and said, "We have a green light. I'll go through the whole detail when we have all the players here. I'm going to take a 4x4 ride now, I'll be back before noon. I'll carry the Midland and leave my cell phone here, it will signal if the surveillance system calls it. Then wake everyone up."

Matt dressed warmly and walked down to the cabin at the quarry that served as a hunting camp. It was the only cabin on the property for a dozen years before Matt built a new house. It was built inside the huge shop building that was used to service the monster steam engines that worked the quarry. It was last filled with workers in the early 30s. The shop walls were thick concrete and the roof was tin over massive iron girders seventy feet above the concrete floor. Besides housing a two story prefab cabin—appropriated by Matt and his cronies from a departing pipeline project, it held and protected multiple boy toys—snowmobiles, 4x4 all terrain vehicles, canoes and junk men couldn't drive or throw away.

Matt gassed up a red Honda 4x4 and drove back up to the house. In the garage he strapped a plastic box to the back deck of the machine. He filled a small Husqvarna chainsaw with mixed gasoline and chain oil, threw in various hand tools, fifty feet of nylon rope and a gallon of Coleman fuel. On the front luggage area he tied down two filled plastic gallon water jugs.

He took his pistol and headed north up the road. The day was gray and cold with the possibility of snow or worse, sleet. He was grateful to have goggles on, the cold air would otherwise make his eyes water. He didn't wear a helmet, his Kromer, a neck scarf and zipped up hunting jacket kept him warm. He substituted his usual hunting gloves—military wool glove liners for leather gloves lined with Gortex and Thinsulate.

Twenty minutes later brought him to a hardly noticeable eastern fork off the two rut road. He worked around several dead falls, opting not to cut the trail clear. Twice he used the rope and reverse on the 4x4 to clear dead falls. He went through a swamp, crossed a rock bottomed stream whose icy water came high enough that he had to pick his feet up. The trail was part of a rail spur to the north, the area across the swamp at one time had rock fill and timbers—all useful materials were taken out when the spur was closed. With a trained eye Matt could see the difference in the size and species of the growth along the eighty year old road bed. The trail on the other side of the swamp became straight and easy going. When Matt had last visited the cabin many years ago he had driven in with a pickup. To duplicate that drive now would take a day of clearing work. There were no signs of travel for many years on the way to the cabin.

Matt reached the little one room cabin. Its owner was now 92 and had told Matt neither he nor his family had been in the place for several years. Matt got off the 4x4, and walked around the cabin. The brush was still cleared away from the cabin. The overlapping red rolled tar paper roof was all in place and debris free, the door was closed as were the shutters, the metal chimney was sound and straight. The key to the door's padlock hung on a nail inside the door of the outhouse. Matt noted some porcupine damage on the outhouse door, but the inside was fine, toilet paper was safe in a plastic topped coffee can.

Matt opened the cabin door carefully, he didn't want to startle a skunk or something else with teeth, claws or wings. The cabin was tight. A roll of paper towels over a sink area was the victim of happy mice who found it great for bedding. Matt knew he would find a shredded mass somewhere in or under something. Matt went outside and opened the shutters. All three windows, two flanking the only door and one on the east side, had glass intact. Next he went to the wood stove central on the far wall. It was a Kalamazoo, its green enamel as perfect as the day it was made. He tapped the stove pipe, no solid sounds, no rust; he worked the damper, left in a closed position, and opened it. There were no nests or creatures in the oven or burn box. There was kindling in a wooden box next to the stove and a larger wood box next to that. He lifted the burner plate that exposed the wood box; it was full of kindling and dry hardwood. There was an old blue coal oil can half full of kerosene. Matt checked the cupboards, red and white checked oilcloth below heavy ceramic cups, bowls and dishes. No mouse droppings. The old man was a stonemason all his life and was fussy about things closing tightly.

Matt found mouse nests in the kindling box, no customers. He lit the balls of chewed up paper to see if the chimney was clear and would draw. Success, the fire burned and the smoke was drawn in and up. He poked the burning mouse chewed paper deeper into the burn box, added kindling. The room would soon be warm.

The bedding was in plastic bags on top of the two bunk beds. The mattresses were covered with heavy plastic sheets. Matt folded up the plastic and checked for mice use. They were clean, but musty. The exposed bed springs were something from WWII, but not rusted. Matt brought in the Coleman fuel and filled the two lanterns, both with intact mantles, and then the two burner Coleman stove. He pumped them all to make sure they held pressure. There was a five cell flashlight—it barely came on, Matt mentally noted the need for D batteries. There were utensils, tools, axes and saws, all useful.

After another hour Matt had cleaned, swept and nailed where needed and removed the mouse droppings and dead flies from the window sills, open shelves, table and counters. He made a note of what was in the pantry and continued with a list of some supplies the women might want for a week or so. During the next hour Matt broke a sweat: finding deadfall hardwood, cutting and dragging the limbs back to the cabin, then sawing them into short blocks, measuring them with a stick he gauged from the firebox so the wood wasn't over fifteen inches. Then with the ax from the cabin he split enough wood to equal what was already stacked outside. He figured it was a lot easier work when there wasn't a foot of snow. His wood was dry and clean, the old stacked wood had a lot that was mossy and punky.

While he cooled down from wood splitting, he walked around the cabin and followed a path down toward a gully. Halfway down into the depression was an outcropping of white, weathered limestone. Matt found the old piece of two-inch well pipe that had been driven horizontally into the hill. A small but steady stream of water poured out of it. A large galvanized moss covered wash tub caught and overflowed with the water. Matt scooped up a handful of the icy liquid, it smelled pure, he tasted it, —pristine. It was gathered from under-ground limestone structures common to the area. Matt splashed his sweaty face with the cold water and thought to add plastic buckets to his list for the next trip.

Walking back to the cabin, he closed up and locked up, letting the fire go out.

He got back on the Honda and tried his radio. It didn't make con-tact. He would try as he returned. A mile back, just before the descent to the stream he contacted the house. So the twenty mile radio works three miles in the woods.

Back for lunch Matt told of his idea for a safe house—or very remote cabin.

Webb liked the idea, Karen didn't like the mice and Carla had never used an outhouse or been without electricity. Tanya had to appear positive, as the odd woman out, and to support Matt.

Webb said, "Being off the grid is good, Matt says no one can get to it without going through here—at least without a helicopter and there's no place to land."

Tanya asked, "What does the cabin owner know?"

Matt said, "I just asked if I could use it through deer season. He said fine, it would be good for someone to open it up. He said if it needed anything to get it and he'd pay me back. His kids are all in California and to his grandkids 50 degrees is freezing. The place goes back to the Forest Service when the old man dies. The property is land locked by National Forest; the Government basically stole it from the fam-ily when it took over the railroad right-of-way. They even outlawed the ATVs driving through the woods. It's a shame; it is a fine cabin in great deer country."

Al came in, looked at Webb, "Phone for you. Koning."

Webb and Carla raced to the motor home. The others stayed at the table.

Koning began, "I've got an update. I sent off the message about Dave Adams being key to finding Carla and that we had the phone under a tap order. Then I sent our best tech person, who happens to be a cute young lady, to Adams' apartment to act as a date for his roommate, he was more than pleased with the plan. She will open the cell phone and put in a GPS that pings on its own. Now we wait for someone to take the bait. I'm running this on an 'only need to know' security, no briefings to the staff. I've got a SWAT team standing by oiling their guns and knives.

"On another subject, I've talked to the visitors you had yesterday. They drove the materials you gave them all the way to our lab. Their report of your activities is very vague, I understand you got the drop on them while they were reconnoitering."

Webb responded, "They were lucky to be alive. I told you to give us warning if you were sending people. In the dark they were Islamic terrorists as far as we were concerned. Let's not have this happen again."

Koning answered, "I hear you and it will be so."

Koning asked, "Is Carla there?"

Carla, her ear near the phone, said, "Yes I am."

Koning said, "Hello young lady. We will do everything possible to help your boyfriend. We'd like you to keep calling the cell phone. Call ten minutes before or after the hour. That way the roommate knows it's probably you. We are expecting Dave or someone to contact the roommate to get the phone. If you talk to Dave don't tell him where you are. If the bad guys know that information they won't need Dave anymore. Keep him talking. Let yourself be as nervous as you probably will be."

Carla said, "I understand, I won't have any trouble being nervous. I'm so worried for Dave. He'll fight them if he gets a chance."

Webb took the phone, "She'll be fine. The plan needs good people on your end to rescue Dave without harming him. Are your people skilled?"

Koning answered, "They are the best hostage rescue team we have available in suits or body armor. They are standing by at the Ann Arbor airport—helicopter and vehicles at the ready. All ex servicemen: fit, smart and trained to perfection. We have the roommate covered and an electrical tracking team working 24/7. I am doing the coordination personally through an FBI inspector I've known for ten years. We want prisoners and Dave rescued. There will be no promiscuous shooting."

Webb and Koning then talked about how he could trap the leak from above. The options were discussed, but nothing was resolved. They hung up.

Webb joined the group that had all gone back to the kitchen. He said, "Well, we have a plan, we have preparation, now we need our enemies to act as we hope they will.

"Now let's talk about that little cabin in the woods."

Matt went over the conditions of the cabin, stressing the quiet beauty of the woods, the creatures that would be wondering around, the flowing well and the old green enameled Kalamazoo woodstove.

Karen seemed interested, "My grandmother had a woodstove, I remember the wonderful pies, rolls and biscuits that came out of it."

Matt said, "With Tanya's permission, she and I will make another trip to the cabin and make it fit for living. If the ladies need to go there, we might not have time to haul supplies."

Tanya brightened at the idea. She and Karen started putting dry foods, flour, sugar, coffee, cans and various breads, bacon, a ham end and more on the kitchen table. Matt drove the Honda down to the tool shop and came back with a small two wheeled cart attached. With Webb's help he loaded the cart full with food and materials for the cabin. He included candles, a portable radio, and a Marlin 30-30 rifle and ammunition. He also remembered plastic pails, 8 D batteries, another flashlight and a hanging battery powered lantern.

Tanya came out with a cooking pot, filled with a bottle of cooking oil, a carton of eggs wrapped in towels and some spices. She also had a small frying pan,

She packed her materials in the cart, the pan going in last, "I won't cook with pans that mice have pooped in."

Matt laughed, "Just pretend they're caraway seeds."

Matt and Tanya, well dressed, headed off to the little cabin. Carla wanted to go, but Matt said the fewer trips the better, he didn't want to make an obvious trail.

They worked all afternoon in and around the cabin. The woodstove made it warm and dried it out, They hung the thin mattresses out on a rope Matt had strung up. Tanya reswept and washed down with hot soapy water all the shelves, counters, tables and chairs.

Matt made the area around the water pipe easier to get to and put down wood to cover the mud around it. He brought in water, filling the reservoir on the far right in the stove.

Matt noted, "This will give you hot water, when we finally leave we'll have to drain this. We can't let it freeze."

Tanya began to make the beds with the freshened mattresses, "This bedding is good. These quilts are beautiful work, too good to be left in an old cabin. The pillows aren't bad either. I thought we would need sleeping bags, we might want to bring them anyway, we should save these quilts."

Matt said, "Ok, but use the quilts, they belong here, in this cabin."

Tanya said, "We could use a cooler to put outside to keep things cold."

Matt said, "The bear will love that. I've lost a lot of food that way. Raccoons can get into coolers too. The pantry, built against the wall, is cool enough this time of year, just keep the door closed.

"Keep the tube loaded in the rifle and keep it by your bed, not by the door. Brace a chair against the door knob. That's for bear, not terrorists. The Muslims don't eat bacon, but a bear can smell it cooking for miles. So can I."

Tanya looked worried, "We had bear in Florida. We had to be careful with fish guts."

Tanya and Matt together cleaned the outhouse. Matt hung up a battery powered lantern.

Matt took Tanya to the flowing well; she was impressed and happy to have good water.

After checking the fire and stocking the inside wood fully, they locked up and journeyed back.

Matt enjoyed Tanya's warmth behind him. The little empty trailer bounced and rattled behind them. A light snow came down as they got back to the house. Matt suggested they leave the Honda in the garage at the house rather than down in the quarry and that they get a half bale of straw for the trailer to pad it, so the three women could get to the little cabin: two on the machine and one in the trailer.

Matt asked Tanya, "Can you find the cabin?"

Tanya answered, "In the daylight, I'd be fine."

Matt said, "I don't want to mark the trail. We use blaze orange ribbons or thumb tacks that shine from a flashlight beam, but those things are like a flag to a bull for some hunters. I don't want the ATVs and the hunters we will be getting in here during the next two weeks tearing up a highway to our hiding place. As it is, I've got friends that will see the little disturbances we have made. I'll tell them truthfully that the far north territory will be my area this year. We don't work another hunter's area without an OK."

Matt and Tanya went into the house, it was snowing harder.

33

Got Your Number

Assistant U.S. Attorney James Koning sipped his cold coffee and fingered up the last crumbs of a Danish roll he had begun to eat twenty minutes ago. He had a momentary fear that he was in the wrong Ann Arbor restaurant. Then the reason for his long early morning drive and clandestine meeting slid into the booth.

Lisa Heffner was small, cute and very, very smart. She was his FBI computer and communication genius. He had assigned her to Dave Adams' roommate. She was an integral part of a complex and bold plan—actually multiple plans.

Koning asked, "How's life with a college kid?"

Lisa answered, "He's nice and very quick, a perfect person for our plans. I need to get back ASAP. We have three cell phones ready and labeled, plus the phone from Carla and the roommate's own phone. I'm wired to our team, sound and video. They think I'm in the shower right now, my bug rig is hanging on the bathroom door, I hope it isn't getting too steamy."

Koning said, "OK, you're doing a fine job. Don't say a phone number or let the roommate refer to or show any of the extra phones. Here are our code names for the various phones."

Koning handed her a paper with three numbers, each followed by the word: dog, cat, bird.

Koning continued, "When you report, use one of these names to tell me the phone which the call came in on.

"With a little luck we'll get Dave back, catch some terrorists and find out what department has a spy, all in one operation."

Lisa, taking the paper, stood up, "Got to go. A call could come in at any time now."

Koning paid his bill and drove back to Detroit.

Koning, back in suit and tie, looked over the three reports he had prepared to send off. His secretary was confused and came into his office to show him he had dictated three different phone numbers for the roommate's cell phone.

Koning looked at her seriously and said, "I'm aware the numbers are different by just transposition. The reports have a purpose, be sure you get the numbers right. This is confidential—the slightest gossip or screw up would mean your job—and probably mine. Are we on the same pages with this?"

The secretary nodded agreement and left with the three printed memos, soon to send their electrical duplicates into federal cyber land.

That afternoon a call came into the apartment to one of the three cell phones lined up on the kitchen counter. The roommate answered as Lisa watched, he said, "Hello."

Dave spoke, "Hey roommate, good to hear your voice. I was glad to use your number. I'm in trouble and need Carla's cell phone. Has she been calling?"

The roommate answered, "I've been worried, where you been? Yes, she's been calling and she's worried."

Dave said, "Can't say right now. I'm fine, but I really need that cell phone. Could you bring it to McDonalds? I'll explain when I see you."

The roommate asked, "You want it right now?"

Dave answered, "Yes, come alone, I'll be waiting."

Dave stopped the call.

Lisa hearing every word from both men, asked, "Where is the McDonalds?

The roommate answered, "Two blocks down, one block over, five or six walking minutes from here."

Lisa, slipping off her sweater, said, "Let's get this on you, we'll have people already there, walk slowly, the camera is very good, so is the mic, face the cars as you go in, maybe make a 360 at the door. We will be recording everything in front of you. Give Dave the cell phone and don't ask too many questions—he's being watched. I'll follow behind you a half block."

Lisa finished rigging the camera, mic, battery pack and transmitter on and in the roommate's jacket, checking with her cell phone that the men in a nearby vehicle were awake, receiving and recording, and on their way to the McDonalds.

Dave's roommate pocketed the cell phone and left through the front door of the apartment building. However, just half a block into his journey, a dark car pulled beside him. Dave's face showed in the rear window.

Dave said, "Give me the phone and don't look into the car. I'm serious. Do it, don't think about it."

The roommate could do nothing except put the cell phone in Dave's outstretched hand. Dave's face was in the dark, but his bruises showed, he was pulled back and the window slid up, the car sped away down the deserted street. By the time he remembered the camera, all the roommate got was tail lights and wisps of exhaust.

Lisa came to him, "Damn, that was quick and smooth."

Lisa used her phone, "Black Buick four door, Michigan plates, no numbers. Follow the GPS as planned. Dave Adams in vehicle."

The roommate and Lisa walked back and into the apartment.

Lisa debriefed the roommate as she retrieved the camera bug. The roommate didn't add anything.

Lisa called Koning's cell phone, when he answered, she confirmed that he was at his home, and she said, "They have the cell phone, we were intercepted on the way to the exchange, Dave was alive in the vehicle, the airport chase team was alerted, our front car team was pulled out of position.

"I'm tired, going home to take my dog for a walk. I'll leave the car team here."

Koning responded, "Send in your report, clean up and go home. Thank the roommate."

Koning hung up. His worst case scenario had just come true. The leak was within the Department of Justice. One of the offices of his bosses was dirty. How was he going to accuse the top law enforcement officials in the nation of multiple crimes? Who could he go to? He had hoped his trap would have been sprung by Homeland Security or even better for him—the ever sneaky and unpopular CIA.

Koning knew he had to be careful and really plan his next move with Justice. He thought of Fast and Furious, several suspicions noninves-tigations, politically motivated wire tapes, leaking classified military information to reporters, internal e-mails getting into the associated press, obtaining illegal phone records and wide spread investigations of people not supportive to the administration. The Attorney General usu-ally put out guidelines if his minions were caught in some wrong-doing. Koning wondered what would be the dire repercussions of the Justice Department being accused of giving highly classified, life threatening information to Islamic terrorists.

Koning put his worries on hold, found his daughter, borrowed her cell phone and punched in Webb's number. Al answered.

Koning asked for Carla.

Carla was on the phone in a minute.

Koning began, "Carla, I have news. We saw Dave this evening. He's alive but still being held by bad guys. In about a half hour, you should call the cell phone you and he agreed to use. Try to go along with any-thing he asks, just keep him talking."

Carla nodded agreement, then found her voice, overwhelmed with emotion she agreed to call.

Koning continued, "Let me talk to your father."

Webb came on the line, "I'm here, you brought good news. What can I do?"

Koning answered, "We need to buy time. We're a long ways from out of the woods, but we are at least in the game now. Stay with Carla when she calls, keep her calm if you can, whatever happens, report it to me on this phone."

Webb asked several questions which Koning avoided, and then the call was over.

Webb, Matt and Al stood or sat behind Carla when she made the call to Dave. Her mother and Tanya watched and listened from down the hall sitting on the bed.

The phone buzzed three times then Dave said, "Hi honey."

Carla said, "Are you alright? I've been worried sick. I couldn't get the phone they sent to work."

Webb and Al gave thumbs up to Carla's rehearsed response.

Dave said, "I'm with people who don't want you to be a witness. They want you to leave the country and not come back. They say when you are gone and there is no trial they will let me go."

Carla responded, "I'll do anything to keep you safe. I don't care about anything else. How will I know you are all right? Will we be able to talk? Can I see you on Skype or something?

"How did you get phone eight, are you back at your apartment? I'm so glad to hear your voice. Talk to me."

Dave answered, "I don't know what they will let me do. I just know you have to go away to keep me safe.

I'm not at home. I don't know where I am."

The phone gave static as if someone was covering the microphone. After ten seconds Dave was back, saying, "I'm not free to say anything about location.

"Are you still with Matt and Tanya?"

Carla, looked at her dad, he indicated yes, she answered, "Yes, we are still here. We can move to Canada to the island cabin in just a few hours. Would that make your captors happy?"

There was a pause again and then someone else came on, saying, "You can stay where you are for now, we will tell you when to go. You will do what we tell you or we will send you more little boxes—inside will be various parts of your boyfriend. He will stay alive, there will just be less of him." There was snickering in the back ground. Then the phone must have been handed back to Dave.

Dave said, "I'm sorry, there isn't much I can do. You need to keep safe…"

There was a large concussive bang, the phone gave a buzzing-ringing tone, it was dropped on a table or floor, there was scuffling and then four gun shots, more scuffling, men yelling, their words incoherent in the obvious tumult that was taking place. The noise of another series of shots blasted through the phone in Carla's hand, then silence.

Twenty anxious seconds passed, after continuous unidentifiable noises, a voice came over the phone, "This still working?"

Webb took the phone from Carla, "Yes, the phone is working. What happened?

Dave yelled into the phone, "Honey, I'm fine. I love you.

"The Muslims are either dead or wounded. I can't hear. A SWAT team just shot the shit out of these four guys."

Webb spoke, "How are you?"

Dave said, "Hi Mr. Webb, I'm fine. They were laughing about mailing out parts of me. Things changed fast, two of them have their brain parts on the wall right next to me now. I'm shaking and my ears are really ringing. They all had pistols, they weren't surrendering.

"I've got to go, they have a medic here. What's Carla's number and can I keep this phone? They smashed my cell phone when they got me in the parking lot. They used a taser, that was bad."

Carla got the phone back and gave the satellite number and said, "Keep the phone, call me back as soon as you can. I love you."

Carla slowly replaced the satellite phone on its cradle.

Everyone came to Carla and hugged her. She cried and laughed.

Webb said, "When we find out where he is, I'd like to send some men to guard him. I don't trust the FBI. And then we get him up here to be with Carla. She has some news for him.

"I've got to call Koning, he should know all about this by now, but I need to compliment him."

Webb tried three calls. Each time he got Koning's daughter's phone mail. He didn't leave any message. His recorded number on the cell phone would say enough to Koning.

Webb joined the celebration in the house.

34

Koning's Dilemma

Koning left the hospital in Ann Arbor. It was 2:00 am. He had time to think as he drove back to his home in an upscale suburb. His emotions were a mixture of joy and accomplishment, coupled with a crushing dread of the knowledge he possessed of collusion with terrorists being carried out within the Department of Justice. In times of war—a condition with Islam many believe we are actually in—the actions of someone or someones would clearly be treason.

Koning snorted a laugh as he envisioned a firing squad dressed in dark three piece suits all with the latest color power tie, formally circling the guilty transgressor. A circular firing squad would be very appropriate. Koning could not make a mental picture of who would say, "Fire."

Back from his reverie, he drove off the highway into his familiar neighborhood. He passed a well lit 7/11 store. He saw an increasingly rare pay phone. Making a u-turn on the deserted street, he pulled into the parking lot of the store. After converting bills to coins he entered the phone booth. He called an operator for help to make a long distant call, paid from his side. After some instructions and a handful of quarters he got Al on the phone.

Koning apologized for the hour of the call.

Al said, "No problem, I had to get up to answer the phone anyway."

Two minutes later Webb reached his phone, "Hello, Mr. Prosecutor, you're up early."

Koning said, "I'm still up from yesterday. I just came from the hospital where we've been questioning two men, still alive, who kidnapped Adams. They are both Syrians with expired visas. They demanded a lawyer as soon as they could mumble. They were both severely wounded; they each took multiple 10mm bullets. Worst case they may live, the doctors say they can't last long. We told them they were being treated as terrorists, enemy combatants, and were not granted our constitutional rights."

Webb interjected, "Sure, they blatantly despise U.S. law but when they get caught, they demand our legal privileges. What did you learn?"

Koning continued, "That's the reason for this call—from a pay phone I might mention—they were tough and arrogant. You will be having company soon. When we mentioned the attempt on Carla they intimated their efforts were not complete yet. We gave the bastards Demerol with just a splash of Pentothal for body. They told us how they would conquer our worthless and godless country. Nothing they said will get to court, but they admitted a team is headed your way. We couldn't get names, numbers or details. They kept talking about virgins—must have been the Demerol. Oh, two vehicles and rifles were mentioned. Also, one mumbled hunting the infidels like wild goats."

Webbs said, "We'll be ready. Thank you. The last time a government person helped us he was from the DEA. He saved my life and that of my family. It was hard for me to like and trust anyone in the government, but I had to change.

"How did you find Dave?"

Koning answered, "We put a GPS pinger in the last cell phone Dave and Carla were using. They had to get it from Dave's roommate."

An automated female voice interrupted, telling Koning to put in more money.

Koning put in the money, took a breath then said, "I'm going to talk to you about a problem I have. It indirectly affects your daughter. I don't know who I can trust. So I'll trust you, a Russian gangster."

Webb chuckled, "The enemy of my enemy is my friend—I think is an old Russian saying. Go ahead—what's your problem. The doctor is in...five cents."

Koning, replied, "OK, Lucy. I sent out my required progress memos regarding the terrorist prosecution to several national departments. I reported that the failure of the explosive cell phone saved Dave Adams, also it made it imperative that Carla contact him if the kidnappers were to use Dave and have any influence. They would obviously need the last of your throw away cell phones, which was in Dave's apartment. I put Dave's roommate's phone number in the memos, except I used three different numbers and sent the memos to three government departments—per the orders of the Patriot Act. They went to Homeland Security, the CIA and the Department of Justice. I set this up like a double blind experiment. My secretary knew the three phone numbers, my FBI agent that was on scene knew which phone got physically called, but she didn't know who got that number. I was the only one to know which agency is involved, and now you share that knowledge with me."

Webb interrupted, "Well played."

Koning went on, "In a matter of hours, the kidnappers called Dave's roommate, to a cell phone with the number I sent to the Department of Justice. I work for Justice. I'm three managerial levels from the President. Above me is the Deputy Director then the Attorney General."

Webb said, "I can appreciate your situation—it sounds like the Soviet Union I left. We couldn't trust anyone either.

"What do you want of me?"

Koning replied, "I don't know right now, I'm too tired to think straight. I know I had to warn you. I can send people to protect you, but I just had a feeling—based upon what you did to my FBI agents, you might not want help.

"My other issue—I just had to tell someone. Your daughter and Adams are in real trouble if there are no secrets from Islamic Terrorists."

Webb added, "Let's talk tomorrow. A known spy can be useful. Let me think and you sleep. We will be ready for tomorrow—which is Election Day I think."

Koning said, "I'll call you from the office, my daughter's phone or from a pay phone depending upon the level of information we will be sharing.

"You sure you don't want federal help up there?"

Webb answered, "No, we can take care of ourselves, thanks to your warning. You can help with the bodies.

"Carla won't be safe while the Imam lives. If the man goes away, the trial goes away, and maybe we can finesse it so the spy gets the blame and he/she goes away. Let me think about it as we prepare for visitors."

Koning said good bye and hung up.

Webb turned to Al who was listening over his shoulder. "Get people up an hour before good light, I want the ladies gone at dawn.

Webb got Matt up, he explained what Koning told him as they made two pots of coffee, Matt mixed up and started making pancakes, after putting a jar of maple syrup in a pan of water to heat up. While Matt flipped pancakes and concentrated on not burning bacon, Webb asked, "Could you guide them into the cabin with another machine?"

Matt answered, "Sure, there are two more ATV's down there. One is a side by side, but they are heavier and leave too much of a track. The other 4x4 hasn't been run for some time. I'll go get it now, you watch the bacon. Don't look away or it burns. Leave the rest of the batter for the ladies to cook."

Matt dressed for hunting, securing his FN 5.7 pistol and holster under his left arm with a belt like a bandoleer. It was concealed inside his down vest and hunting jacket. The weapon would be easier to get to than on his belt. He also got out his rifle and its scabbard to be attached to the 4x4. He picked his old Browning hunting jacket—all Real Tree Camouflage. He took the matching Kromer and his light face mask. Walking quickly to the quarry floor, using a flashlight he found the green 4x4 had gas and the tires were inflated, the battery barely turned the engine. Matt pulled the choke and the manual pull starter, the machine came to mechanical life. Matt raced back to the house and put the machine in the garage where he had light and warmth to prepare it for a trip to the little cabin. He would have Carla ride with him, Tanya would ride with Karen holding on. They now had the little two wheeled cart behind a 4x4 as a bonus for hauling gear.

Matt loaded the little trailer with three sleeping bags, various foods he plucked from the garage freezer, and left the rest of the space for the ladies to fill. He also added his Browning semi auto shotgun and a box of number 4 lead shot. In its case it was safe from harm. He had shown Tanya how to load and fire it. She didn't like duck hunting for a half dozen clearly articulated reasons, but she could use the weapon. Matt thought that five number 4 three inch magnums would be lots of firepower. He couldn't find any buck shot.

In the kitchen, the ladies were up and excited about their journey to a hidden cabin. They understood the wisdom of their going into hiding.

Carla asked, "How do you wash up or brush your teeth?"

As she finished her breakfast Matt explained, "There is a high table outside, you use a cup or glass, brush and rinse, you spit on the ground. You can wash inside or outside from a large wash pan you'll find hanging on the wall, you throw your water out the door—its fun, watch the wind—don't spit or anything into the wind. The water is warm or sometimes hot in the reservoir on the right side of the woodstove, lift the lid and dip it out."

Tanya added, "It will be nice, get a couple books. We can play cards, checkers and chess."

Karen said, "We've got iPads with many books. How do we keep them charged?"

Matt responded, "I should have thought of that. I'll send along my solar charger, it has ends for Tanya's cell phone and the iPad. It is slow, but you have lots of time. The two windows face south, you'll get sun. The Midland won't reach here anyway. We'll use Tanya's phone if we need to, but keep it for emergencies. The idea here is to be off the grid."

Tanya added, "I'll have all the privacy options off. Beside removing the battery I don't know what else we can do."

Webb looked outside, "We've got light out there, you should be going."

Tanya and Karen added more toilet paper, paper towels, another flashlight and a box that cleaned the refrigerator of eggs, milk, and salad materials.

Tanya, carrying the box out, said, "You guys just drink beer and eat chips anyway."

Matt led the two 4x4's to the cabin. While the ladies were building a fire and inspecting the little cabin, he unloaded everything and hid the machines in the pines.

In the short time Matt was gone, the ladies had the cabin warming, the pantry organized, and water heating on the stove for tea. Matt showed Carla and Karen the flowing well. They came back with two buckets of clear, cold water.

Carla drank from the old black and white enamel dipper, "This is wonderful water. This place is beautiful. Are there bears?"

Matt answered, "Yes there are bears, but unless you smell like garbage you'll be fine. Watch what you throw out or leave out. They have great noses. This time of year they need food to fatten up for winter. Use common sense, you won't be bothered."

Matt showed them how to close the shutters and block the door. He filled the sconces on the walls with candles. They each had a mirror behind the candle, he commented, "Keep shuttered and locked up at night, watch your smoke in the daytime. Get your fire going at night and keep it going with larger blocks. Be sure the wood is dry, only burn paper at night, watch your damper, don't make any more smoke than you have to. Watch where you throw the ashes—don't start a forest fire."

The ladies asked a few more questions, but seemed eager for Matt to leave so they could get on with their cabin life.

Matt kissed Tanya from the 4x4, checking his watch, said, "I feel like Gary Cooper going to fight what's his name—Frank Miller, in High Noon.

Tanya gave him another warm kiss, "I wish I was with you. Remember Grace Kelly shot one bad guy for her man."

Matt said, "You take care of Webb's ladies." Then he realized what he said.

Tanya winked, "We will do just fine. You keep your head down.

"We're not getting to vote today."

Matt agreed, "I'll cover tracks going back, but you should be able to come out if you need to. I'll be back when we have things settled. If you don't hear from us in a few days, drive back to the creek and use the Midland, if that doesn't work use your cell phone. Keep the guns loaded. I'll call out when I come back, if you see anyone else, fort up and point weapons.

"Worry about snipers, watch your silhouettes at night. Worry about planes; get inside by the stove—only one heat signature. We're two weeks before deer season but hunters still roam around. I can't imagine a stray hunter coming in this far on foot, and you'll hear a machine a mile away. Remember, watch your light and smoke.

"That's all I can think of."

One more kiss and Matt drove back to base camp, covering up tire marks on the way. He spent fifteen minutes where the cabin trail met the two ruts. He used dead falls, leaves and rubbed out tracks with pine branches. Then he drove past the turn several times. Satisfied, he went toward the house.

35

Hunting Hunters

Matt motored to the house. He came up slowly, ready for anything. In the driveway was a big red GMC pickup truck. Matt recognized it—the Ferr brothers were here. They had left their big mink farm and had come to prepare their hunting areas.

Matt had the garage opener zip-tied to his 4x4 handle bar. He put the garage door up and maneuvered around the pickup and then put the door down. He thought, *Sam and Will may get more hunting than they figured on today.*

Sam met Matt at the kitchen door. He was drinking coffee, a deviation from the usual prehunting mid-morning beer. His brother Will was seated at the table, looking at a topographic map of the area. Webb was listening to him. Their expressions were serious.

Webb said, "Your friends came at a good time. I was going to tell them nothing, they are here to set up blinds. However, they could get hurt if they didn't know what was going to happen. I told them men were coming to kill my daughter and I explained why, then I said they should leave. They laughed."

Will Ferr said, "We were here when you had a shoot out with Canadians, now you pissed off Islamic terrorists. You run an exciting camp Matt. I remember we put bodies in a car trunk. We have a history with Webb. Plus, we can't have towel heads ruining our deer hunt."

Sam Ferr added, "We didn't expect gun play when we got up today. But we both made it through Vietnam and protecting a brave little girl seems a worthy use of our military talents."

Will pointed at the map with a capped magic marker, "The county paved road is here, your dirt road starts here, north, straight as a string for almost a mile."

Matt interrupted, "It is on the old railroad bed, the road turns but the bed runs another couple hundred yards right to the south side of the quarry."

Will went on, "True, but here the gravel road turns east to go around the quarry. Webb said you have cameras up at the forks, here." He pointed at the junctions of several trails and rutted roads that converged at the north east corner of the massive quarry. That's good, but you'd be wise to have eyes on the long road, a mile before the cameras warn you."

Matt explained, "The wireless system only works for 400 feet or so. We can't go down the road."

Sam spoke, "We just happen to have a brand new hunting stand in the truck. That's what we were going to put up today. If we put it in the woods at the curve, we can watch your main driveway, and a quarter mile of road before it turns north. There is no good place to hide a vehicle along the road. Anyone dropping off people would have to fart around on the road. We can put the stand here at the corner up on this little rise," He pointed to a spot where several topographic lines looped closer together. "With a little work we can hide the stand in the thick trees."

Sam said, "We didn't bring any rifles, just an old shotgun in the truck and only bird shot."

Matt said, "Not to worry, I'll get you an M16 and my dad's old 30-06, also 12 gauge slugs."

Webb said, "We don't know when our fundamentalist friends are coming, so we need to move along. We will go with you to help set up your stand and also be guards. Let's move."

Matt got the black M16, and two gray metal magazines. Sam took it, looked it over, broke it open, dropped out the firing mechanism, eye balled the bore up to the light and had it back together in one minute flat. He inspected the military full metal jacket shells in the two magazines he was handed after hitting one thirty-shell magazine on his palm, and slamming it into the weapon, he pulled and released the charging mechanism and clicked a lever to S for safe.

Sam, looking at the selection lever area, asked, "What's the R for?"

Matt answered, "This is a Canadian Colt, R is for repetition, northern neighbor talk for semi-automatic. It has full auto also—like you had in 'Nam."

Will asked, "You got a couple of warmer jackets? If we are going to be up in a stand for hours, we'll get cold."

Matt went to the garage, opened a big closet filled to capacity with hunting clothes.

Matt pulled out two of his insulated duck hunting jackets, one lighter than the other—both camouflaged like weeds and leaves. He had head gear to match.

Matt handed Will his Midland, "Use this—just turn it on and talk, it's all set. We will only answer you with whispers, only if you call."

Will said, "I know this radio, we'll keep it off until we see something. We have cell phones too. We need to call our wives if we stay late. We told them we might stay over in your hunting camp if we have too much brush to cut or a bear eats our truck."

Matt added, "Or we get into some bad brandy that had turned."

Matt also handed them a red box of Federal slug shotgun shells and a rifle in an old canvas case.

Matt said, "There is a full shell folder in with the rifle—twelve 30-06, the four-power scope has seen a lot of deer go down."

Matt's Yukon and the Ferr pickup drove back to the sharp curve. Webb stood by the vehicles as a watchman. The Ferr brothers unloaded the new stand. Matt helped them make several trips with the dark green metal tubing, decking and plastic sides. They threw away the instruction manual after realizing they couldn't understand the English version of the Chinese instructions that didn't seem to need verbs. After some discussion about location and some judicious limb trimming, they finally set up their elevated blind with views south and east behind and between maples and forest edge pines and cedars. The taller background of oaks and beech behind their 4 foot square elevated platform hid their outline. They could see fairly well around the curve and had a perfect view of Matt's north-south road all the way to the paved county road. They were undetectable after they added some pine boughs and leafy branches. With water, their lunches, radio, weapons and heavy coats they said good luck. Webb drove their truck and followed Matt back. They put both vehicles in the garage after Matt moved the green 4x4.

Matt went into the RV where he met with Al and Webb.

Matt said, "I can't see how any group could find us, let alone attack us without coming up from the south. We've got good camera coverage up the north trail."

Al asked, "What about parachute or helicopter?"

Webb said, "We need to stay loose, let's check our weapons and clothes. Matt did a good job making us some hiding areas for several situations."

Al, who sat at the computer, said, "I can make it record now, see here you are coming back."

Matt said, "We are lucky to have Sam and Will on our side. They are where one of us would have to have been stationed, alone and without a platform. We can count on them."

Al said, "I hope they don't get hurt."

Matt answered, "They fought in jungles they never saw before. They are on their home court now. We have all chased deer through these woods and swamps. A person will go through easier paths, and we know all those paths. I've already shown you where people coming in from any side would most likely come out. The woods are noisy, lots of leaves, no snow and there isn't much wind, if you're still, they will sound like a herd of buffalo, particularly if they get down in the bad stuff.

The Midland on the counter by the computer issued a click and a whisper, "Radio check, you read?"

Matt picked it up, thumbed the talk button, "Read you Will. Comfortable?"

Will replied, "We could have shot a nice ten point, walked right by us on the old road bed trail. Sam wished we had a bayonet with the M16.

"We have a question—do we kill or capture?"

Matt looked at Webb, who drew his finger across his neck.

Matt reported, "No prisoners, they are here to kill. The FBI and a U.S. Attorney are witness to their plans. Let's not take any chances. If we get a wounding and he is no threat play it by ear, don't take any chances. These guys are fanatics."

Sam came on, "Any thoughts about how long we are going to be out here?"

Matt answered, "We think they will come in the daytime, dressed like hunters. We aren't going to deploy until we know how they are coming in. It might be a Keystone Kops attack, where they come driving in and rush us, or they may try to sneak up on us. In any case let them come in, we have a lot of fire power. We are mobile; with the women safe, we don't have to defend the house. Just don't let them out."

Will said, "Roger and out."

Al, Webb and Matt had their weapons loaded and ready, their boots on and their jackets ready.

At 2:00 pm Will called in, "Dark SUV stopped out by the county road, got the rifle scope on it. Now it's pulling to the side, here comes a big truck. I think it's a UPS van, turning in on your road. The SUV is following it."

Matt and Al didn't wait for more information. They got on their coats and ran out of the motor home to take up prepared positions on the other side of their road.

Webb got his coat on and listened as Will reported in a whisper that the SUV pulled to the side of the road at the curve, and three armed men got out.

Will whispered, now barely audible, "They're fifty feet from us, one in car, three going north through woods. Can't talk."

Webb wanted to update Matt and Al. He whispered back to Will, "Good luck, got to go."

On a hunch, Webb hit the scan button on the CB radio base station, it ran through the wavelengths, and stopped, excited Arabic came from the speaker. As he thought, men in the UPS van and three on foot coming in from the quarry side. Webb went out of the motor home. He couldn't see Matt or Al but knew they were in ear shot. He announced the information he had heard.

Finally Webb said, "We take the truck first then worry about the three coming across the quarry."

Then Webb found a friendly bush south of the house on the opposite side of the road from Al and Matt. They had discussed their lines of fire. Crouching out of sight, he could hear the truck's springs and the crunch of its tires on the bumpy graveled road.

Matt set his loaded and locked rifle by the tree he was hiding behind, in his hand he had his pistol with a full magazine of twenty cartridges, another full magazine was in his left jacket patch pocket. Matt thought, *The UPS lady would be a good hostage for the bastards; she would know his location, be a familiar sight and the van would provide an enclosed hiding place for many terrorists.*

Matt heard Webb's warning, he then said, speaking in a firm level voice, "The UPS driver is a blond lady, brown uniform. Don't shoot her."

Matt thought, *If they are coming up the old railroad bed, they must be using aerial maps or Google Earth. They don't know they can't get up the north quarry edge. They will have to use the east road to get out. Good plan, but you got to know the territory.*

The van slowly came closer. Matt pushed the safety lever down with his right index finger, he then used the other index finger to touch the little chrome pin that stuck slightly up on the left top of the pistol when a shell was chambered, he tried to relax his double hand grip. Finally, he remembered to breathe.

36

The Wrath of the 5.7

The brown UPS van moved at walking speed up the road. Matt had on his face covering and knew he was invisible with the afternoon sun shining into the van's large window as he crouched in the shade of the bushes. The driver was not the usual pretty blond lady. A bearded man in a brown UPS uniform was at the wheel, he was studying Matt's house intently. Matt could see another man lurking in the shelving area behind the driver.

The van passed Matt by ten feet and turned into the driveway, rolling almost to the cement apron of the garage. Matt moved to the other side of the tree where his rifle rested. There was a little used van door on Matt's side, but he and Al now had the double back doors within twenty feet and Webb had the side door perfectly covered.

The two back doors swung open. Three men with short AK pistols, magazines longer than their barrels, hopped out. Matt knelt to make his shots stay off the van's floor where the UPS lady might be tied up.

Matt found the trigger and locked into a thumb to thumb two hand grip, as he aimed, Al opened up with his P90. The sound of the machine gun hurt Matt's ears and seemed to squeeze his head and stomach. Matt didn't shoot. The three men that Matt could see over his sights were cut down as wheat before a scythe. Their arms flopped up, their weapons flying; they did a puppet dance before crumbling down against the steps of the UPS truck.

Matt swept the bodies with his sights, there was twitching and some leg movements, but Matt couldn't identify a target that would represent any threat.

Matt couldn't see the driver come out of the van from his right side door, he just heard the angry staccato rip of Webb's weapon. He saw glass and metal parts fly from the left side of the big vehicle. The blast lasted several seconds. It was noticeably longer than Al's burst. Matt sensed vindictiveness in the angry cracks of the small deadly shells.

After the woods absorbed the sound of Webb's volley, Al said, "They're all done. Stay back while I check."

Al slowly advanced. He fired three more times when one body twitched.

Matt moved around the left side of the van, there were several holes erupting outward from the dark brown paint. He looked in the window, no one visible. He completed the journey around the front of the truck and came to the crumpled corpse of the driver, it looked like an execution by ax not firearm, the man was almost cut in half. All of Webb's shots were held within a yard's width. Matt doubted if even three of Webb's thirty or forty shots missed shredding the man. Matt had seen a road kill come out from under multiple 18 wheelers with less damage. He could smell feces and guts along with the sweet coppery odor of blood.

Stepping into the van, Matt found the UPS lady bound and gagged on the floor. She was blinking back tears and moaning. She had suffered, at least, a blow to the temple, where an angry cut trickled blood and was puffing up. Matt took his jack knife and cut through the clear packaging tape that was binding the driver. The tape on her head came off painfully, pulling skin and blond hair. She also had a wad of cloth in her mouth.

Her frightened eyes cleared and focused on Matt. She spoke, "They asked directions, then some guy hit me." She suddenly realized she was only dressed in a shirt, long underwear and socks. Her boots were off.

Matt helped her up, asking if she could walk, she steadied herself on the shelves, testing her legs and nodded yes. He helped her out of the truck, trying to get her turned away from the gruesome sight at the base of the steps. She looked and it didn't seem to register for a few seconds, then she said, "He took my uniform."

Matt helped her toward the house, he observed, "You're going to need a new one.

"We have more of these bad guys coming, I'm sorry, can't stay with you. Can you walk enough to get into the kitchen and get some ice on your head? There's aspirin in our bedroom medicine cabinet."

She said, "I can walk, go, I'll call the police."

Matt said, "Don't do that right now, this is a complicated situation. Trust me, we don't need police right now. Go on in. Help yourself to clothes and shoes, in the bedroom closet or the garage."

Webb and Al came up, already reloaded. They looked at the bodies. Al looked sad, Webb didn't show any emotion.

Webb said, "So much for questioning anyone. I've never shot anything like this weapon, you see it in the sight, pull the trigger and it's gone. We've got four down, four to go."

Matt said, "I didn't even get off a shot. I was squeezing when Al wiped them out."

Al added, "Reactions get better with experience, the problem is sometimes getting the experience also gets you dead. As a cop I would have had to identify myself, lots of guys died doing that. In Vietnam I never saw anyone that shot at me."

Matt went back to look at the three sprawled out at the back of the truck, Al followed him.

Matt had multiple feelings go through him at the sight of the dead bodies. Al sensed his feelings and said, "They would have cut you down just as dead if they were given a chance."

Webb came up to them, looking impatient.

They heard a strange sound, Webb had a Midland, it was on, he took it from a jacket pocket and Sam whispered. "Can you talk?"

Matt, recognizing his friend, took the radio, "The Muslims are toast, actually more like chop suey. What do you see?"

Sam, still in a whisper, said, "Three men with AK's walked almost under us toward the quarry. They are out of sight. The one in the SUV is talking on a radio, I can't see him but I'm close enough to hear him. What in hell did you shoot up there? Anyway, they are trained and moved and carried their weapons liked they have been around battle."

Matt said, "Don't let the SUV leave. We'll be ready for the other three."

Webb took back the Midland, none to gently, "I want a prisoner that can talk before he suffers greatly at my hands. I may be able to screw up their radio man. See if you can take him alive. Be careful."

Sam replied, "Message received and understood, I don't think I can sneak up on the vehicle. If he gets out I can pop him. Out."

Then he came back on, "Hey, don't shoot Will, he's on the ground with the M16. He grabbed the rifle and was gone before I could talk sense to him, a damn horse to the bugle. No jacket, in a gray hooded sweatshirt, camo cap... I glanced at his eyes; my little brother is back in the green machine. He won't take prisoners. He's got AK scars on his legs from 'Nam. He's liable to kill them all. He will probably wait until they're down in the quarry, in the open."

Matt took the phone back, giving Webb a hard took, "We all hear, we're fanning out and working south. We won't go past the fork. Sound OK?"

Sam said, "Yes, I'm open on 5, be quiet, over and out."

Matt handed the Midland back to Webb. "We have three terrorists to take out. The quarry approach looks good on a map, but it's exposed and this edge is about impossible to climb."

Looking at Webb he said, "I'd suggest you and Al go down this road then fan out to the right, covering the only road that comes up from the quarry. The quarry area is open, no cover. I'll take my rifle down to the cliff, between Will and me they won't have any good place to hide. We have them boxed in. I hope they can't get to any of the buildings for cover."

Webb said, "Sounds good. Go ahead, I'll be right behind you. I'm going to take a minute and screw up their communication. The guys in the truck had ear radios."

Al started down the road, Matt went south on an old path toward the quarry edge overlooking the old crusher and shop building. He stood where there were steps, now gone for eighty years. He swept the area with his Leopold telescopic sight.

Webb went into the motor home, selected the terrorist's frequency on the base station, locked down the send key and turned up the gain to its top setting. He also turned on the RV's stereo system. Grabbing another P90 magazine, he hurried down the road after Al.

The sun was getting lower, thick clouds mitigated its brilliance. Shadows of brush and large boulders made it difficult to pick out men. Nothing could be seen moving. Matt kept looking carefully, starting from where he knew the southern railroad bed met the quarry.

A rifle shot boomed and echoed from the south. Matt knew it was his grandfather's 30-06. He visualized someone dead on the road. Then he heard five measured shots from the M16. Matt knew it had to be from Will. The Ferr brothers were taking their toll on the body of Islam.

Matt jogged east along the quarry edge, working between trees and brush for a better view of the quarry's massive gray expanse. Five more shots came from the south rim. Matt couldn't see a flash or locate the sound.

Then Matt heard a different automatic weapon fire a burst. Matt saw the flash of fire, the sound wasn't much of a help for a location, it seemed to bounce all around.

Matt cranked the adjustable power to 9X, he leaned against a tree to hold the rifle steady. He saw a black speck move. After scoping the area he identified two men. He also identified one spread out on the quarry floor. They were wearing hunting jackets, the one that was down had blaze orange on his shoulders and collar. The men Matt could see were two hundred yards away. They had rifles, weapons with long barrels.

Neither Matt nor Will had radios. Matt had stupidly left his on the kitchen counter. However, the two old friends had hunted together as boys and men for nearly forty years, they knew how to work a hunting situation, they knew how each other thought and moved. Matt understood Will's excitement, he could be impulsive, he was very skilled in the woods and he was a deadly shot, with years of combat experience. Matt was the novice, never trained in military skills, he had to be careful that he did the right things, the expected moves that a vet would take for granted.

Men weren't deer. Matt didn't know if Will would go down after the terrorists. The open space was a two edged sword. We could see them and they could see us if we went into the quarry. The terrorists were about equal distance between Will and Matt. There were locations where they were hidden by blocks from both sides.

Matt decided he was suffering from paralysis through analysis. He thought, *Find 'em and shoot 'em. They will shit when I start firing shells at them from this side.*

Matt moved further east, found a low branch to rest his Remington and scoped for a target. He found a target, a man hiding from Will but exposing himself to Matt. Matt's brain programmed with a lifetime of rifle shooting, calculated his elevated position, the lack of wind, the distance to a stationary target and the negligible drop of this bullet at 200 yards.

Matt eased off the safety, took two deep breaths, steadied the rifle, and put the cross hairs between the man's shoulder blades. Breathing slowly out, then holding his breath he gently squeezed the trigger to and then past the break point, the 7mm magnum shell exploded and drove the 150 grain red plastic tipped Nosler bullet out of the barrel at over 3,000 feet per second. The 9-pound weapon kicked into Matt's shoulder, the man slumped before the sound came back off the quarry walls.

A few seconds later, Will fired four measured shots. There was a time lapse of ten seconds then Matt heard him let out a whoop. Matt scoped the area toward Will's yell, there, only fifty yards in front of Will's side of the quarry was a man, he held his hands up over his head, unarmed, he stood in the open.

Matt swept the area for another minute. Nothing moved, he still couldn't see Will in the weeds, the brush and the shadows of the far side.

To be in the open, the target of an unseen marksman brings a helplessness Matt hoped he would never experience. Matt thought, *The terror of the sniper is almost as deadly as the bullet.*

Matt yelled, "I'm coming down with a 4x4." He repeated his message several times, spacing the words so the echoes didn't wreck the message.

Will yelled some words, Matt couldn't understand him.

Back at the garage, Matt checked on the UPS lady. Lying on the couch, she had ice on her head and was wearing sweatpants and a hooded sweatshirt. She was still in her socks.

Matt said, "I think we are out of danger, but we've got to take a prisoner and check on the bodies. How do you feel?"

As he talked, Matt looked down at her eyes, which seems to track, her pupils were equal. He lifted the ice cube filled washcloth off her injury. It looked mean and might need a stitch or two.

When Matt said bodies, the UPS lady looked shocked again. She said her head and jaw hurt.

Matt patted her shoulder and said, "Be patient a little longer and you'll have a great story to tell."

Matt retrieved his Midland where it was charging on the kitchen counter and went out to the green 4x4. It was the only usable transportation; the other vehicles were blocked by the UPS van. Using his sling to strap his rifle over his back, then pushing the garage opening button, Matt maneuvered out. He backed carefully past the open van with four dead men dreadfully splattered or festooned at its doors and then headed for the quarry.

37

Body Count

Matt steered and throttled the 4x4 with his right hand, his left hand worked his Midland radio. He announced, "I'm driving the 4x4 down to the quarry floor. Will has a prisoner. I think seven bad guys are accounted for. Where is number eight? Over."

Sam came on, "I got him. His radio wouldn't work. He got out of his vehicle, took a rifle from the back and went toward the quarry; he was going to come in behind Will. Over."

Webb came on, "Matt, hear you, I'm where the quarry road cuts along the hill. Pick me up. I'll let Al know we got eight for eight. Sam, keep watch on the road, in case they have reserves."

Matt drove slowly, alert, his coat and down vest open, exposing his pistol. He was sweating from nerves and movement. He went around to his right on the fork that led to the quarry. Another hundred yards and he came to Webb standing on the side of the trail. Webb got on the machine, its springs appreciating his weight. He had his back to Matt.

Webb announced, "I'm on, go slow. Al is up on the hill somewhere."

Matt saw Al step forward, he was in the trees, up on the hill that the quarry trail cut through on one side. Matt appreciated his choice of position, anyone coming up the road from the quarry would be in his sights before they could see him, he would be shooting down at them.

Webb had Matt turn off the machine, he spoke to Al who stood on the edge of the cut, "I'll go with Matt, go back and call Koning, have him call you back on a secure phone. Get some help with the clean up. The FBI will want to know who these guys were. We may be a while. We will take the prisoner to the hunting cabin in the quarry. Don't mention we have a prisoner."

Webb hopped off the 4x4, got out his radio and tossed it to Al, saying, "Here, have this, we've got Matt's."

Webb got back on the machine, Matt drove down onto the floor of the quarry.

It was a long, slow trip to the far side of the quarry.

Will met them as they drove over. He had a man ahead of him. The man had his hands behind his head. Will carried two rifles; the sinister compensator at the end of the M16 barrel pointed unwaveringly at the man, the other weapon, the prisoner's, was held by a sling over his shoulder.

The man was more of a boy.

Webb pushed the prisoner to the limestone floor, he searched him from the back, then turned him over, opening his clothing and searched him right down to his skin.

As Webb inspected the prisoner, he asked if he spoke English. The man responded in the negative in what Matt supposed was Arabic. Webb gave the man a vicious back hand blow, and asked again. The scenario played two more times then the man gave a very articulate, "Yes, I do."

They escorted the man to Matt's hunting cabin, enclosed within the huge shop building. It had an open area with kitchen, couch and chairs on the main floor, broken only by a bathroom in one corner and a staircase in the middle. The second story had an open sleeping area.

Matt turned up the propane heat in the building, Webb did the same with the prisoner by taping him securely to an old captain's chair, carefully wrapping his hands and isolating his fingers over the chair's arms. Then he found a propane torch that Matt had under the kitchen sink area.

Webb moved a chair directly in front of the prisoner, he turned the regulator knob, and used a metal sparker to ignite the torch. Webb carefully regulated the flame until it was a sharp yellow and blue arrow head that hissed like a deadly snake. Webb waved his hand in front of the flame to gauge its intensity. He passed the flame past the prisoner, who had to turn his head away from the searing heat.

Webb held the touch, its sound and heat shot menacingly into the space between the two men. Webb said in a calm voice, "I'm going to ask you questions. If you answer them quickly and honestly you will not be hurt. If you hesitate, I'll burn your fingers, if you lie, I'll burn your fingers off, one at a time. Do you understand what I just said?"

The man nodded yes.

Matt sat behind the man at the kitchen table; he had a pad of notebook paper and a yellow pencil.

Will moved behind the man, and leaned on the end of the couch. Matt knew Will wanted to talk about his experience. When Webb started to get the torch close to the prisoner's little finger, Will asked for Matt's radio and said, "I'm going to call Sam, see if he's OK."

Will went outside.

In a half hour, with only one little finger blistered, Webb had learned the man's name, his Pakistani boyhood and family who now lived in Detroit. Matt was forced to hurriedly scribble as the young man's information filled three pages. The man was a U.S. citizen, He gave up all the names of the others, admitted that the man in the SUV was their leader, they were ordered to kill the girl and everyone that opposed them. He didn't know who sent them—that question and no answer cost him a blistered finger tip. He didn't know the Imam but he knew the girl was a key witness against him. He had been back to Pakistan twice, once with his family as a young boy and again with a training group that was dedicated to Jihad. They have a second vehicle parked back at Rexton.

The torch finally sputtered and went out. It was out of gas and so was the prisoner.

Webb had Matt bandage the prisoner's finger. He was given some water. Then his hands were bound in front. Will had got the side-by—side Polaris going so they all could ride up to the house. Webb, again back to back with Matt on the 4x4, held his weapon pointed at the prisoner, as Matt led the parade up the hill.

At the house Al had moved the bodies. Matt could see they had been dragged into the woods. There were major dark stains on the driveway dirt. The UPS van had been moved and was in the road.

Al met the group as they came into the driveway. Matt and Webb went up to him as Will guarded his prisoner who remained in the Polaris, out of hearing range.

Al reported, "I called and got called back by Koning. There will be people here in an hour or so. They're coming from St. Ignace. I told them to get a van or a pickup. The UPS lady is up and feeling OK. I got her boots back. All the bodies are in the woods across the road. I searched them, I got four knives, four pistols. All had AK automatic pistols with thirty cartridge magazines. A bag in the truck had two grenades and back up magazines. They had no IDs, their radios were top level commercial or police grade. Oh, I turned off your radio interference in the Ambassador. They are… were all young—twenties I'd say. The three I shot didn't even have their safeties off. I'd say they expected to catch us cold.

"Sam is still on watch. He went through the SUV parked at the corner and searched the man he shot. His guy had ID, a wallet full of money, his driver's license says he is forty-five and lives in Virginia. The SUV had maps, satellite printouts and papers in Arabic and English. He had a cell phone and a powerful CB set. They all had Motorola professional level gear. He was their leader and control. This was organized like a military operation.

"Sam said his only weapon was a like new scoped hunting rifle."

Webb asked, "Where is the UPS lady?"

"I'm here, "said the woman, carrying a large box from her van. "This is what I was delivering. No holes in it. I need to scan it, but my scanner is shot. The van runs. I will have some explaining to do. We get barked at by dogs but never get hijacked. There are holes all over, including my driver's seat. Your friend says the FBI is coming. I had to call in because the GPS in the van told my headquarters I wasn't driving. I said I have equipment trouble and would be on the road again soon. That was almost three hours ago. Al explained these were terrorists and I'm lucky to be alive."

Matt asked, "How's the head?"

The lady answered, "It hurts to the touch, but the headache is gone."

Webb said, "You should stay a little longer to make sure you are OK, and the FBI people may want to keep this under wraps. They will want to know about the men. Your four are all done talking. What were their accents, what did they talk about? Just about anything you can remember will be useful. We'll let the FBI be responsible for any cover story. Al is right, you're lucky to be alive, between terrorists and all our bullets, just having a bang on the head isn't too bad."

Al and Webb put the P90's back into their hiding areas in the motor home. They had reloaded all the weapons and extra magazines just in case Sam gave them a heads up about more hostile visitors.

Matt assembled all the terrorists' weapons and put them on the garage workbench.

Al opened the UPS box. It contained various laser sights and three night vision goggles and their battery chargers. Al closed up the box and pushed it under the workbench.

Matt made up some sandwiches, got some beers and headed out on the green 4x4 to see his friend Sam. Will stayed with the prisoner, who was also given some food and drink.

At the corner, Sam stood by the terrorists' vehicle. He was thirsty and greeted the beer with a smile. Matt went alone down the trail to inspect the body of the leader.

Matt found the dead terrorist in the middle of the trail, just thirty yards from the blind. He was spread eagled on his chest, one shot entering from the back. Matt didn't need to roll him over, bloody material had sprayed down the path, the red and pink chunks had to be exploded heart and lung tissue, the result of a Remington Core-lock lead bullet at close range. A 30-06 at any range is a formidable shell, testimony to its use by U.S. forces in two world wars. The man was not dressed for the woods or hunting. His shoes, jacket and no hat meant he had planned to remain in the vehicle while he directed the killings.

Matt thought, *I wish Webb had a chance to use his finger burning technique on this sorry bastard.*

Matt heard a whistle, Sam was calling him.

Part way back he saw Sam wave from the elevated blind. Then he pointed down the road.

Matt stood below the blind, he could hear the motor and tire crunch of a vehicle coming up the long straight roadway.

Matt realized the 4x4 was in sight, parked by the terrorists' SUV. He worked toward the road, staying low and hidden. Car doors slammed. Whoever they were, they were not sneaking.

Matt drew his pistol and crouched behind heavy brush.

A man yelled, "FBI. Anyone here?"

Matt stepped out from behind cover and said, "Keep your hands empty of weapons and show some badges."

The man on the other side of the vehicle said, "I was here before— remember, you shot me and my boot."

Matt recognized the man named Stan. He put the pistol back into its holster.

Matt said, "Glad you're here in the daytime. We have a customer for you and seven bodies."

Matt went on to shake Stan's hand. It showed good faith and also signaled Sam they were not targets. Matt thought, *Stan, you wouldn't be smiling if you knew Sam had your head in the cross hairs.*

Matt pointed at the SUV, then the path north, "We checked it out from outside, gloves on. Their leader is down that trail, dead. We have two more down on the quarry floor and four at the house.

"You'll need something bigger than this car."

Stan said, "My partner will be here soon with a paneled van. He is driving because he can find this place."

Both FBI men looked into the SUV.

Matt watched, then said, "We may as well go to the house and get on with what you need to do."

Sam stepped silently out of the bushes, rifle cradled in his arms, startling the FBI men, "Can I get a ride, I'm tired and my feet are cold."

Stan drove the terrorist SUV, Sam got in the FBI vehicle and Matt followed on the 4X4.

38

Crime Scene Investigation

Five vehicles clogged the road and driveway of Matt's house, white artificial lights flooded the area as the golden rays of the sun went behind the western trees, power cords ran into the lighted garage. Crime scene technicians in white lab coats outnumbered the FBI labeled jackets and the blue uniformed state policemen. Al and Webb withdrew to the motor home, out of the way and yet able to view the activity.

Webb watched two men picking up shell casings, one swabbing up yellow numbered blood samples, others loading stretchers with sheet covered bodies into a windowless step van. He said, "Matt denied them the right to search his house, if they bring a warrant they won't find anything anyway. They know the agents of Islam were machine gunned, quite effectively I might say. And those not machine gunned where shot in the back. They can say we were not sporting, but we are not the ones being put into a meat wagon."

Al added, "I gave them all a full report, also, Matt's notes from your talk with the prisoner. They took a hundred pictures. They want the blood stains to match the bodies and then to match our stories. And I walked them through the house as a courtesy. Stan is the officer in charge as first on the scene, he's being cooperative and understanding. He also had the cell phone from the leader. He thinks they will get information from it. They are going to fly it, blood and DNA samples to Detroit tonight.

"Where's Matt?"

Webb answered, "In the kitchen, drinking beer with Sam and Will."

Matt took the last three beers out of the garage refrigerator. He handed two to Sam and Will who were perched on the workbench, the terrorist weapons had been taken away.

Will took a drink, burped, and said, "Well, we never expected to have the day we did. I felt I was back in the jungle, creeping through weeds, looking through a peep sight and getting in a fire fight. I got the one guy at over a hundred yards. The one you got had fired back at me, it got real when I heard the shells snapping through the brush near me."

Sam took his drink and added, "OK if we stay down at the quarry cabin tonight? We've given our statements, but they may want to ask us some more questions and we just as soon not have them come to our houses. We want to keep our wives out of this."

Matt answered, "Sure, I think the road's blocked by the state police anyway. You can sleep here if you want."

Will answered, "I think we want the little cabin. It is quiet and peaceful. We figured on staying over anyway. We have some food in the truck, and our sleeping bags."

Sam hopped off the workbench, "Let's go, I'm pooped. Oh, I think we should leave the blind where it is. I saw two more bucks while I was cooling my feet."

The Ferr brothers carried their beers and went to their truck, a patrol vehicle had to move so they could get out of the garage. They spoke to Stan explaining they were not leaving the area, but going down to the cabin in the quarry for the night.

Stan came into the garage. He spoke to Matt, "I've sent the cell phone off to Detroit. It will get to Lisa—she's the best there is on cellular tracing and computers. We also sent all the papers in the terrorist SUV, along with fingerprints and pictures. We're driving the prisoner down to Detroit tonight. He isn't much help so far, but we should know a lot more by this time tomorrow. Koning said he will call you."

Matt asked, "We need our weapons back. The threat isn't over."

Stan answered, "It isn't standard practice, but I cleared it with Koning, there will be no criminal charges, just a detailed report. When we leave you'll have your rifles and pistols.

"By the way, where did you hide the little machine guns?"

Matt grinned, "I'll take the fifth. M16 is illegal too, but we need it. The 30-06 was my grandfather's. The pistols are very accurate, as you know."

Stan said, "This is a special situation, we are cutting you a lot of slack. We need the state police to go before you get them back.

"Where is Carla?"

Matt answered, "That's the fifth again. We sent our women to a safe place, and I'm sorry we can't trust you with the information. Your leaks gave away this place."

Stan said, "I understand and so does Koning. The bodies and most of us will be out of here in another hour or so. What would you say if we put people at the corner where you had Sam? Maybe even use the blind that is there?"

Matt said, "I think it is a good idea, but let me talk with Webb."

Matt went to the motor home. Al and Webb were watching news on the TV, there were dishes in the sink, they must have eaten something.

Matt explained about the weapons and the FBI's offer to post guards, Webb agreed that it was a good idea.

Al said, "Maybe we can get some sleep."

Webb said, "You can sleep well tonight, your National Guard is!"

Matt laughed, "It will give us two more armed men. We will give our guards a list of my hunting buddies that will be showing up between now and the 14th. We will have to kick out the guards for opening day—Sam wants the blind."

Webb asked, "How about the women?"

Matt answered, "They might have heard the shots, but I doubt it. Anyway, I'll pay them a visit tomorrow. I'll make sure they are doing alright and give them a report."

Webb said, "Don't lie or evade, let them know the game we play. They need to be tough and alert."

Matt asked, "Do you want to go along? We could take the side by side, just spending some time covering up our tracks."

Webb said, "No, I've got work to do. Koning and I need to do some talking."

At midnight the last of the official tail lights eased down the road. One vehicle with two men would be posted on guard at the corner. The next day Matt said he would cut an area for them to park out of sight.

Matt closed the garage door, then he went outside. Dim lights were on in the Ambassador, the rest of his world was dark. The night sky was full of stars. Matt took deep breaths of the pure, cold air. He went back into the garage, still too keyed up to sleep. He met Webb standing in the kitchen doorway.

Webb said, "Can't sleep, I'm still shooting people."

Matt went to the gun cabinet, he took out a large wooden cleaning kit, which he placed on the work bench by the weapons the FBI had finally returned.

Matt said, "Find some of your expensive vodka and two glasses, and we can clean guns."

Webb returned with the vodka cold from the freezer, Matt had the pistols apart and was working on the M16.

Webb took a sip of the clear cold liquid, picked up the grip of the FN 5.7 he said, "This is all plastic, do we oil it or put it in the dishwasher?"

Matt answered, "There's springs inside, clean and oil it lightly, they really don't get dirty, but I don't like strange people handling my firearms."

A half an hour and half a bottle later, they left clean and shiny weapons smelling of Hopper's solvent and gun oil, turned off the fluorescent light over the workbench and found their beds.

39

Cabin Trip

Matt approached the cabin carefully. It was 10:00 in the morning. He could detect the faint smell of smoke from the wood stove. The door and shutters were closed. There was no sign of life. Matt yelled, "Hello the camp. Come out, come out, wherever you are!"

Tanya stepped out from behind a spruce tree twenty feet behind him. She carried the 30-30 and was wearing her new deer hunting cap and jacket that Matt had suggested.

Tanya walked over and kissed Matt as he got off the 4x4. "We heard gun shots yesterday, we buttoned up and kept the fire low. I thought I could be more useful out here. I made a hiding space inside the branches of that big tree, it's like a room inside after I sawed off some limbs.

"What happened?"

Matt answered, "Let's go inside, make some tea and I'll tell you all at one time."

In an hour the shutters were open, the tea was brewed and Matt went through all the events of the previous day.

Carla was sad, blaming herself, "All those men dead and poor Kate. Dave beat up and living under a guard. It is awful."

She lost her ability to make words, she choked, her eyes flooded. The beautiful smile and perfect features were replaced by a trembling narrow bitten lower lip and a furrowed brow. Her head bowed in sorrow.

Tanya, brought her some honey for her tea, and said, "You know we talked this all out. We're all here together. You are doing what has to be done. You can't turn your back on your duty. Everyone knows we are doing the right thing."

Karen added, "She's tough enough, it comes with her breeding. Hormones make her cry I think."

Carla dried her eyes, got up and went to the pantry, returning with a plate of biscuits. She served them to Matt with a tub of butter and pushed the honey to him.

Matt split the fluffy biscuit, buttered it and added a coating of honey. He enjoyed the texture, aroma and taste.

Carla said, "This is our third batch, we finally realized we needed to rotate the baking pan or they wouldn't cook evenly. Most of the heat comes from one side. Our first batch was burnt on one side and dough on the other. They all tilted."

Tanya added, "The animals loved them. We've got raccoons, squirrels, blue jays and deer drinking from the wash tub."

Carla asked, "When can we go back? I want to call Dave. I'd really like to be back in school."

Matt answered, "We are working on a plan to end our hiding. We've got an FBI guard now. Your dad wants you here for a while longer.

"Do you have enough food for another week?"

Tanya answered, "We're fine. A week is no problem. We just needed to know it wasn't forever."

Matt split more kindling and filled both wood boxes. He also lugged water. He said he wouldn't stay for supper because they didn't have that much food to spare. He said he would be back in a few days. The hunters would be coming in and they would be very safe at home.

Back home, Matt learned that the Ferr brothers had gone home for a few days and would return two days before opening morning. They said Dick and Billy had told them they planned to come at the same time. There would only be the four this year. The word had gotten out there was strange goings on at the quarry. Matt knew the stories were too good for a secret to last through the third beer. Too many people had seen too many official vehicles go up and down the county road. Matt could imagine what the UPS van generated in the form of rumors and gossip. The state troopers also had ties to locals.

As Matt drove back, the snow started, wet, the kind that stuck to the trees. It covered the ground by the time Matt drove into the garage. He felt his tracks would be well covered coming from the little cabin.

Al and Webb were finishing lunch.

Matt made himself a sandwich and reported the women were doing fine.

Webb reported, "Koning called, he's in a dither. They have a lot of information, Washington big wigs from the Justice department are now on sight, FBI bureau chiefs are scheduling meetings, the elections went to the Republicans in the house and senate, so the administration had three months of lame duck ass covering to perform. Lots of jobs will be lost or scuffled around. Koning feels the general mood is to keep the lid on the Imam trial until the new congress can have terrorist activity associated with their watch."

Matt said, "Carla wants to call Dave. She's feeling a lot of responsibility and pregnancy doesn't make things any easier for her."

Webb winced with the word pregnancy, and got up from the table, "I'm going to get Dave up here. They need to be together."

Matt was about to speak, but stifled himself with a big bite of sandwich, and thought, *Some fathers use a shotgun, Webb has a machine gun. Dave better be ready for the big "I do."*

Webb went to the motor home while Matt finished lunch and cleaned up the kitchen.

Al went out with a broom to sweep the snow out of the path between the garage and the Ambassador. Matt was pleased the blood on the driveway was covered.

Webb returned to the garage as Matt finished gassing up the 4x4 and Al finally realized that sweeping during a snow storm is dumb.

Webb said, "Dave will be up here by morning. I've got two men bringing him, we will slip him out same way the Muslims did. The FBI is still just sitting in their vehicle outside.

"Do you think Carla will be happy with Dave up here—I'm thinking she needs to stay in the cabin another week or two."

Matt nodded, "It will help a lot. They will need supplies."

Webb looked at Al, "You and I are going down state. I've set up a meeting with Koning, too sensitive for any kind of phone communication. Let's plan on leaving tomorrow after Dave gets here. I'll have two more men to take our place, you show them the security system. They don't need to know about the cabin."

Webb turned to Matt, "Can you go into town and get food for them? At least another week on top of what they have. Dave won't have winter clothes, I hope he can use yours."

Matt answered, "No problem with clothes. I would like to bring Tanya back, four is a lot in the little cabin. Dave seems capable and Karen can chaperone."

That word brought a glare from Webb, who forgot he was in no moral position to throw stones.

Al said, "What do we use for wheels?"

Matt answered, "The Yukon is yours. We have everyone coming here in a few days. I'll do a big grocery and booze run right now, gassing up too. We always have more than enough food provided by the wives for the first week of hunting.

"The important thing is only one more run in and out of the cabin. Let's hope we get more snow in the next week. I'll take Dave and supplies in and bring Tanya out."

Matt left for Naubinway, the closest town with groceries and gasoline. He brought and filled three five gallon plastic gas containers and added a cooler for the cold food.

Webb and Al went to the trailer and made plans for their meeting with Koning and several other nefarious doings.

40

Movement

The morning was very busy. Dave had arrived with the pink sky of dawn and two short Slavic types in a dark SUV, not unlike the FBI style. Webb had previously gone to the FBI guards to explain people would be joining them and they didn't want undue scrutiny. This made the FBI want to scrutinize all the more. A call to Koning, and some heated discussion, got the situation fixed. The FBI didn't know their charge had been spirited away—again. The Russian accents and shifting eyes of the two men with Dave didn't help the discomfort level of the FBI guards. Koning wasn't pleased with another witness being out of his control, but possession is 10 points of the law in this situation. Webb's men had clearly shown that FBI protection sucked.

At the house, Webb and Dave had a lengthy discussion in the living room. Matt didn't hear any loud noises or the sounds of impact or of limb breakage. In thirty minutes they came back to the kitchen in a friendly mood, a much relieved bridegroom-to-be and his prospective father-in-law, a Russian crime boss, who Dave knew could make use of a 55-gallon drum for more than transporting hydraulic fluid.

Al and Webb left after an hour of turnover instructions, mostly in Russian, had been given to the two men that came with Dave. This included a nonfiring familiarization with the two P90s. Webb dynamically described his use and effect of the weapon on the Muslim driver. Matt observed that Russian little boys didn't seem to make the same gun sounds as he and his friends did at ages ten or so, Webb make a repetitive "R" sound not an "Ack" sound. This cultural difference was overshadowed as Matt watched the eyes of the two new guards as they bonded with the little six pound plastic weapons; the men aimed and dry fired the weapons, they resembled the same ten year old kids with brand new bicycles, standing in a garage watching a heavy rainstorm. Matt resolved to remind himself and all his friends to clearly identify themselves around the house and along the northern road.

Dave was happy to be closer to Carla and seemed to Matt to be agreeable with the cabin plan. He was happy to have gotten past the meeting with his father-in-law to be. Matt learned that he was competent with rifles and had hunted small game and deer. Matt outfitted him well with winter clothes. Matt had a closet full of excellent hunting outfits that had mysteriously shrunk over the last ten years. When Dave was ready, a full backpack made up of clothes, toilet products, and some food went on his back; Matt tied a plastic milk carton container on the front deck of the 4x4 and heaped it with supplies. Astride the heavily loaded machine, they set off for the cabin before 9:00 in the morning.

There had been another two inches of snow—the 15 degree fluffy kind. It would be hard to hide their deep tracks without more snow or a general thaw.

Matt created a different route to the cabin, cross country, working through deadfalls and thick brush. He rejoined the trail at the creek. Dave was a sport through the whole bouncy journey and a willing help with clearing their way and concealing or blocking their back trail.

They drove right up to the little cabin, it was a picture, framed by the snowy woods, with a plume of gray-white smoke and soft yellow light from candles coming from the windows.

Carla was hugging and kissing Dave before he could get the backpack off.

Tanya was glad to see Matt also. Her kiss was a lot more than perfunctory; it was a promise of things to come. Matt thought the essence of the lonely little cabin, primitive living and sexual isolation should be bottled.

Karen gave Dave a warm hug. Then all the supplies were carried into the cabin. Webb had sent Karen several books. She greeted his thoughtfulness with glee, saying, "I've read everything printed in this cabin—even the old calendars and some of the yellowed newspapers used for fire starting."

They made coffee in the old aluminum percolator. Cinnamon rolls came with the hot brew. All the news was shared for over two hours. Karen was worried when she learned that Al and her husband had gone down state. She said, "There will be trouble. When my husband gets involved in this type of planning, someone generally gets hurt."

Matt took Dave for an outside tour. He showed him several fresh deer runs and where they came in to drink along the ravine that led to the wash tub.

Matt asked, "You ever dressed a deer"

Dave answered, "Many, my father had me hunting with him before I could carry a rifle."

Matt gave Dave his Marble hunting knife, "Here, I've got others, if you got a camp deer it would help with the food supply. I'll show you where they have a hanging pole. We'll check it to make sure it is still strong. It is cold enough you can take what you need. You want to keep it high so critters don't get at it. Bobcats and fishers are impossible to keep away, but they may not come around.

Matt asked, "Do you know about just killed deer meat?"

Dave answered, "Yes, it should hang a day or so, enzymes in the fresh meat give you the runs."

Matt said, "Right, the same enzymes will make the meat tenderer, that's why they age beef for the best quality. I'd like Carla and Karen to have a good experience with venison.

"Also, use only one shot if you can. One shot is hard to get a direction on. You're at least three miles from the nearest hunting camp. Shots before season always draw some discussion. It usually means the hunter was too dumb to sight in before camp or it was for camp meat.

"Be watchful; keep the 30-30 near you. Close up tight at night. Make a patrol, look for prints, listen for birds and red squirrels—they announce predators and hunters. Be suspicious of sounds, or of no sounds or motors. Don't leave tracks that can be seen from the air."

Back in the cabin, Karen said she knew how to cook venison, and different types of game Webb occasionally brought home. She wished she had some wine for cooking and from time to time, sipping on.

Matt brought out a gallon of Carlo Rossi's best and only Burgundy. From the bottom of the plastic box he had carried in.

Karen poured a glass for everyone and they toasted to being together in the warm, snug cabin.

Matt drew attention to the renewed snowfall. "We should go, the snow will cover our tracks if it keeps up. I wish we could have communication but Webb said no. As he and Al were driving off, he said the big dogs are in the game now—I didn't know what he was talking about—maybe the NSA, satellites, who knows, but we will stay off the grid for a little longer. I'm leaving the little cart, so you three could get out if you had to. Basically south and a little west will get you to the road. There is enough of a trail to follow and past the creek you will hit the road coming in from your right in about a mile."

As the day got warmer it started snowing harder, Matt and Tanya left the three standing in the doorway, a picture of early pioneers in their forest home.

Tanya and Matt were bundled up against the cold and the showers of snow that fell from disturbed boughs and branches. Matt enjoyed the hugs Tanya gave him. They enjoyed touching each other and being apart had been a strain on them both.

Back at the house it was quiet. Tanya made a bee line to the steamy shower while Matt thawed out steak. She had prioritized her return in three words: shower, steak and you.

Matt made sure the two guards knew the house was off limits that evening. They were confined to the motor home. They understood and were happy with the luxurious RV home and their security duties. The FBI guards took care of themselves and used the cabin in the quarry. When deer hunting opened, they would have to go to town for rooms. That time was just a few days off.

Webb and Al met Koning in a motel room off I-75, equal distant between Detroit and the Bridge. Al had brought in fast food and coffee from a nearby Burger King then left for another room in the suite. Koning swept the room with a bug detecting device. He turned on the TV and looked for cameras. The blinds were already closed.

Satisfied he and Webb were alone and not being recorded, Koning started, "Officially we are meeting to discuss your daughter's and Dave Adam's testimony and availability to testify.

"We didn't get anything useful from your prisoner, which you didn't already know: dedicated Islamic fundamentalist, a mindless follower, truly believing in converting the world to Islam or destroying it. He will be sent to a prison where, I'm afraid he will just have his actions and beliefs praised and strengthened by his Islamic Brothers—all at public expense."

Webb asked, "What about the cell phone and the papers in the leader's vehicle?"

Koning answered, "Still working on that, lots of overseas traffic, Europe and the Middle East. He lived in Virginia, his wife works for Virginia Social Services and he heads some kind of consulting group for various shipping concerns. His actions here show him as radical Islam as you can get and he is running around loose—actually flying around. Home Land Security and the FBI didn't have him on any hot lists, he is a US citizen and has all the papers. He doesn't attend a local mosque, or its leaders won't admit it."

Webb listened then said, "We're chasing little shadows, we need to expose the lack of attention at the highest government levels, cut through the politically correct crap and get people to realize there is a war going on."

Koning asked, "What's your idea?"

Webb answered, "Can you get the Imam out of Terre Haute and to some interview location?"

Koning nodded, "Yes, in fact we should be having meetings regarding pretrial motions and admission of evidence."

Webb said, "Good, arrange a meeting, schedule it to take several days, put all the information into your usual memos. Have three sets of guards and three rooms on different floors. Leave the room and floor information off the memos. Have the FBI watch who asks question about rooms and floors. I'd be surprised if others aren't interested. However, I will have the Imam kidnapped. We will put the evidence and blame on the Justice department. You can be incredulous, use the cell phone incident, couple it with the abduction and throw up your hands at the leaks from the highest law enforcement office in our country."

Koning looked sick, "I don't know, too many things can go wrong. I'm breaking laws."

Webb countered, "Self preservation is an ancient law. The country's leaders are betraying your office and their pledge to uphold the Constitution. They are either conspiring with Islamic terrorists or allowing them to infiltrate and suborn our agencies.

"Anyway, when the stuff hits the fan and if we get some new tough investigators, maybe the fallout will expose the sinister face of our Muslim government workers and Imam allies. You can be a hero, get promoted by the next political party and help safeguard the country."

Koning asked, "What if you get caught?"

Webb answered, "We won't be caught. We will probably be just ahead of a hit team from the government or Islam. There is no way they can allow the Imam to get to trial. Our biggest risk will be passing them in a hallway."

Koning nervously asked, "What are you going to do with the Imam?"

Webb paused, then answered, "I'm going to destroy him in multiple, horrible ways, you can know nothing about. I'm sorry I even told you that much.

"Someone once said of a bad man, "The best thing he did in life was the leaving of it."

Koning said, "I'm not convinced we need to do this."

Webb leaned closer to Koning, "People have died, more are going to die. The Imam should be killed. Islamic terrorists don't care if they die, the government in power will lie and have or let people be killed to stay out of negative headlines and to keep their power, my daughter and the father of my grandchild won't live through the trial, you will be the fall guy when the trial comes apart—another of a long line of federal prosecutors with an unlimited budget, aided by multiple federal agencies, an air tight case and you blow the conviction."

Koning got up, he paused and turned to Webb, "I've heard enough, actually too much. I see Kate dying over and over in my nightmares. I get out of bed and go to my daughters' rooms just to hear them breathing. I fantasize about killing the Imam in various ways with just my bare hands... I'll schedule the pretrial meetings, I'll put the information out as we agreed, I'll call you with the time and place as soon as it is finalized. I'll make sure you get several days advance notice over anyone else. That should help you. I'll make that call myself. After that, all communication between us will be through my secretary. I need to distance myself from you."

Koning took his cold, stilled wrapped, burger and left.

Webb said to the empty room, "You can come in now."

Al opened the bedroom door and laughed, "On his drive back the phony SOB will eat that burger and be planning how he will be the next Attorney General."

Webb asked, "Your recording equipment work OK? Who would have thought you could have a whole camera, mic and wireless transmitter in a button, which I could turn on with a squeeze?"

Al smiled, "Video and audio are perfect."

Webb touched the sport coat button, "We may find a record of this meeting to be very valuable in years to come.

"Now we need to get people ready for the next phase."

41

The Arbitration of the Sword

The weather was perfect. Wind, rain and snow pelted the dark alley in downtown Detroit. No one was disturbing the large dumpsters that lined one side of the road that ran by the back of the large office buildings that spent their money on the façade not where they deposited their garbage. Two vehicles had found room to park between the dumpsters.

Webb lectured two men in hats and long dark raincoats who were seated in the back of his rental car. Al was at the wheel, Webb turned to face his subjects, "Check your watches, it is 6:15 in 30 seconds. The food will be delivered in the next fifteen minutes. Plan your entrance to room 310 for 7:00. The meal will include coffee and tea. The Imam drinks tea. The coffee will take out the two guards if they even drink a half cup. The tea will make the Imam compliant but able to walk with some assistance. Use the last of the four elevators."

Al handed back an envelope, "Here is the room card. Only touch it with gloves on, destroy the envelope. Don't look up, keep your hats pulled down while you are in the hallway, elevator and in the garage.

There are cameras covering all these areas, we want you recorded but not a good face shot. We will have had the lenses sprayed with motorcycle chain oil. They will be a little out of focus, but to a bored security officer they shouldn't be alarming."

Webb continued, "Speak in Arabic only. The most important part is in the garage, your voices will be easily heard, say "You are fortunate to have such powerful friends, they work to make you free."

Al broke in, "That will play well in the press room."

On of the men asked, "What if the guards are not asleep?"

Webb answered, "Then use your weapons to gain control any way you must. The Imam, your speech and the timetable are the critical factors. "

Al added, "The room service delivery is by their regular person, he doesn't know we have drugged the coffee and tea. There should be no suspicion. We have a hotel employee helping us, you do not know, and will not see the person. Also, we have arranged for three of the elevators to be either inoperable or very slow. Hit all the floor keys when you leave the elevator in the garage. It is a kids' trick, but it will foil pursuit. We will be distracting the security area from 7:00 to 7:10 with a pizza delivery. They should be more interested in who sent them a pizza than their out-of-focus monitors. Helping a staggering man into a van in the garage area might be interesting to them, but they won't stop your leaving."

The men nodded understanding, "We are prepared with our other vehicle. And we meet you in the old house out in the marshland. We know how you wish us to secure the Imam."

Al said, "Good luck," as the men left the car.

Webb said to Al, "Let's get out of this area, drive north and find a bar."

Al smiled, "I know a good cop bar, $3.00 boiler-makers, free popcorn."

As they drove Webb commented, "I like settling issues out of court. We are conducting a form of arbitration tonight. It makes me think of one of my heroes, Winston Churchill, he once described the actions of Britain in the Sudan in the last of the 19th century when they avenged the killing of their General Gordon by the Dervishes, led by the Mahdi. The British force offered no terms but fight or die. They accepted no reparation, apology or treaty, they just killed the Dervishes. Churchill said, "They offered only the arbitration of the sword."

42

Captured Imam

Webb looked down at the sleeping, securely bound Imam. While drugged, he had been clean shaven. He looked younger, less severe. His skin was blotchy and pale. He was spread eagled on the bare, musty single bed. Even his neck was secured with towels and ropes. The restraints were to secure him and keep him from self-inflicted wounds or bruises. The room was small, the faded wall paper showed mold and water stains, the ceiling sagged where a light or fan had once hung. An old floor lamp without a shade gave light and a *film noir* atmosphere to the room. The house was located in an isolated marsh north of Detroit, a weeded channel snaked to its attached boat house, once housing a fast mahogany speedboat that smuggled liquor from Canada during prohibition.

Webb checked his watch, 5:00 am, he shook the bed with his foot on the chipped white metal frame. The Imam opened his eyes. Webb snapped his fingers. A man seated near the Imam spoke in Arabic, telling the Imam he was safe, the restraints were to keep him from falling from the bed as he came out of the drug he was given. He went on to explain that the hotel room service had provided drugged coffee and tea for him and his guards.

The Imam looked around and tugged against his bonds. He hissed in English, "Get me out of these you fool. I didn't need or wanted to be rescued. We will have the witnesses against me eliminated. It is all planned; our man will stalk and kill them. You make me look guilty, afraid.

"Who are you? Who is he?"

The Imam moved his head within the limits of his ropes, gesturing toward Webb.

Webb spoke, "I am the father of the girl you are trying to kill. You will soon die at my hand. I am sorry it will not be slow and very painful as I would have liked, but you will die in disgrace, a symbol of all that your twisted religion despises."

Webb nodded at the man near the Imam. The man grabbed the Imam's right bicep and jammed it down, immobile against the bed, the force of his grip brought up the veins on the Imam's forearm. Next came a narrow syringe containing a yellowish liquid. The injection was swift and practiced. The syringe empty before the Imam realized what had happened.

Immediately the Imam seemed to fight for breath, his eyes widened, he tried and failed to focus on his surroundings. He finally relaxed and grinned, saying, "Your daughter will die. Our hunter is well trained, he never fails. He is the arm of Allah."

Webb immediately left the room, going outside to use a newly purchased throw away phone. He called for Matt, to alert him of the new danger. The satellite phone buzzed unanswered. With great frustration Webb returned to the house. Al and two men met him in the screened porch of the disheveled property. Webb said, "We need to leave. You two can handle things from here. You know the plan. Be sure there are no marks on him, other than needle marks. Use rubber gloves, no finger prints, none of your hair, nothing transferable. Don't contact me unless everything goes to hell. He needs to be worked on, eye brows plucked, make up, perfume, special diet, silk and jewels, take your time, do it right. Pop him at the bar after hours, no witnesses, the janitor will find him in the stall. Follow up on the publicity, get pictures on the internet as well as in the press and news television. Then go swim in the Caribbean for a month—my treat—the Turks are great."

Webb gave one man a business card for a Detroit travel agency.

Al had the Yukon started, its lights went across the weeds and hummocks of the vast marsh area. The glow of Detroit lit the southern sky. The northern sky was clear and full of stars.

Webb got in after trying his cell phone again. No luck.

As they drove, Webb said, "If I can't get through soon, I'll have to call the FBI and that could become complicated. We don't want to be anywhere around this part of the state for the next few days.

"Drive fast, but don't get picked up."

43

Deer Camp

November 15 is the high holy day of the Michigan Upper
Peninsula. Most schools are closed and for the three or four
across the peninsula that aren't, plagued by misguided tree
hugging administrations too dumb to recognize the importance of the
day, the absent students are usually excused without consequence. To
many, looking over a rifle barrel as the dawn turns the eastern sky from
lavender to pink to yellow is a near religious experience. The hunter
feels his or her connection to all the hunters through all the annals of
the earth's history, unless his or her feet are cold.

Matt was given many, almost daily, reports from Koning's secretary. The FBI had identified all the terrorists as practicing Muslims.
The leader was named and had ties and communications with several
Islamic terrorist groups here and abroad. The live prisoner was an
informational dead end. The reports were perfunctory and seemed
as a courtesy, fulfilling an obligation. There was no word of Al and
Webb, as days passed.

Two days before the season opened, the boys arrived: Dick and Billy Lamoreaux and the Ferr brothers, Sam and Will. The FBI was ordered out of the hunting cabin. Tanya had a big supper for the hunters. The talk was more about terrorists than the rut or blind placements.

Billy brought in an old M14 with a scope. He passed it around the table, saying, "I've had this for years, too big and heavy, but it holds twenty .308 shells—it is civilian, semi auto—with its scope it's a tack pounder. I decided to lug it around this year seeing how you never know what kind of game is running or sneaking around in your woods."

Dick spoke up, "The UPS driver is my wife's cousin, the driver said you may never get another package delivered. She will just throw it out on your road as she drives by."

Matt invited in the two Russians—or whatever they were, he made it clear that the six around the table were friends, not to be shot. They were the only ones hunting during the first week. He also explained that people dropped by occasionally during hunting season. They were to be directed to the house or the quarry cabin. They were not to go on the north road, which was closed for hunting season.

The men took their work seriously; they looked carefully at each man. They were already in love with Tanya and knew all her features in their dreams. They inspected Billy's military style rifle, determining it was too heavy and had too much wood on it. They were invited to sit and eat, but declined. They were on the job and Webb expected their best efforts at all times. They left to continue the surveillance of the road and area around the house. They had visited the FBI guards each day just for the fun of sneaking up on them.

Sam Ferr spoke, "I can't bring myself to kick the FBI out of the blind, and they've got it canvassed up and have a heater in it. We insulted them enough by booting them out of the cabin."

Tanya asked, "I've got my blind comfortable, and I'm excited to be going out on opening day—or rather morning."

Matt squeezed her hand, "It will be cold and clear, you're on two good trails and there are rubs all around you. You'll have to walk in alone, we don't want any more people or, movement than we need to."

Around the house kitchen table various camp stories got retold, the movement of deer by place and times, the strategies for the opening day and the next several days were settled.

The two sets of brothers said good night and moved down to the cabin where they had set up housekeeping for at least a week of hunting.

Opening morning saw Matt and Tanya at the quarry cabin, eating a 5:30 am breakfast of eggs, bacon, pancakes, coffee and juice. Lunches were packed and the hunters disbursed. They were linked by radios and their familiarity with each other's hunting methods.

The rifle shot came at 7:38, first good light, and was from Tanya. She dropped a large buck. She excitedly whispered into her Midland Radio, as she looked down at the animal, "I got him, one shot, eight point."

Matt whispered back, "Be sure it's dead, then get back in the blind, give me an hour and I'll field dress it, we don't want to move around much before 8:30, congratulations honey."

No other shots were heard, the morning got brighter and colder. Matt stood, stiff legs recovering from his near catatonic hunting posture, he worked his way out of the brush encircled stump where he greeted the dawn. The crisp 16 degree air felt invigorating as he took deep breaths. His radio broadcasted a hiss and some static, someone had pushed the talk button. Matt paused, took the radio from his coat pocket, expecting to hear from Tanya.

A loud accented voice said, "Immediately come to trailer, come fast."

Matt knew all the hunters had heard the urgent message. He heard two 4x4's start up across the quarry as he walked and jogged toward the house. He was the closest hunter to the house. Tanya was the other way, north west of him, he spoke into the Midland, "Honey, stay where you are."

One of Webb's guards was waiting outside the RV. He carried his pistol. He walked to meet Matt, "My friend has been killed, someone, a killer, is in woods."

Matt heard the 4x4's coming up the road, it would be the Ferr brothers, they were close. However, Billy and Dick were deep into a swampy area, driving out nearly a mile by pick up, they would be a few more minutes at best.

The four assembled and were led by the Russian down a trail behind the RV, they found the other Russian face up, sprawled dead on the trail. He had cuts on his face and multiple wounds to his stomach and chest. The snow left signs of a struggle that took place over a hundred square feet. Matt noted the dead man's boots and quickly picked out the killer's different tracks that came in from the east and led off to the west.

Sam and Will, rifles at the ready, crouched, fanned out and circled the area.

Matt knelt beside the dead man, he had cloth material in his right hand. Matt pulled it away from his death grip, "This is like burlap or wrapping material."

Sam returned from his brief scout and knelt beside Matt, "That's may be camouflage from a Ghillie suit. Turn the guy over."

Matt rolled the man over; a puncture wound was outlined in blood on his right side just below his short ribs.

Sam touched the wound with two fingers, and then exposed bruise marks on the dead man's neck. He added, "Military training, grab jaw and neck, bend back, blade in side, in and up, takes out the diaphragm, no sound, polished him off with a heart shot. Text book silent kill."

Will came back to the group, "He's gone, went northwest, not a big man—boots about a 9. He put his rifle down by a tree back there, to free his hands for knife work. He knelt behind that bush."

Sam asked, "Show me where he hid."

The brothers went and returned from their inspection of the packed snow, Sam said, "Like I thought, sneaky bastard, his knee print shows he was wearing a Ghillie Suit."

Matt stood up, "Let's get back to the house."

Dick and Billy were waiting by the motor home its door open. Matt explained what had happened. During the explanation they heard the angry buzzing of the satellite phone. It was Webb.

Webb angrily said, "I've been calling for an hour. What's going on?"

Matt explained, the Russian interrupted, "We saw something on camera screen, Bodo went to check, he was killed."

Webb listened than said, "Matt, I was trying to warn you, the Imam boasted he had sent a single killer to get Carla. I'll explain how I know later, in person. Al and I are on our way back up there—we're seven hours away. You need to protect Carla, Dave and my wife."

Matt answered, "We are on it. No more time to talk, see you when you get here."

Billy spoke, "Let's get after the bastard. Track him down and plug him."

Sam raised his hand, "Billy, following a killer more than likely gets you killed."

The Russian called from inside the motor home, "I've got a picture. We can see the fight."

The men rushed into the big RV. The screen showed blurred images rolling in and out of the trail. The actual killing was not shown, but the man standing over the Russian and returning his knife to its sheath was clear. His camouflage Ghillie hood was pushed back. He then took out something and looked at it, then pulled out a compass attached by a cord around his neck from inside his suit. When he turned back to get his rifle, they could briefly see his face. He was young, clean shaven, with hard, tired eyes.

Matt took the control mouse for the computer, he froze the frame and then backed up to the frames just before the compass was shown.

Matt stopped the frame, then zoomed in on the grainy screen. He said, "Look, that glow is light coming from his hand, it's a cell phone. It's not a map or a photograph. He is using a satellite picture, like Google Earth, a Geological Survey topographic map or maybe a picture from a plane."

Sam said, "I bet he knows about the little cabin."

Will added, "They could have gotten some info from my prisoner, he could have heard us talking about the women going into hiding."

Matt agreed, "The red of that old rolled roof is a giveaway from the summer satellite views , or if he's got recent pictures, the cabin heat could have melted the snow off. I know he can't see the roads or trails because of the snow and tree cover if he has new aerial pictures. Also, if he is using satellite pictures—they're old—1995 I think—there isn't much need or demand to keep this area updated. The pictures are from the summer. He can see a road here and there, but not trails or the old railway grade."

Sam looked at his watch, "He's got at least a twenty-minute start on us."

Will asked, "What's our plan brother?"

Matt said, "Sam you were the sergeant, what do you think?"

Sam thought for a few seconds, then said, "The first rule is—don't do anything stupid. Second, prepare and third, use our resources. I suggest we flank him, box him in, then ambush his sorry ass..."

Matt added, "He's got four miles as the crow flies to the cabin, but the crow wouldn't have to go through two miles of cedar swamp, steep walled gullies and flowing streams. We have a road and an RV trail on both sides of him if he is going by a compass bearing. We have five men that know every creek and gully between here and the cabin."

The Russian spoke, "You have me; I fight in Afghanistan and Balkans. We have two machine guns. He kill my friend."

Matt didn't respond to the Russian, instead he got a pad of paper and made a square for the house, cabin and lines indicating the old road going north and the trail along the railroad grade that got to the cabin from the north east. He had their attention when he said, "I'm no general, Sam is the combat expert, but let's think about this, "Sam and I will go in on the 4x4, get to the cabin. We'll take one machine gun and set up in case the killer comes in on the regular trail."

Sam broke in, "An experienced soldier knows to stay off regular trails, he will probably swing wide and not leave tracks. I suggest Will, Billy and Dick take our pickup north. Drop off Will and Dick in the timber above the swamp, they work east along the ridge, easy walking, go slow and quiet, single file, stopping to listen every hundred yards. If he's down in the swamp, between breaking ice and snapping cedar he should sound like a herd of buffalo. The road winds east, you'll be less than two miles from the cabin. Billy can take the pickup truck all the way north to the road above the cabin. Matt and I will send the women and Dave north along the old railroad grade to where it crosses the old road, that way they're out of the war zone. Rifle bullets will go right through that old cabin's cedar logs, the cabin will burn or can be blown up—it isn't a safe place. Billy, you'll get in position before we get to the cabin, unless the road is blocked, let us know by radio if the road is blocked and where. The 4x4s can come to you."

Matt added, "We should look for signs of more terrorists. I can't see them locating the old north road, or coming down from the north. The woods are just too thick and the swamps are just impossible."

The Russian asked, "What about me?"

Matt said, "Get Tanya back here, Dick will point out her blind as they drive north. Then get back here, watch the cameras. You guard the house, protect Tanya, keep her with you and tell the FBI what we are doing. Maybe they can find the killer's vehicle out on the road. Webb could call us too. We don't want you in the woods. We intend to shoot anyone we don't know."

The Russian heard Matt's words, thought about the logic, he didn't argue. He nodded his head in agreement.

Matt turned to Sam, "What do you think, are we ready?"

Sam said, "Our plan is solid, if we hurry. Remember, a trained man is smarter and deadlier than any deer. Be ready for anything, plans can change in a hurry. Our radios are a big advantage. But you said it will not be heard back in the house."

Matt agreed, "The radios will work for us, Tanya and the Russian may be able to hear from the base station—it's more powerful than the hand radios, but we shouldn't talk much. We are used to whispering and being very quiet, "Let's get moving."

44

Man Hunt

Matt and Sam made themselves ready on the 4x4. The Russian and Will got in the back of the pickup driven by Billy with Dick riding shotgun, or more exactly—heavily armed with his and Billy's rifles. All were in their hunting clothes with camouflaged caps, the blaze orange vests and caps left back in the garage. They had all checked their radios for channel and battery. The plan was a flanking and pincer action to intercept the killer and then a deadly ambush. As a further action, the witnesses, Carla and Dave with Webb's wife, Karen, would be sent to a little used road some miles north of the little cabin where Billy would meet them and return them to the main house.

Sam had his rifle slung over his back, Matt had his rifle secured to the front of the ATV. He also carried the 5.7 pistol and had bungee cords holding the P90 machine gun and a second fifty round magazine for it. Sam declined to carry the machine gun, he said he would be better with his old Winchester 30-30.

Full of firepower and resolve to stop the threat of the terrorist-killer, Matt and Sam headed out. They followed the pickup that was faster at loading up and was expected to drop off the Russian to go to Tanya and accompany her back to the house from her blind. Matt would leave the main road and work trails east to the old railroad grade, then north toward the little cabin.

Matt watched the pickup move slowly west then north on the road from his house. He wanted to alert Tanya that the Russian would be coming to help her.

Using the radio, realizing all the men with radios could hear him, he said, "Tanya, we're going hunting again. The Russian is coming to escort you back to the house. He'll explain what has happened. He should be at your blind in a few minutes. Over."

Tanya spoke back, "Matt, what's happening? I started field dressing the deer, it is a lot harder and heavier than doing a big fish. Lots of blood and smell, I didn't like doing it."

Matt waited for her to finish then said, "Forget the deer, we have bigger problems. Keep alert, you should hear the truck in a minute or so, start walking toward the road. Over."

Tanya said, "OK, I can hear it, I'm on my way."

Matt tucked the radio in his jacket pocket and gunned the 4x4 up the road. As he turned the curve to go north, there was a flash followed by a dull boom. Sam reacted instantly, he dove off the ATV, grabbing Matt and pulling him off the machine.

Sam whispered, "That was a grenade. Let's work our way up the road, stay behind me and on the other side of the road—stay on the edge, don't shoot me."

Matt took the P90, chambered a round and began to follow Sam, who was crouched and alert going toward the sound.

Matt's radio hissed, Dick's voice came from the speaker, "I think we were hit with a grenade. The Russian is down in the truck bed, Will has an arm wound, the truck is full of holes and a tire is shredded. We are in the woods. We didn't see or hear anyone. Be careful."

Matt responded, "We are coming on foot, Sam is leading. Don't shoot us."

In two minutes Matt got to the pickup. It was stopped in the middle of the road, steam came from a ruptured radiator, it tilted slightly toward its left. Sam had heard the message and had sprinted to the scene. Sam checked his brother, then the Russian. Dick and Billy stood on guard on both sides of the road, rifles at the ready.

Matt got to the truck, Sam spoke, "The Russian has a chest wound that's bad and some slices on his arm and shoulder. Will has a gash on his forearm."

Will said, "Tape me up, my arm works. I've got holes in my coat from shrapnel: went up and through my sleeve, most missed me. I had just stood up, holding onto the cab. We were stopping, the Russian was about to hop off."

Dick came up to them, "Billy has glass cuts, and a cut on his leg, but nothing bad. The explosion came from the left side. The truck is toast or Swiss cheese. I had my window taken out too, the stock of Billy's rifle stopped a big chunk that would have taken off my leg."

Sam said to his brother, "We need our truck, the Russian needs a hospital, you need stitches. I haven't looked at Billy yet."

Tanya ran up to the group, out of breath she spoke between pants, "Can I help? What blew up?"

Sam answered, "A grenade, probably a trip wire set it off. Our killer just chewed up our time and several of our people. Good tactics."

Matt suggested, "Honey can you drive Will down to get his truck, then come back. Sam and I need the 4x4. We need to hurry, the folks in the cabin are in real danger."

Billy had a first-aid kit taken from the truck. Matt worked on Will's wound first, applying a bandage and taping it up tightly. Will said he was fine and could do his part to hunt down the killer. Then he got on the ATV with Tanya. They hurried down the road toward the quarry cabin and the Ferr brothers' pickup.

During their absence, Sam and Matt inspected the area. They found wire wrapped and twisted securely around a small tree on the far side of the road. They found footprints that were brushed out and covered with leaves and twigs. Matt said, "The guy is good. He went northeast, leaving tracks we couldn't see from the road."

Matt looked at the chunk blown out of the tree where the grenade had been tied, he speculated, "If we had been first down this road we'd be dead. It was set low for a 4x4 not a pickup."

Sam looked at his watch, "If we take the Russian to the FBI, they can help. We need to get back on our plan. This could cost us nearly an hour and one man."

Matt said, "Tanya can take up the slack—she can man the radio, we can give the Russian's machine gun to Dick, between it and Will's M16, that's a lot of firepower up on the ridge above the swamp."

Matt used the first aid kit material on all the cuts and wounds of Billy and Dick, the Russian was conscious, but had difficulty breathing. The wound had hit a rib and probably a lung. Matt packed the wound with the help of Sam. The Russian didn't complain. He wasn't bubbling blood, but he was laboring to breath. He didn't talk, just watched with sad eyes. They got him propped up and his breathing improved.

Sam called Matt aside, "That's a bad chest wound, but I've seen a lot worse. He has one lung working, but if the bad one fills up with blood he will be in trouble."

Will was back in fifteen minutes. He backed up to the damaged vehicle and they moved the Russian. Tanya came as they were ready to pull away.

Sam stopped everyone for a plan check, "OK, Matt and I will take off, following our plan. We will be careful, looking for wires and foot prints. Take the Russian to the FBI people at the curve stake out. Let them know what we are doing. Then bring the truck back, and get back on plan."

Tanya asked, "What about me?"

Matt said, "Man the security system, use the radio, keep us informed, whisper, repeat messages. Answer the phone. Keep a weapon with you. Webb and Al will be here this afternoon.

"We all need to be careful, this guy is deadly, he may be just stalking us, saving the cabin until we are out of the way."

Sam spoke, "I still say he is going for the cabin now. It is too risky to take us all on. He could be wounded or killed. Let's get moving. Dick, say the word, "Ready," when you are on the ridge. We will know our west flank is being covered."

Matt and Sam loaded on the machine and headed up the road. Sam road backwards, pushing against Matt's back. He watched their back trail. Matt drove carefully, looking for wires or branches across the road, they soon came to the fork to the east. The two-rut trail was snow covered and showed no fresh tracks. Twice Matt stopped and they inspected branches that had fallen across the trail. They also scouted into the woods looking for footprints. They came to the railroad grade and right-a-way. They could see down into the woods and swamp area. Tracks would have plainly showed themselves. Matt drove as fast as he could while keeping Sam on the machine. They covered several miles in just a few minutes. When they approached the fording area, they dismounted and scouted the area on foot. Finding no sign of the intruder; they brought the machine across and back up to the cleared track area. They got to the cabin to find Dave and Carla waiting, both were armed.

Matt noted a small deer skinned and hanging. Matt answered their questions and told them to bundle up and be ready to move north. Sam was scouting the area for any signs of the killer. He was also looking for ambush positions. He had hunted the area for many years.

In a few minutes the two 4x4's were ready, Dave leading on one and Carla driving the other with her mother on the back. Dave had the 30-30 and Carla had the shotgun strapped to their machine.

Matt had made a map, and gave them his compass, he instructed them all, "Go north on the railroad grade, stay on it until you come to a road that crosses it. It is a little more than two miles. Billy should be there in a big truck. Use your radio only if you get in trouble, we don't know if the terrorist killer is scanning our frequency."

As a last thought, Matt strapped an old Finn saw and a coil of rope on Dave's machine. Matt instructed, "There could be dead falls across the trail, cut them and pull them out of the way, try to stay on the level area. If you see anyone other than Billy, be ready to shoot. Be quiet, your engine noises are bad enough."

Matt listened to the two-machine caravan heading north, the thick woods and snow quickly muffling their sounds.

Sam came up to Matt, he whispered, "No strange tracks within a hundred yards."

Matt thought a moment, "Let's make the cabin look inviting, and then stake it out, watching trails from the south west coming out of the swamp."

Sam nodded, "OK, I'll stay outside. I found a tree that someone had made into a blind and there are good places along the ridge. He would be too smart to come up a trail, he might even come up and work down the ridge, bad luck for us if he gets between Will and us, he would have the first shot advantage. I'll end up on the ridge, in the big pines, looking down into the swamp."

Matt said, "The tree you mentioned, Tanya did that. I'll work in the cabin, then go there. You work the ridge. Let me see you when I set up so I don't shoot at you."

Sam slipped away, Matt went to the cabin.

In the cabin he built up the fire, turned on a Coleman lamp, put some bacon in a cast-iron fry pan, placing it on a warming area of the woodstove and turned on the radio, getting mostly static with some music and talk fading in and out.

Matt went out and settled into the space inside the big spruce tree, he saw Sam wave on the ridge, about fifty yards on the other side of the cabin.

An hour went by. Matt jumped from his crude seat when his muted radio made a hiss and Wills voice whispered, "Ready."

A series of clicks followed, each an indication the radio's owner had heard and understood the message.

Another half hour went by, the sounds of ice cracking came from the swamp. All of Matt's attention focused on them. He put down the machine gun and picked up his familiar rifle.

Suddenly from the swamp came the sound of breaking ice coupled with the popping sound of twigs and branches. Then two large does broke cover and bounded up the slope. They raced through the opening that fronted the cabin, then went down into the ravine behind it.

Their movement and speed could be read several ways: a buck was chasing them, someone was driving them, or they wanted to run just for the hell of it.

Matt slipped the rifle's safety back on.

There were clicks on the radio. Alert signals from the men on the ridge. Everyone was awake and ready for anything.

If a buck was chasing the does, he would have been making noise following them. No sound was ominous. It could mean a stealthy man was approaching. The southwest wind was increasing, it might have carried the foreign smell of a sweating man in a Ghillie suit to the deer.

Matt continued the watch, leaning against his branch seat, his rifle leaning against the tree, he moved the P90 in his lap and felt the weight of his pistol in a shoulder holster under his left arm. He was waiting to kill a moving mass of strings and ribbons, hoping he would see or hear the killer before the killer could draw a bead on him.

Then Matt heard a splash and the sounds of gravel grinding, not the normal gurgle of the stream. Someone was working down the stream. Not stepping on the growing ice shelves, fragile and noisy as thin glass, he also was avoiding the breaking of the dead wood branches that stick out of the cedars. The sounds were faint but definitely coming closer. It was not a deer. The man came slowly and steadily down the stream. Matt figured he was looking for a good place to leave the stream and work up the bank. For a stalker there was just enough snow to reduce some of the leaf noise, but the subfreezing temperatures still made a step give a noticeable crunch.

Matt thought randomly, *If he goes all the way to where we forded the stream, he will see the fresh tracks and be warned we are ahead of him. If he has a scanner with an ear piece, he could hear our brief radio traffic. The ford was several hundred yards away. These sounds were thirty yards down the bank. He must have a GPS system. No one could go through miles of dense cedar swamp with multiple streams and come out dead on with just a compass and a picture.*

Ten minutes after the last gravel sounds, Matt saw movement along the ridge of the stream bank. He didn't move because he couldn't identify a specific target. He would have liked to scan the area with his telescopic sight, but movement is your enemy when you are being stalked.

Matt identified movement in a specific red osier dogwood brush, next came a boom and rapid firing. Sam was being attacked.

Matt was unsure of his next move. He could see steam rising above the thin red spears of the dead leaf-filled bush. Matt could see the dark, thicker hot barrel of an automatic weapon. Sliding off the safety, Matt brought the short P90 to his shoulder, he placed the red dot of its optical sight on the bush and pulled the trigger. He fired in short bursts, fighting the short weapon that wanted to rise with each shot. He used the whole magazine in a half dozen volleys. Each burst cut into the bush, the sound was deafening after so many hours of stillness and anxious listening. When the machine gun clicked on an empty chamber there was only a rolling echo and a painful ringing in Matt's ears.

With great relief he heard Sam's 30-30 fire four measured shots. Then there was more silence.

Matt pushed his Midland call button, "Sam, you OK?"

Sam replied, "Fine, but I may have soiled myself. You hit him, I'm not sure of my shots, he tumbled down the bank like a load of dirty laundry. Let's bring up reinforcements. We need to be very careful. He was off by ten feet with his grenade and only ten inches with his shooting. A big pine saved me."

Will and Dick checked in. They were working along the ridge, slowly, listening as they came. Matt put a full magazine into the P90. He saw Sam working down the ridge, using trees as cover. Matt followed suit, working toward the spot where they had seen the killer.

Even with his hearing diminished by the pain and ringing from the loud explosions of the powerful little 5.7 cartridges right next to his ear, he heard ice breaking and dry branches popping in the swamp. Stealth was forgotten as their target worked to get away.

The ground behind the bush was a mixture of snow, leaves and blood. Some spatters of blood were bright red—lung blood. Sam picked up a leaf with a piece of tissue on it. Matt found shell casings—AK 7.62 millimeter.

Sam got on the radio, "He's wounded badly, spread out he's heading south. Stay on high ground, we won't go after him. Let him bleed and get cold."

Matt got on his radio, "Billy, can you read me?"

There was no answer.

45

A Day Around the Swamp

Billy's excited voice came over the radio, "We're OK. We're at a tent deer camp setup along the north road, we are all getting hydrated. We got an escort bringing us back to you guys. It's a long story, I had to tell them what's going on or they wouldn't let me go by. I'm glad I'm not with the Forest Service, I'll explain later. We have eight men coming back to the house. Hope you got enough beer and brandy, least we can do for interrupting their opening day. See you in a half hour, where I dropped Will and Dick off."

Matt spoke back, "We shot the terrorist, he's wounded bad, headed into the big swamp. We are going to watch the ridge, maybe you can have a few of your friends watch along the road and the trail that goes east on the south side of the swamp. We don't want anyone going in after him. He killed a Russian bodyguard with a knife. We want to watch the swamp area. It's going to take some time."

Sam spoke next, "Are you guys sober? You don't mess with this guy, he almost got me before I even saw him. I'm just lucky to be alive. I say get everyone back to the house, send your escort back with some beer and our thanks, then you come back and pick up Will and Dick."

Matt came on the radio, "We do what Sam says, he's our field general, otherwise we might have people shooting each other."

Dick spoke, "OK, Will and I hear you, we'll work back, get picked up and go to the house and guard it. We'll keep our eyes peeled for a person or tracks."

Sam replied, "Yes, Matt and I will get together and make plans. We will assume the killer is listening to us. We'll check in with radio clicks every half hour. A scanner won't have time to pick up anything."

Billy agreed with the plan.

Matt could imagine several pickups and some ATVs with rifles sticking up like a bunch of wild Sandinistas working their way back to his house. "Who you with? Sorry to be bothering them."

Billy answered, "You'll know them all. Most got their deer last week anyway. I told them the whole story. They want to hunt the bastard down."

Sam looked at Matt and shook his head.

Matt and Sam stood by the ridge that overlooked the stream. Matt had brought a gallon of the cold flowing well water to satisfy the thirst that follows the adrenalin rush of combat.

They watched and listened for a half hour. No abnormal sounds came from the swamp area.

Matt took more water and spoke in a whisper, "I think we should walk out, staying in the woods, slow and low. If he is alive, he has to be hurting. I don't think he would go north, no future there. He will go south then either west to the quarry or east to go around the house. His tracks showed he came in from the highway."

"I agree," said Sam. "We can work around the swamp from the east. Use the old trail, easy walking and quieter than crashing through brush. We can use a stalking hunt, we stop every hundred yards or so and listen."

Matt and Sam made sandwiches at the cabin, took some hard candy for their pockets and started south. Sam went first, Matt followed thirty yards behind, the machine gun at the ready, his rifle strapped on his back.

Two hours later they stood together on the east-west trail, never seeing a track that wasn't theirs and never hearing a sound they couldn't identify. They were both hot and thirsty. Matt was tired, stalking a wounded killer is nerve wracking. Every mound, bush or deadfall looked like a man in a Ghillie suit pointing a rifle. Every moving pine branch became an arm tossing a hand grenade.

Sam waited for Matt to join him as they looked down the open trail, undisturbed except for the 4x4 tracks from earlier in the morning. They found a dead fall to sit on.

Matt asked, "How long were you in Viet Nam?"

Sam answered, "Twenty-two months. In a forward base ten months."

Matt said, "I don't know how you could stand it. I'm wiped out in just two hours of worrying about being shot, blown up or knifed in the back by a mound of moss."

Sam snorted, "I understand, but really this is nothing: one enemy in an open woods, a noisy woods at that. We fought thousands of the clever little bastards in a jungle where most of the time you couldn't see or hear anything outside twenty feet, sometimes ten feet. If you got used to it and got sloppy, you got yourself or your buddies hurt. Some guys could smell them. We had dogs. Still sometimes they would sneak into your wire and turn our claymores around."

Sam and Matt sat for another five minutes.

Matt looked at his watch and pulled out his radio, giving the send button two presses.

Static came back, Tanya's whisper came out of the little speaker, "Matt, that you?"

"Yes, honey," said Matt.

Tanya continued, "We are all safe at home, guards posted, the FBI wants to talk to you."

There was a pause, "Matt this is Stan—I'm here with a SWAT team. Where are you, over."

Matt started to reply, Sam held up his hand and shook his head, indicating—no. Matt answered, "I don't want to say. The killer may be listening. You go to the red pickup that got blown up. Stay there. You can see up the road, keep your eyes open, check the tracks; he could be coming out right there."

Sam smiled and nodded his head in agreement.

Stan answered, "I understand, see you when you get there."

Sam took the radio, "Bring cold beers."

An hour and a half later, not deviating from the quiet and careful stalk they had been practicing for many hours, Sam and Matt arrived at the disabled truck. Two black SUVs and a dark gray step van blocked the road. Men dressed in black stood up from bush concealment positions. Automatic weapons, helmets, armored vests, tactical goggles and knee pads were the dress of the day.

Sam and Matt were directed to the back of the van. They sat heavily on the bumper and were presented with Coor's Light cans. After drinking almost all of the wonderful liquid, Matt asked, "What do you want?"

Stan explained, "The SWAT guys want to follow the tracks the killer left. We will be out of light in a couple for hours. I held them back because we didn't know where you were. They are a little pissed off."

Matt looked around and found another beer in the van, he popped it open, "I totally understand, but if we told you where we were and the killer could figure the opening in our coverage he could have slipped through to the south and go to the highway.

"Did you find a vehicle he might have come in?"

Stan answered, "Opening day—lots of vehicles parked along the paved road. We checked all their plates, no suspicious or rental hits. We think someone dropped him off. We are looking for any unexplained tourists in a several mile radius. Again, it is hard with all the hunters new in the area. And he might have been planning a one way trip, par for a lot of these terrorists. We have extra people at the bridge, checking anyone suspicious going south."

The leader of the SWAT unit came over. He was small, Matt thought he would have made a tough 132-pound high school wrestler, twenty pounds and years earlier. He looked at Matt and at his weapon and said impatiently, "Now we know where you are, we are going to track down the killer. You shoot him with that little weapon?"

Matt hadn't thought of the illegal machine gun he had on his lap, "Yes, I got him with several hits from thirty yards."

The SWAT man asked, "You sure he was wounded."

Sam burped and answered the question, "Lung tissue and blood, dark blood on the ground he rolled down. He still was able to scurry into the swamp and was making good progress. We decided to let the wound, cold water and miles of cedar swamp soften him up, if not kill him. He was in a ghillie suit, had an automatic telescopic rifle and knew how to use two grenades."

The SWAT man looked at Sam, "You been in combat?"

Sam said, "Yes."

The SWAT man asked, "When was he shot—how long ago?"

Matt looked at his watch, "Maybe 10:30—so that's a little more than six hours."

The SWAT man put on his tiny head mic and ear piece. He broadcasted, "We're going in, get to the positions we outlined. The man's wounded; he's armed with an automatic scoped rifle and may have hand grenades. He is in a sniper suit, and knows how to use a knife."

Matt said, "You have less than an hour of light, it gets real dark in the swamp. Do you want my help, I know these woods."

The SWAT man thought, then said, "If you're up to it. You can be with me, I've got younger, quicker people ahead."

Matt looked at Sam, Sam said, "He's all yours. I've done enough hunting for today. Maybe I can get some help for Tanya and her buck. I'm about two quarts low on beer. See you later Matt, don't be the first down any paths."

Matt got up, heard a scraping sound, it was his ass dragging. He was happy to leave the nine pounds of his Remington 700 deer rifle with

Sam. He had the P90 strapped over his right shoulder. The SWAT team saw it, no one asked any questions. The SWAT leader was named Kevin, the last name on his vest said: Hill. Matt didn't feel good about saying either of his names, so he didn't. Matt was fitted with a head mic and ear piece. His ears still rang from firing the P90.

Matt and Hill stayed thirty yards behind a "V" formation of seven SWAT members. They moved easily, ducking and hopping over obstacles. Matt stumbled along, going around obstacles to save the energy needed to go over or under them. The half of mile of hard wood travel was easy going, the killer's steps in the snow kept a bee line toward the cabin.

Then they hit the first of the ravines and small creeks. Hill helped Matt down the steeper slopes, Matt took the help.

Matt turned off and lifted his microphone, commenting to Hill, "Your guys are fit and move well in the woods. I can hardly hear them, but my ears are still bad from shooting this piece of plastic. My uncovered ear was right next to the breech and firing mechanism."

The SWAT leader whispered, "We use ear protection, the H&Ks and SIGs are loud too. How much more of this swamp."

Matt replied, "We just started in the bad stuff. We have almost two miles. We will never get through it before it's too dark to see."

Hill asked, "Let us know when we should go back so we can get out without using lights for every step."

Matt nodded.

They went down into an area of meandering creeks with iced edges, steep banks, dead falls, sphagnum hummocks, weeds and brush. The natural twisting and twining of thick cedars made the going hard and slow. They were tracking the killer, Matt saw where he also had trouble with the terrain. Occasionally a piece of the Ghillie suit was found on a protruding branch or on a root where he had worked up a bank.

At 5:00 Matt suggested they stop. "You won't see your hand in front of you down here in another half hour. Up in the hardwood we will be able to follow our prints out. If the killer wasn't wounded badly he would have gotten back this far. He may be too hurt to move much. Anyway, we shouldn't go any further."

Hill broadcast, "Stop the pursuit, we can start going back now, be careful, cover your retreat." He started to get confirmation of his order from each member.

Matt and Hill waited for their lead teams to come back to them. The rest flanked them, dark images moving silently among the cedars.

As Hill was again doing a people check, ensuring all his people were accounted for and he had his extraction organized, there was a percussive boom, seconds later another. Yellow lights flashed in the dark trees. All the men instantly got low or prone. The explosion was fifty yards to their east. Several of the SWAT team took a compass reading. Matt instinctively knew the way to the area would be along a stream edge on a worn deer trail.

Matt spoke, "I think I can lead you to the area. We just have to follow this stream. It is the easiest walking—or hopping or squirming. This is about the worst area in the whole swamp."

Hill directed his people; he had some follow the stream, some in the gravel bottomed foot deep stream, and two on each side watching from the higher banks. He and Matt followed.

Next to the stream it was dark, the deer path mud and moss made for quiet walking, the only sound was the stream bubbling around and over ice and fallen branches. Then Matt heard someone on the headset say, "Shit, what a mess."

Matt's ear radio picked up more expressions of surprise and consternation. Hill was listening too. He allowed Matt to lead him along the path. Lights came out and came on. The men had flashlights on their weapons and some they attached as head lamps.

Matt had problems with loss of night vision when he looked at the bright beams playing around the trees and creek. In a few minutes Matt arrived at a circle of several men whose lights illuminated a gruesome scenario.

The ghillie suit was blown open, stomach, liver, intestines, lung, ribs, and a twisted arm came out of it. A part of the man's head had one eye staring up toward what little sky showed through the thick foliage, reflecting a faint red glow from the sun that was already over the horizon. The tangled mound that once was the killer steamed, pieces of the suit smoldered. The smell was rank with blood, fecal material and explosive.

Matt moved closer and stepped on something soft and yielding. Matt looked down, it was a tail and leg of a large wolf. Lights played around the little valley formed by the creek and steep banks, another wolf lay on its side. It moved, its side was cut open and its back legs and back were mangled and broken, it growled in pain and defiance. A red dot appeared on its forehead, a pistol cracked, the animal's head dropped out of the lights. A SWAT member had dispatched the horribly wounded animal.

Hill ordered, "Film all this, then move back. Don't touch anything."

Digital cameras came out, still and motion pictures were taken, men spoke into microphones. Matt stayed out of the way, trying to make sense of what he was looking at.

Hill made sure everyone was out of the immediate area and behind cover. Then he began to inspect the body. In a coat pocket he found and displayed two grenade pull pins. He circled the body, then got on his knees, and began carefully probing under it. He spoke as he worked. "The grenades were under the killer's arm or arm pit. The blood pool under him indicates he bled out here. I'd guess he used two hand grenades to booby-trap himself. The wolves smelled the blood, came in, pulled on his arm... Bang and bang!"

Hill took out a coil of rope, tied it to the still connected arm, played the rope out, added another rope and the SWAT men pulled the body over from eighty feet away while they were safely behind some large trees. No booms.

It was now completely dark in the middle of the cedar swamp. A little snow came down through the trees. Hill talked with his men. They needed to move the body and they discussed how they could do it.

Matt suggested, "If it were a deer we'd either float it or drag it out to where we could get an ATV to the bank, or we'd put it on a pole. This guy is such a mess you couldn't drag it, he's too ripped up to float—like a deer would. So let's cut a good pole and carry him out.

The men talked among themselves and then started to use their sheath knives to chip and chop at the base of a tall and straight cedar tree, six inches at its base. Matt watched their pitiful efforts for a minute.

Then Matt said, "Stand back, I'll show you a real lumberjack in action." Matt got down on his knees, three feet from the tree's base, when holding the weapon low, he pointed the P90 and slid off the safety, everyone moved back. A two second burst on full automatic sliced the tree as effectively as a chain saw. The eruption of sound rolled through the swamp.

The tough cadre of law men provided a satisfied series of grunts and gloved muffled applause as the tree fell. It hung up among other cedars, but was quickly pulled down and stripped of lower branches. Matt cut the top off just as effectively as he had done the base, his ears now painfully ringing.

The SWAT members worked to bundle and tightly tie the body to the pole. Matt heard the men gag and complain as they worked to secure the gruesome cargo. Next, two men carried the dead terrorist on a pole. It was a grueling task. Others carried their weapons and pistol heavy belts as well as the killer's rifle and what little was left of his gear.

As fit as the SWAT members were, they still had to change bearers three times before the group got back to their trucks in the forest area.

Hill and Matt were leading the procession, through the dark woods, following their dark prints on the white forest floor. Hill said, "There will be people criticizing me for moving the body. I wasn't going to leave men in that swamp and I'm sure that other wolves would have caught the scent of the kill and finished the meal. We need what's left of the face and his remaining fingers."

As Matt approached the vehicle he smelled a pleasant and familiar perfume, Tanya was near. Matt saw her leaning against the SWAT team van, Webb was with her.

Tanya walked to him, she looked up to him, her eyes glistened in what little light was cast from the vehicles and many flashlights working the area. She kissed him on the lips, then hugged him. Matt felt so tired he wished they would carry him home on a pole.

Tanya said, "I've listened to almost everything that was said. Webb and Al got here two hours ago. Webb has been talking nonstop to the FBI, he is very concerned about the Imam being on the loose. He is very upset about Bodo being killed, they have known each other for many years. He finally agreed to walk me down here to get some fresh air and to calm down.

"I'm so glad you're not hurt. Sam said it was some fight. He said you might have saved his life."

Matt hugged her and smelled her hair and felt her warmth. "I wasn't being shot at. The terrorist never knew where I was—I was hidden in the big white spruce tree you made into a blind. Congratulations on getting a buck. I'm sorry I wasn't there to field dress it and get it on the pole."

Tanya laughed, "I've had help from everyone. Billy's bunch came in with Carla and Dave, drank all the beer they brought, then almost all our beer in the refrigerator and garage, took care of my deer, even took pictures with it. After lots of beers, they wanted to fight the SWAT team. They hate the U.S. Forest people for closing off the road where they have been hunting for thirty years. We could have had a war. Anyone in a uniform was the enemy, lots of weapons and beer and their hatred of government bullying. The boys had opened the road the feds had dropped trees across, when Billy was trying to maneuver through, they stopped him until they saw who he was, they didn't recognize the Ferr's pickup."

Webb came up to Matt, "I'm glad you're OK. I understand the P90 did a good job on the killer and works as a chain saw too."

Matt looked down at the short weapon, "Yes it did, we need to get it out of sight before someone realizes how many laws it breaks."

Webb took the weapon, removed the magazine, cleared the chamber, put the still partially loaded magazine back on the weapon, then removed his long coat, put the weapon over his shoulder and put on his coat, "*Voilà*, gone. Let's walk back to the house. It has been a long day. Karen is organizing supper, your friends are bringing up some food from the quarry cabin—we'll all eat together."

Matt would have liked a ride back, but the FBI and SWAT people seemed to be busy with what they considered important discussions and duties, stowing all their gear and poking around the dead man. They were not in any hurry to leave the area.

Matt held Tanya's gloved hand and the three walked slowly down the dark road, back to the house.

46

Actions At Home

I n the kitchen of his home Matt enjoyed being with Tanya and his friends. His initial tiredness was overcome by a warm shower, comfortable indoor clothes and a very busy household full of people. Most had already eaten from a buffet arranged on the kitchen counter. Webb was holding court by the fireplace in the living room with Carla, Dave, Karen and Al. Three FBI agents, led by Stan, had just finished questioning them, then filling their plates, they listened and talked between forkfuls with the rest of the men in the kitchen. When the lawmen had cleaned their plates and were satisfied with the stories they heard, Tanya and Matt escorted the FBI team out through the garage.

Tanya asked them, "Will you be going back tonight?"

Stan answered, "Yes, but we've got an hour or so of work to do yet this evening. The Russian's body and the terrorist remains need a coroner and forensic examination. The SWAT team is heading back downstate. We've left double guards on the road, adding U.S. Marshals. The Imam's escape has everyone embarrassed and on edge. We've worked with the Muslim community and put out All Points Bulletins, press releases and TV interviews by the Assistant U.S. Attorney Koning. We got zip for responses."

Matt added, "Webb is very upset, he said he heard that the people that took the Imam from the hotel were speaking in Arabic."

Stan replied, "That's true, but it isn't common knowledge. Webb must have gotten that from Koning. We actually have surveillance recordings from the parking garage of the hotel that show two men hustling the Imam into a van. We found the van a few blocks away on a side street. The Imam's prints were identified."

The FBI group walked to their vehicle, Tanya spoke to Stan as he got into the back of the SUV, "You know Webb has threatened to take Carla out of the country now that your people have been shown to be incapable of keeping a secret, guarding a witness or protecting Carla from killers."

Stan took a long breath, looking sad, and said, "I'm sorry to admit that everything you said is true. I warned Webb that he had already broken laws, and we looked the other way, but if he tries to flee the country with Carla, we will arrest and prosecute him, and anyone who aids him. The law is the law. We don't make it, we enforce it. Prosecutor Koning made this very clear in a conference call we had today with Webb."

Back at the kitchen, Matt ate a second helping of venison stew that Will's wife had sent with him for deer camp. Matt had had three beers and was full, satisfied he would recover from the stress of the day. He and Sam had repeated their battle with the killer at least four times. The account of the booby trapped dead terrorist and blown up wolves Matt had told Webb and Tanya on their walk back from the SWAT truck, but he was saving that first hand gory tale for the rest of his guests until well after dinner or better yet, the next day.

Tanya sat next to Matt, touching him occasionally as they listened to the table talk about hunting a killer, Tanya's buck, tomorrow's plans to get Billy's truck moving, the danger of another attack, the celebrity of the SWAT team, FBI agents and news reporters trying to get information about what was happening on Matt's land. Will, Sam, Dick and Billy agreed it was like living in a news documentary. They finally succumbed to the long day, physical injuries, life threatening danger, a big meal and liberal partaking of alcoholic beverages. The medical expert with the SWAT team had done a professional job on their cuts and injuries. They didn't feel a multi-hour trip to a clinic would be worth the effort or expense, plus there were too many interesting happenings at Matt's camp.

With the hunters gone, the house finally got quiet, Carla and Karen went to their bedrooms. Dave began to make a place on the sofa. Neither Carla nor Dave wanted to approach Webb on the subject of their sleeping together. Webb noted the arrangement, went up the stairs to his bedroom with Karen, after a few minutes he came back down and took Dave's pillow, then went back up the stairs and tossed it into Carla's bedroom.

Matt and Tanya were cleaning up the kitchen and enjoyed the unspoken drama.

Matt went out to the motor home to check on Al and the Russian who were manning the security system. They were also doing walking patrols, coordinating their activity with the two FBI or US Marshals assigned as working teams at the main entrance.

Finally in bed, Matt held Tanya, they could see snow coming down illuminated by a three-quarter moon glowing through scattered clouds. On the other side of their bedroom the fireplace cast a red glow. Matt whispered, "That was a good decision by Webb with Dave and Carla."

Tanya agreed, "Yes, Carla needs love and support. She and Dave are a good match."

Matt changed the subject, "Did you find out what Webb and Al were doing downstate?"

Tanya answered, "Webb said he was meeting with Muslims and working with the prosecutor. He wanted to get guarantees that Carla would be safe if she went back to school. He didn't go into details.

Knowing him he probably made threats they couldn't refuse. But today he was mostly upset about his friend getting killed. He's known Bodo for twenty years."

Matt felt Tanya push against him, he suggested, "Let's sleep in tomorrow, seeing how you provided the deer meat for the house."

Matt was dreaming about being lost, splashing around in a cedar swamp chased by snarling giant glowing eyed wolves, when he heard a close rifle shot. He was immediately wide awake. The shot was real; he could still hear the echo. He looked at the red digital display of the clock by his bed: 8:15 am.

Tanya was still sleeping, they had enjoyed each other the evening before and both had fallen asleep very contented. The shot brought Matt back to the realities of the complex world that surrounded them. Then Matt remembered it was the second day of rifle hunting season. The sound was south, maybe within a half mile. Matt guessed it was Billy or Dick in their familiar area of swamp southeast from the quarry.

Matt smelled coffee. He was mentally awake so he quietly slid from the mess of covers and left the bed.

Webb was in the kitchen, Matt padded in, barefoot, wearing sweat pants and a long sleeved t-shirt. Webb, in an old bathrobe, handed him a cup of coffee. Matt tasted it—it could be chewed. Without a complaint he put in some milk. It was now drinkable, but it made his heart race.

Webb sipped his coffee and looked at the snowy scene out the window. He said, "I have a feeling it will be a busy day. We should be hearing news from Koning. That Imam can't stay hidden forever.

"Let's make breakfast for everyone, have our whole family at the table."

Matt and Webb got busy in the kitchen. Matt began mixing up pancake batter, Webb worked on chopping onions, cheese and green peppers for omelets. Bread was ready for the toaster. They made lots of noise and extended the influence of their activities with the aroma from pans of sausage and bacon cooking on the stove. The noise and smells were irresistible to the rest of the household.

In twenty minutes the table was filled with food and the chairs with hungry people.

After some time to get the first plateful of breakfast eaten, Webb took his second cup of strong coffee and addressed the morning assembly.

Webb waited until all at the table understood he had something to say, "I want to tell you what Al and I got accomplished while we were down state. We couldn't say anything last evening with all the law around.

"I worked with many powerful and influential Muslims during my time in Detroit. Within the illegal framework of moving material and people clandestinely they were trustworthy and reliable. I used these contacts to arrange a meeting with the leaders in the Ann Arbor area. My goal was to impress upon them the concern I had with the safety of my daughter and her soon to be husband."

Carla interrupted, "We talked last night, we want to be married at the University Chapel."

Webb added, "Actually, Dave said that to me before we left. I didn't want to say anything until you agreed to a wedding and to a place to perform it."

Tanya asked, "What did you say to the Muslims?"

Webb took a sip of coffee, "I'll answer that, but I have a pre-ramble to go through…I've spent nearly fifty years dealing with threats and terror. Working in the government of the old Soviet Union you needed a balance of coercion and collusion to stay in any important position, I was in a Soviet prison for involvement in a fatal bar fight, there the niceties of civilization are stripped away, you never bluff, you counter force with greater force. In the invisible business I ran for a quarter century we used bribery, blackmail, and gruesome consequences for disloyalty. I have never seen acquiescence or appeasement work against a determined enemy.

"So I had been previously introduced by my former Muslim business acquaintances as a serious person and I proceeded to explain that if anything happened to my daughter or her husband I would rain destruction on them, their families and turn their mosque to rubble."

Carla asked, "Did they believe you?"

Webb went on, "They did after I told them to look at their hands."

Matt said, "Hands?"

Webb smiled, "Remember when you make a threat you need to establish yourself as able to accomplish the threat.

"I had them notice that the cracks of their skin, on their hands, their necks, around their eyes. I pointing out they were stained. They all noticed the discoloration. It was subtle and looked just a little dirty."

Carla asked, "Did you poison them?"

Webb smiled, "They thought so for a few seconds and looked shocked. One doctor mentioned he had dark stains between his toes, he thought it was from new socks.

"They were very relieved when I said it was a harmless chemical I had put into the water of their mosque. It was silver nitrate—a clear, odorless liquid that reacts with light and turns dark. It was used in photography, on the eyes of newborns, and is actually a disinfectant. I explained it was a stain, but would wear off with time. I went on to say the chemical could have been one of many very deadly compounds that could bring lingering and painful death—much like the Polonium their Imam attempted to drop on the crowd at the stadium."

Tanya asked, "What did they say to that?"

Webb continued, "They said they had nothing to do with the plot or attack and shouldn't be held responsible for the Imam's actions. They insisted it was unfair to blame them and their peaceful religion. They didn't even know where the Imam had gone when he escaped from the FBI.

"I said they had better help with the search and hope the man is found. I made it clear that we would not meet again, my retaliation would come without any further discussion. If I learned of any plots or fatwa being issued against me or mine, then they specifically, and an uncountable number of their members would die. Then I told them the meeting was over."

Tanya asked, "How did they take your threats."

Webb answered, "They continued to argue and even plead as to the unfairness of my position and action. I had Al move them out of the meeting room."

Matt asked, "What are they going to do with the silver nitrate in their water?"

Webb snorted a laugh, "They will have a hard time figuring how it is getting into their water. It is in their water softener salt. They have bags and bags of it. A percentage of their salt pellets are really nitric acid silver salt, it is a white crystal pressed to exactly match the rest of the little white pellets. We had used this pressing and concealment technique to smuggle many chemicals.

"The dilution is so much, the effect of darkening the skin is more a product of accumulation than a onetime thing. They will find the most devout will be most affected."

Carla asked, "Father, you wouldn't really kill them, would you?"

Webb looked at Carla and Dave, "Oh yes I would, if they harmed you. I don't just talk of consequences. I already have plans in place that would take action in days of any further attacks."

A minute went by as these serious words were spoken. No one asked about Webb's horrible plan. Matt stood, got the coffee carafe and offered refills. After serving Tanya and Dave and then himself he said, "The Imam is the loose cannon on the ship. We don't know what he will do."

Webb spoke, "We need to wait and see how all the searches come out."

Matt finished his coffee, "I'm getting dressed and going to check on the hunters."

The group broke up and started their day.

47

Amen Imam

The second day of rifle season was cold, snowy and unpleasant out in the woods. The snow turned to torrents of sleet just before noon: cold, loud, miserable for man and beast. After the buck shot that morning was hauled out and hung up, the four hunters drove up from the quarry cabin to Matt's house for lunch or brandy or just to enjoy seeing what Carla, Karen and Tanya were wearing.

They said that Billy's buck was so big its twelve point rack stuck above the swing set cross bar and its hooves dragged in the dirt. Tanya's eight point hanging next to it was a small cousin.

Over a beer and some reheated stew Billy said, "I've never shot such a big deer during the season, in daylight."

His brother Dick said, "You won't be able to stick a fork in its gravy."

Billy said, "You're bad mouthing it because you were asleep when it walked by you. It will cost you a beer to have your picture taken with it."

Dick said, "I was still tired from stalking a Muslim killer while you were drinking beers up on the north road."

Sam Ferr stood up, drank his coffee and looked outside, "Crappy weather, we got to get that truck moving if it lets up some."

Matt said, "I walked down by the truck this morning, we were lucky you were not all killed. When you get on a good tire, put it in the heated garage while we figure out what parts to order."

Will added, "You guys start on the tire, we'll use our truck to tow it back, a warm, dry garage sounds good."

Matt said, "Sure, tow it up here and I'll help push it in. Right now I need to check on Webb, he's in the RV."

As the brothers prepared to head out into the wind and sleet, Matt went to the big RV.

Webb was engaged in a phone call with Stan the FBI agent, the speaker phone was on so Al could hear, Matt recognized Stan's voice. Stan was the agent he had shot during the night battle.

Webb was saying, "That's good news, I appreciate you calling us. When will Koning call?"

Stan said, "Later in the afternoon, when the finger prints are confirmed. He's upset about the publicity and the fact that the news knows more than he does, and they have lots of pictures. He's also upset with you because he knows about your threats to the Muslims. I'm giving you a heads up on that issue, don't say I said anything."

Webb said, "Thanks for your call and the information; if we don't see you again, we all appreciate your help."

The phone link was broken and the hissing speaker turned off.

Al gave Webb a high five.

Webb turned in the swivel chair where he was sitting, "I've got news, they found the Imam. He's very, very dead."

Matt gave a fist pump, "Great, what's the story?"

Webb got up, "Let's get everyone together; it is a complex situation and a delicious story with a surprising ending."

Webb assembled his family and Matt and Tanya in the living room. Al loomed in the doorway while Webb sat on the stones fronting the fireplace, more or less in the center of the surrounding furniture of the room.

Webb began, "I just talked to Stan, the FBI agent. He was kind enough to inform us of significant happenings down state. He said we will have official confirmation from prosecutor Koning this afternoon. "

Carla asked, "Confirming what?"

Webb answered, "Confirming that the Imam is dead. Also he can inform us if there will be no trial and you will be able to return to your school and your lives."

Dave sitting next to Carla on the couch gave her a hug.

Matt asked, "How did the Imam die?"

Webb, looking around the room, gaining a dramatic pause, began his story, "The Imam, leader of his vicious terrorist group, was found dead, sprawled in a filthy bathroom stall, at a very disreputable Detroit bar, of a heroin overdose."

Webb's audience looked more shocked than pleased. All except Al who said, "It gets a lot better."

Webb continued, "We are waiting for positive identification from fingerprint comparison and DNA evidence. He was clean shaven, had on makeup, jewelry and was dressed as a woman. The needle was still in his arm. He was found by an early morning janitor."

Al spoke, "There will be pictures at five, lots of pictures."

"I understand there will be publicity." Webb added. "Somehow the press was alerted as well as the local police, before the Feds could put their usual lid on the investigation. Before the first FBI agents got on the scene, all the city news sources had their leads written, including motion and still pictures."

Tanya asked, "What does this mean?"

Webb answered, "We need Koning to confirm what the justice department and the federal system will do. We believe there will be no trial and if the pattern of federal actions on terrorist prosecutions continues, nothing official will be heard of this attack from the government, time and distractions are their ally."

Matt said, "This will be a great shock to the Islamic community."

Webb added, "Very much so, the manner and conditions of the death violates many Islamic laws and edicts. To Muslims the Imam will be an anathema instead of a symbol of Jihad."

Koning's call came in the late afternoon. The household had been expecting it for several hours and everyone milled around between the kitchen and the motor home. Dave and Carla were the most excited, their talk ranging widely between wedding plans, catching up on class work and school projects, life among shops and shopping centers, pizza and seeing their friends again and even baby names.

Webb didn't announce to Koning he was on a speaker phone and that the motor home was crowded with a very interested audience.

After Koning confirmed he was speaking with Webb, he began, "I understand you have previously talked to my man Stanley, he probably told you too much, he's still glad he lived through his gun fight with you guys. Anyway, the identification of the body found this morning was that of Ahmed Hussin Saleem Alikhan. According to the coroner, who tends to wax lyrical on his descriptions, the deceased died of a very pure heroin overdose. He said Alikhan was dressed fetchingly in a red silk peasant blouse with a black velvet vest and matching slacks, his accessories of gold all matched his heeled sandals and painted toe nails. The dark wig, plucked eyebrows and make up made it hard to identify the individual as a man let alone an Imam. The hooked nose remained the same."

Matt listened, he thought, *Four beers and some men overlook a big nose.*

Koning went on, "He died between midnight and three a.m.. The steam heaters in the bathroom were set high, their heat confuses the time of death."

Webb broke in, "So the bastard is dead, what happens now?"

Koning answered, "Yes, he's dead, but not forgotten. There will be publicity, it is bad for everyone. Right now we wouldn't confirm his identity, but when they get the official report with forensic evidence and fingerprints the stories will run wild, out of our control."

Webb asked, "Where do you stand on the trial?"

Koning answered, "There is agreement from all parties involved, there will be no trial, an investigation will continue, the guy you sent back on a stick was a foreigner, no record or fingerprints on file, the man you captured in the quarry will go to Guantanamo where he will be with his Muslim brothers and away from any publicity."

Matt stayed silent, and thought, *The most expensive prison on earth, it cost us over a million dollars per year per prisoner.*

Koning, sounding official, went on, "I have an official question for you. What part did you play in all this?"

Webb, holding the phone in front of him with one hand and the fingers of his other hand spread on his chest in shock, answered, "Absolutely nothing, I was here for the last two days complaining to your people about the Imam's escape. I left the Muslims and we came straight back, you can ask Al, my friend, and former sworn police officer, he drove. Check the film at the bridge, if you take any."

Koning replied, "You mentioned the Muslim leaders, you threatened them, they don't know how you poisoned their water, they have been forced into bringing in trucks of water to wash in. They are really upset."

Webb said, "If they had killed people in the stadium they would have been more than upset. They would have been hunted down and killed. Jihad can work both ways. A realistic understanding of consequences is good for the Islamic faithful. The water won't hurt them and it's good for them to have a problem to work on."

Koning said, "Why don't you go back to the Dominican Republic and grow sugar cane."

Webb replied, "I'd be very happy to do that—and it is bananas and chocolate, a wonderful combination. I just had to protect my daughter, her soon-to-be husband and my coming soon grandchild. Your system of justice and protection has been useless, even dangerous to us."

Koning retorted, "We, the Federal System, and I personally, did all we could, we stretched and even ignored the law at times in your favor."

Webb asked, "What are you going to do about the collusion between the Department of Justice and the Muslim community?"

Koning answered, "We won't allow defendants and their lawyers to be alone anymore. That will keep men like the Imam from directing retaliation from prison. The passing of information from the Grand Jury system is more complex and is still a problem. I have proof of the information movement, but no specific names. The Attorney General, my boss's boss, won't investigate the IRS, Benghazi, Fast and

Furious, NSA spying or voter fraud, so there is absolutely no chance of an inquiry over a suspected Grand Jury infraction or of cell phone numbers being passed around."

Webb asked, "So you aren't going forward with your information or complaints?"

Koning answered, "No, not at this time."

A silence followed.

Webb finally said before he hung up the phone, "Well that about sums up our business together. I wish you and your family a nice holiday season."

The mood in the motor home was one of joy.

Carla asked, "How are we going to see the news, I've got to see the Imam in drag. I hope Kate in heaven knows this; I've got to get it to her parents. Why would he do that? He seemed so mean and dedicated."

Webb answered, "No telling what's in the mind of such a hate filled person. You know Santa Anna, the Mexican general at the Alamo? Well, later, when the Texans slaughtered or captures all his troops in 18 minutes at San Jacinto, the big cheese general cowered in the woods dressed as a woman."

Everyone left the motor home except Matt, Webb and Al. The Russian body guard, a skilled mechanic, was in the garage working on the truck.

Matt asked Webb, "You arranged all this didn't you?"

Webb said, "Maybe I helped, the TV and newspaper reports are important. I must admit, when I moved all these chess pieces around, I hadn't thought Koning would cave in like he did. He had so much power in his hands, but he lacks the courage to use it. He just had to follow the tide of the Imam publicity with his proof of Justice Department corruption and he would be nationally recognized as an honest government official. All this proves that the power of the Federal political machine is not to be underestimated. I planned moves that, sadly, will never happen.

"I wonder what we can get for this motor home. We should get Carla and Dave back to Ann Arbor. I hope they can live in the house we have there, if not we'll get another. It may have too many memories of Kate."

Al, looking tired, opened the door of the RV, saying, "I'm dry."

As the afternoon turned to evening the weather cleared, Tanya walked Carla down to see her deer. Carla told of the success that Dave had had with getting them meat for the cabin. They also talked about a wedding. Carla asked Tanya to be her matron-of-honor. Tanya agreed with happiness. As they carefully walked in the few inches of crusty snow and ice down the lonely road, Tanya told Carla she would have a sister as well as a loving friend standing with her before the altar. Carla cried and hugged Tanya.

Then Carla said, "I felt this between us for many years, I saw the pictures of your mother when she was young. I saw pictures of my father in Miami years ago too. I saw how beautiful and kind you are and I wanted to be like you."

Tanya said, "I won't mention this again, we will hold our knowledge in our hearts."

Matt watched from the driveway as the two lovely women walked together. He knew what they were talking about.

Matt turned toward the garage when he heard the pickup start. They had gotten the radiator patched enough to test it, maybe good enough to get it to a repair shop. He looked around his property, the sun was almost gone, the sleet had stopped hours ago, the trees, rocks and fields glistened with a coating of ice. He heard a wolf call to the north. It was calling for some company. Matt understood the feeling.

He heard a crunch behind him and turned to see Webb coming from the garage.

Webb stopped beside Matt and together they watched Carla and Tanya pass out of sight down the road to the quarry.

In a low voice, almost a whisper, Matt asked, "What happens now?"

Webb watched the empty road for several more seconds, then said, "We can leave in a few days. The Muslims will reel from the news reports directed at them. They don't take ridicule or insults well. On the other hand they know they are not immune from vengeance. We may have a balance of terror or terrorism for a time. I'm sure sooner or later some Islamic fundamentalists will strike again, heedless of any consequence to themselves or to others. It is the nature of Islam."

Matt added, "Too bad they can't learn from nature—a badger and a wolf will almost never fight each other, they can sense the risks would be too great for them both."

Webb, ignoring the biology lesson, continued, "I need to confess that when I hear you say wolves, I feel guilty for what I did with Dave. I had that knife stuck in the door in Ann Arbor. All I cared about was getting Carla out of town and giving her better security. I threw poor Dave to the wolves. It was a mistake. I didn't know then he was the father of my grandchild. The more I'm around him, the worse I feel about my actions. I also put you and Tanya in danger and I got a good Russian friend killed.

"I never used to second guess my actions, I must be getting old."

As on cue, the lone wolf howled again to the north.

Matt suggested, "Let's go down and walk the girls back, it will be real dark soon and they may like the companionship."

Webb said, "Fine, we have lots to plan: a wedding, getting a new household going, new security people and the miracle of a baby."

Matt spoke as they walked, "Dave and Carla may have some ideas too."

Webb hunched into his jacket as the evening got colder, "Sure, I don't want to interfere."

The northern wolf called again, and then another wolf answered from the west, across the quarry, close and throaty. The men picked up their pace.

THE END

Acknowledgements

I t is difficult to make plots more convoluted and horrible than those delivered by the never ending, repetitious, news services. I may need to go to science fiction, historical or super hero genre to bring the reader respite from reality.

My wife, Ann, is always the first and last to help produce this novel. My dear friend, August (Augie) Altese did the major editing: a 92-year-old with a brain and attitude to be admired at any age. He found mistakes in book three, so I put him to work. Other contributors to the novel-making process were: John Lachat, Father Frank Lenz, and James Koning. (I borrowed Koning's name for my prosecutor.)

Walt Shiel is still my mentor, guide, production manager, typesetter and friend. His wife, Kerrie, does the wonderful oil paintings that become the covers. Their talented daughter, Lisa, a successful author, shares some of her time to act as my webmaster.

Research included: reading the complete J. M. Rodwell translation of the *Koran* (from the original Arabic by G. Sale), Winston Churchill's notes and book, *The River War*, hundreds of pages on the Patriot Act and the grand jury system. I accumulated a three-inch folder on Islam: historic and current, dress to *jihad*. (I suggest our nation's leaders should do the same.) Nuclear facts radiated from the deep and wide knowledge within the Internet. The weapons and locations in the novel are all real and with which I am familiar.

The words and actions of my characters are all their own, fitting their situation and experiences. I never could control Webb.

About the Author

Field Research: Yes, the little 5.7x28 mm cartridge can cut through a cedar tree, verifying a little piece of the story's action. The Belgium FN Five seveN makes the chips fly and the bad guys die in J.C. Hager's fourth novel.

He and his wife, Ann, live on Little Bay de Noc in Michigan's Upper Peninsula. Before retiring from 27 years with IBM, John was a science teacher, coaching wrestling and football at Gladstone High School. He has BA and MA degrees in Biology and Science Education.

Looking for the perfect gift for an outdoorsman, a fan of adventure thrillers, or somebody in need of a great "summer read"?

The Matt Hunter Adventures can be purchased:
- At your local bookstore
- At online book retailers
- Direct from the author at *www.JCHager.com*

Available in popular eBook formats, too!

The Matt Hunter Adventures
by J.C. Hager

Hunter's Choice

With the sound of snapping pine tops and tortured metal skidding across a frozen lake, a peaceful deer hunt becomes a rescue mission. Hunter's choices quickly become life-and-death decisions as a barrage of life-changing events thrust him into a fast-paced, page-turning adventure.

> "A powerful and intelligent thriller!"—Steve Hamilton, author of the Alex McKnight novels

Hunter's Secret

Diving into the cold depths of Lake Superior, Matt and Tanya follow the algae-coated links of an old anchor chain to a mysterious shipwreck. The discovery locks them in a vicious struggle with powerful, and deadly, businessmen determined to keep the past buried and catapults them into a wicked world of kidnapping, bribes, corporate subterfuge, and murder.

> "The locales depicted are bang-on, the human characters are well-crafted and many return as the reader's old friends."—Joseph Greenleaf, Publisher, Swordpoint Intercontinental Ltd

Hunter's Escape

Cruising in the motor yacht *Reefer* toward a Mexican honeymoon, Matt and Tanya Hunter discover and rescue a wounded Cuban refugee, bloody, dehydrated, and clinging to life on the broken mast of a shot-up catamaran. Helping the Cuban in his quest for freedom catapults them into battles at sea and the horrors of Cuban prisons.

> "You will definitely enjoy the read, but watch out for ricochets!"—Joseph A. Greenleaf, Author, *Sudden Light: Donegal's Novel*